Secrets in the Storm

Secrets in the Storm

Dana Lindsley

ISBN: 1539871495
ISBN 13: 9781539871491
Library of Congress Control Number: 2016918589
CreateSpace Independent Publishing Platform
North Charleston, South Carolina

To Janet

Prologue

New Amsterdam
New Netherlands
1648

In those days when the island of Manhattan had not yet had its hills removed nor its rivers and marshes filled, a young boy could quickly make a name for himself. Newly arrived from Beverwyck, the tiny northern trading post with a palisaded fort at the confluence of the North and Mohawk Rivers, six-year-old Johann was an expert at rolling hoops. He had already explored the far reaches of New Amsterdam rolling his hoop as he went: the shell beaches along Pearl Street, the small wharf on the East River where the ferry crossed, around the gibbet with it's hanging noose in the main square, and even beyond the Wall on Maiden Lane where the family washed their laundry. In a short time every-one in New Amsterdam, there were only a thousand souls at the time, could recognize and name the boy with the hoop.

Other children rolled the hoop but none as expertly as Johann. He could keep the hoop going through the mud in the streets, the soft sand on the beaches, and up and down the stepped bridges that crossed the canals. There was one challenge he had not yet mastered: the foot, horse and cart traffic that clogged the roads of that bustling port.

Here, in the New World hub of the Dutch West India Company, one of the most powerful multi-nation corporations ever to exist, the streets were never quiet even after the curfew the Director General imposed upon the town. New Amsterdam was the main trading post for the lucrative fur trade, so at all hours, Native Indians, who were called wicken by the Dutch, arrived by the dozens carrying beaver, mink, or stoat pelts upon their backs or on crude travois. Buyers descended upon the laden wicken with offers to pur-chase the furry skins at a tiny fraction of what they could get from the factors or dealers of the ships that moored in the harbor.

Sailors from ports all over the world, Java, Spain, Finland, Brazil, and Curacao, made the most of their short layover and bustled around town looking for the best beer and the fastest women. Also on the streets, wild pheasants, deer, pigs, and chickens roamed freely having been fenced out of homeowners veg-etable and flower gardens. These were the obstacles that Johan had yet to master.

Nevertheless, he was a confident young lad, as it would turn out overly so, and he went here and there showing off the speed with which he could roll his hoop. His father, recently hired by the Company despite his desire to return home to Egmont-aan-Zee in Holland, told Johann to be more careful. "There is no need to rush," he said to him, "it can be dangerous on those streets." They were admonishments that his young son rarely heeded.

On this particular day, he was proud of himself for managing the bumpy and root covered bouwerie trail. It went through primeval woods with dark passageways, overhanging leafiness, and massive trunks grown over several hundred years. Only once did he need to pick up his fallen hoop when a hidden deer startled him when it bolted. He had gone as far as the directors bouwerie where slaves meticulously cared for the grand house, manicured gardens and orchards. Once there he turned around and went southward returning from where he had come. He relished the thought of being back home to tell his family all about his grand escapade.

He thought his last challenge was to navigate Little Angola, just outside New Amsterdam where free black Africans lived in their neighborhood of haphazard huts and bumpy, pocketed streets. He managed well then went through the Wall at the west gate. His path merged at that point with the main road that followed the banks of the North River and served as the land thoroughfare for trade into the interior.

The guard hired by the Company to ensure that the English from New England did not invade the Dutch settlement observed him. Johan waved without pausing his hoop rolling and started down De Heere Street, now known as the Broad Way. It was the busiest street in town if you don't count Het Marckvelt on market day or the harbor at the wharf near Schreijiers Hock when ships arrived. The guard waved back, and Johan rolled his hoop into the hubbub of the busy trading town.

He was not far from home at this point. All he needed to do was go straight down the street toward the Fort, past bouwerie number one known as The Company Garden, and travel a few blocks to his home. It stood tall, cheek by jowl next to its neighbors and was painted light blue. The top front-facing gable, above the three floors of the house, was built with a flourish of white bordered curlicues and a center fleur-de-lis to which was attached a fancy letter "M" in a shield. It was the initial of the family name, Meckelenburg.

But Johann never got that far. A large part of his success was keeping his eye steadfastly on the hoop to ensure firm and steady contact with it. He did not see the horse and rider that rapidly approached him from the rear. When he swerved to avoid a pile of dung on the road he cut in front of the horse's path. The rider's shout was too late, and Johann bounced off the horse's chest, his hoop going one way and he the other.

The hoop found it's way safely to the ground but Johann did not. The impact thrust him into the path of a slow-moving cart filled with timber from what would become New Haarlem. As the young boy reached for the ground to brace his fall, his arm went through the spokes of the cart's wheel. The wheel continued to turn, and Johann's whole body was lifted and spun around. His head did not end up being crushed by the wheel, but it was sufficiently in the way that the side of his head was scraped off, ear and all.

In an instant, a crowd gathered around him, and it was evident that if he were to live at all, it would be with disfigurement and likely without the arm that now lay askew from his body attached only by muscle and tendons. The boy wasn't crying, but his eyes were wide open in shock and fear.

This happened a couple of blocks north of the home of a certain doctor of medicine, Teunis Nyssen, a well-known physician in New Netherlands. In the confusion following the accident, a runner was dispatched to fetch Dr. Nyssen, who, as fate would have it, was home that day and not visiting a sick patient. He rushed to the scene, examined the boy, and had him carried to his home where he could tend to him in the front parlor.

But what was also true was that the doctor asked a shaman who lived in Little Angola to attend the boy when the doctor responded to another medical emergency. The shaman was from the Tortugas and was as black as could be and had facial skin marked by deep scars drawn in patterns. This man filled the parlor full of smoke and heathen songs to which he danced in wild and pagan ways appealing to his gods for the boy's recovery.

Afterward, during the inquiry, Dr. Nyssen explained that he, as a trained and experienced physician, had done all he could for the boy. He cleaned and bandaged the head wounds and realizing there was no hope for the arm removed it. He gave Johann laudanum for his pain and made sure he was as comfortable as possible before handing over his care to the shaman whom he believed to be "as skilled as he was in the arts of healing."

He also said that he summoned the boy's parents immediately but that they were not at home. In the hours following the accident, the shaman, unbeknownst to the doctor, took the weakening child to the nearby river to wash his wounds. While there Johann died whether from his injuries or from drowning was never known.

They hanged the shaman for his part in the affair and the doctor was fined five guilders and reprimanded for his "negligence" in not attending to the boy properly, but he was permitted freedom to continue his medical practice. Johann's family blamed the doctor for his death and after that sought to discredit him and had other physicians attend to their needs.

Of little note during the day of the accident nor the inquiry was the presence of a young girl about Johann's age. She was the doctor's daughter, who shadowed him wherever he went and assisted him as she could. Her blue eyes framed by her braided blonde hair saw it all. Her name was Elsje.

Part I

One

Long Island
New Netherlands
October 3, 1666

Her mother woke her before the sun rose.

"Elsje, he's soiled his bed again," she whispered as she shook her shoulder.

Elsje's father slept in the common room near the fireplace ever since his strokes limited his ability to climb stairs to his bedroom or go to the outhouse. The feather mattress had a foul odor and needed changing. Extra bedding was available in the backyard shed specifically for this purpose.

When the two of them had changed the mattress, Elsje went back to bed knowing that her mother would awaken her when it was her turn to watch him. But she couldn't sleep so she arose and walked outside into the cold air of autumn. A red morning sky greeted her yet she took no notice of its message.

As she pumped water to wash her face, a gust of wind swirled around her, grabbed her unbraided hair and tossed her nightdress. She used both her hands to keep the skirt dress from flying over her head. The wind was violently removing leaves from their summer homes on once-colorful trees.

"Well," she said to the wind," I guess you bring the end of summer!" It would be a day that would end more than that.

The left side of her father's face sagged, and the family could no longer understand the garbled words he spoke. When he heard the wind outside and saw the first drops of rain splattered against the windows, Elsje read the anxiety in his eyes.

"I know," she said to him. "I remember. It will be all right. We'll stay right beside you."

On stormy days memories returned to him of when he was nine years old, and his father wanted him to follow in the grand tradition of Dutch seamanship. He forced Elsje's father into a small sailboat alone. The wind rose rapidly and pushed him far out into the Zee and out of sight of his father. He sped past boats capsized around him and far more experienced sailors were floundering. He applauded himself as a naturally skilled sailor until the cotter pin for his rudder broke, and he could no longer steer. The boat spun and heeled wildly with the terrified boy alone onboard. Eventually, the boat crashed into the side of a merchant ship, and sailors hauled him aboard.

Ever since he felt the same terror whenever the wind rose and rain splashed on streets and against windows. That night he lay powerless in bed, an invalid, hearing the wind and rain of the tempest outside. His only comfort was having someone beside him.

As the winds rose and the deluge increased, Elsje, who was twenty-three, and her mother took turns soothing their father and husband. A branch tossed by the wind shattered one of the windows and rain came through the opening and dampened the floor. When he started trembling, they covered him with blankets, and he shut his eyes trying to distance himself from the events unfolding around him.

They nailed a piece of duck cloth over the window, yet it flapped from the force of the wind outside. The loud snapping unsettled them, and they embraced each other amid the noises and the uncertainties.

"Do you think he will be all right?" Elsje asked her mother. "At least for a while? I'm exhausted and need to go back to sleep."

"I'll watch him," she answered. "You go get some rest."

Elsje went to the distant quiet of the basement instead of her bedroom where the rough foundation stones would deaden the sound of the tempest outside. A cubbyhole bed had been built among the shelves of foodstuffs to accommodate visitors. She closed the trap door that led from the basement to the kitchen. The pumpkins and squash, the large canvas bags of barley, the canisters and pots sealed with cloth, the miscellaneous items of the house on the shelves encircled her with their familiarity. Wrapping a quilt around her shoulders, she laid down and closed her eyes.

A shuddering sound awakened her, and her body felt the aftereffects of a violent tremor. The roaring wind was louder and closer than ever. When she saw water trickling down the steps, her first thought was that a jar of fruit had broken open spilling its contents.

Cautiously she walked up the steps and opened the trap door which was immediately wrenched from her hand by a raging wind. All she could see were tree branches outlined by roiling clouds in the early morning light. Twigs flew through the air and leaves swirled erratically in the gusts of wind. She scrambled through the branches to find her family. She lifted her arm to protect her face.

Her home no longer existed. The large oak tree that shaded their home in summer had crushed the full length of the house. The roof had collapsed, and there was little left of the walls. Most of the chimney remained standing, but the wind scattered embers and coals from the fireplace fanned them into small flames.

The tangle of branches rising before her was impenetrable. Her body wanted to escape to the field behind the house, but her heart pulled her inward to help her family. She shouted: "Alice!" "Father!" "Mother!" "Where are you?" "God, God, help me!" She stumbled frantically over tree limbs, collapsed walls and crushed furniture not sure which way to go.

She saw an entire spinning wheel standing undamaged. She picked it up and carried it with her trying to save something. She stepped over embers and debris balancing the spinning wheel. Her foot stepped on a Delft pitcher and crushed it.

She ran into the open field carrying the wheel, put it down and spun around to return to the house to save her family. The wind and smoke from embers swirled over collapsed walls and splintered furniture. She coughed violently to remove a hitch of smoke that had caught in her throat. Her clothes whipped and fluttered in the wind. She felt as though this was happening to someone she did not know.

Her sister Hannah stood near the far side of the house holding her hand over her mouth. Elsje rushed to her.

"Where are they?" she shouted. "We have to save them!"

"Elsje, thank God you're alive." They embraced each other and then Hannah pointed to Elsje's foot. "You're bleeding!" She started to reach her hand to her leg when Hannah restrained her.

Elsje looked at her dumbfounded and unable to think. She was shaking.

"The men will do all they can," Hannah said as she turned and looked at her husband, Theodorus, and his father, Rev. Polhemus, who were desperately trying to lift a broken timber of the house.

"I have to help them!" Elsje said tears streaming down her face. Her body was trembling, and her knees shook.

"Come with me, Elsje. You are in no shape to be out here. There is nothing we can do."

Elsje stood where she was hoping to see Theodorus or the minister guiding someone from the rubble. She saw no one. Gently Hannah guided her sister away from the destruction and toward Mary's undamaged house next door. When she saw their destination, Elsje was stunned. She couldn't comprehend how her house could be gone when her sister's house was just as it always had been.

Hannah draped her shawl over Elsje's head, encircled her with her arms, and led her away.

Part II
Gerret

Two

Amsterdam
The Netherlands
Eight Years After the Storm

Above the settlement of New Amsterdam not far north of the Wall, there is a tiny spit of a beach on the North River that is down in a hollow and hidden by the salt rushes. I walked there when I was young to be alone. I roamed the Island and explored the primeval forest and the ancient rivers unknown to Netherlanders. The beach was my secret place -- every boy has to have a secret place. I sat on a flat rock that was the right height for my legs. When the afternoon sun shone, I laid down on that rock and absorbed the warmth the sun had gifted to me and the rock.

Mostly what I did on my beach was look across the river at the cliffs, the ones the Indians call *Weehawken*, "rocks like rows of trees." To me, they were an impenetrable wall that separated where I was from whatever was over there. I imagined it was the wall of a grand fortress, and the river was the moat that challenged anyone assailing the wall. I conjured up battalions of courageous soldiers who launched wave after wave of attacks at those cliffs. Their cannonballs hurled from an armada of galleons arced their futile path toward those walls. I knew that real people, Indians mostly, lived there, but it was a place I could never go. So here was here and there was there, divided forever from each other.

The October tempest of 1666 is like that for me. A hinge in my life that separates what 'was' from what 'is'. The past is protected by a wall higher than the *Weehawken* and a moat wider than the river. No amount of wishing or praying to Almighty God will ever get me back to the way life was before the storm. I imagine it is that way for her also. I will tell you about the tempest and how it divided my life, but first I'll tell you how I met her.

There is a tavern on the Haarlemmerstraat Canal not far from the West India House where we can talk. It's quiet there, and the keeper will let us dawdle over our drinks and stay as long as we like. Let's go there and I will tell you everything you need to know to be prepared.

Three

New Amsterdam
Eight Years Before the Storm

My story with her began under the earthen wall of Fort Amsterdam that brooded over my father's tavern where I saw forbidden things. The weather on this particular day couldn't decide between driving rain and bright clearness. So it stitched itself together with a wind that could rip a coat off your back. Days like that made our tavern warm and womb-like. A cocoon in the world's storms. New life can incubate in such places. Or be transformed.

Our long and narrow tavern was on the East end of Pearl Street where the bay doesn't lap up against its edges. The single window, a perfect square carved out of the log walls, begged for cleaning and filtered dirty light to the interior. The entry was a narrow slit of a door penetrated by refugees from the storm and the vicissitudes of life at the edge of civilization.

My father presided at a seven-foot bar stained by years of use and carved with initials and designs made by customers. He kept casks of ale beneath the bar and brandy bottles, glasses and leathern tankards on top. A dozen chairs and a few small tables sat scattered haphazardly around the room to be arranged as customers wished. My father patched narrow flat stones over the old wooden chimney when the Dutch West India Company required a changeover to all stone to prevent fires. It worked well enough, and no one was the wiser for his deception. He was proud of his secret rebellion.

Candles in sconces on the walls gave an intimate feel to the tavern. "The better to do private business," he said. "They stay longer." And they did, raising their tankards and smoking their thin-stemmed, clay pipes with tiny bowls at the end. Two tables in the dark end of the tavern, we called them the "trysting tables," hosted lovers or merchants who leaned into each other and gave birth to dreams. On busy days when night fell, haloed points of candlelight pierced pipe and fireplace smoke giving our tavern the feel of an isolated ship in a thick fog.

My father came to New Netherlands as a cadet for the Dutch West Indies Company. He signed up after a slick-talking factor came to his neighborhood on the Elandsgracht canal in Amsterdam promising adventure and a bright future for those willing to soldier for three years. At the time he was apprenticing to be a shoemaker and said: "Anything was better than shoeing those pompous, opulent, overdressed burghers!"

The Company stationed him in New Amsterdam although it could have been Curacao or Brazil or any other of the dozens of ports where they traded. With his contract as cadet in hand, he brought his family, my mother Annette, my sister and me to the slice of land on Pearl Street granted to him. We lived there while he did his duty in the Fort two or three days a week. To beat the winter he hastily built our home with the help of self-made carpenters and borrowed slaves. The supporting timbers were robust enough, but the clapboards were roughly hewn and did not fit well with their neighbors. The roof and walls leaked.

When I was younger than you are now, I waited on customers. I squeezed through the tight spaces between tables, stretched out legs and coats thrown carelessly on the floor while carrying tankards of ale. More than once I stumbled casting a frothy brew over a sailor's lap or a matron's shoulder. There was adventure in it for a small boy, of course. Customers cuddled, tickled and teased me or gave me gifts: a wooden toy, musical reed, a stick, and ball.

Our tavern attracted the one hundred fifty or so soldiers barracked at the Fort and young women escorted by their brothers. On feast days, when we were allowed to sell our beer and brandy late into the night, many of our patrons drank too much. Men approached women and flirted and teased them, sometimes by lifting up their pipe stems suggestively and then thrusting their finger in and out of the bowl. Or they would stand in front of women and open an oyster and slurp it into their mouths and lick the shell. Every object at hand was an obscene tool to bring forth boisterous laughter. Some women were offended, or at least pretended to be so, but many had their own wanton behavior: exposing their shoulders, lifting their skirts, handling their breasts, or licking their lips. When one of the dead drunks was a woman, men openly fondled her or peered under her petticoats daring each other to reach into her nether parts.

Those were the things I should not have seen as a boy. But outside the settlement away from the tavern the primeval forest seduced me and embraced me with its ancient trees, meadows of ferns, and gurgling streams. We lived beside a paradise and my earliest memories were exploring beyond the Wall along the Indian paths watching beavers diving into their homes, sitting on my beach watching fish jumping the North River, or if I was lucky, a black bear foraging berries in the woodlands.

———

I was nineteen years old, about your age, when I met her. I awakened that morning with a sty in my left eye. Each blink was excruciating. It was a feast day, and we expected many patrons would find appeal in our dark tavern and the meal my mother was preparing. I managed my duties half-blind by squeezing the offending eye closed.

Downpours of rain kept people at home, and only a few of our regular customers were there. Pieter, the tailor from next door whose wife had died years ago, came as he did every day, seeking solace for his loneliness. Several cadets from the Fort drank prodigious amounts of beer saddened by their separation from family. Bravely they put on glad rags and noisily sang to their camaraderie. Old Van Doorn, who paused each day to take his ale before retiring for the night, sat near the fire to calm his aching joints. "Always worse on cold rainy days!" he complained. His ears could not hear our answers.

My mother prepared the feast: pork, root soup, vegetables and fruits, dozens of eggs, haunches of venison, and, of course, olykoeks or doughnuts. These she put on the table along with a candelabrum of twelve tapers next to the large punch bowl filled with caudle wine. We thought her work would be in vain because so few people braved leaving home on account of the rain.

In the late afternoon, there appeared at the door Teunis Nyssen, a physician. Like my father, he had been granted one of the original land grants on De Heere Street in Manhattan. He hadn't been to our tavern before, likely considering it too rowdy and unsavory. He thrust his head inside and peered about holding the door wide open. A refreshing wind raced down the length of the warm and stuffy tavern. Apparently satisfied with what he saw, he motioned for others to follow as he stepped within. To our astonishment, his six daughters accompanied him followed by his English wife, Phoebe. Each held a tattered piece of sailcloth over her head as a shield from wind and rain. Shaking off wetness, they removed their muddied clogs and laid aside the sailcloths. The two older daughters each carried a bundle: sleeping babies.

"We'll have our feast here!" the father announced.

"Of course, Mr. Nyssen!" I replied peering at him with my one good eye. I ushered his family to the large table.

I was familiar with the Nyssen's, of course. It was a small town. Their house on upper De Heere Street across from the large Company farm had a small garden to feed the growing family: vegetables, a single cow, some chickens, a few fruit trees. His specialty though was growing medicinal herbs, prized rarities and much in demand. Old, sick or injured people visited him for advice and treatment and paid for his services in seawan, the beaded seashells we used as money.

I overheard the family talking about the collapse of the thatch roof on the house where they were to have their holiday gathering. The torrential rain and wind caused the roof to collapse onto their meal prepared for the day. The family, none of whom was injured, decided to observe the feast somewhere else, where others cooked the meal.

I tapped a barrel of ale and handed them tankards with a livelier step than usual pleased by having so many attractive girls at the table.

"The feast is yours," I said to them indicating the foods spread in the center of the tavern.

"That eye looks uncomfortable, young man," Mr. Nyssen said to me.

"Yes, sir," I replied. "A speck has refused to be dislodged. It will pass in time." The girls giggled. I was embarrassed to have attention drawn to my clinched up face.

"It is more than that," he said authoritatively. "It needs attention."

"Yes, sir, I shall do that," I said turning away to look after other customers.

"The pain can be relieved quickly!" one of the girls said in an urgent tone. Again the girls laughed.

I paused.

"Let me, Father." It was one of the girls, younger than I by a year or two. She invited me to sit beside her. Her father drew a candle to the edge of the table and nodded toward me.

All eyes were on me. My cheeks flushed. The promise of relief from my pain was sufficient for me to overcome my shyness and to pick up a chair and carry it to their table.

As I did so, I looked at her. Her once-starched bonnet was limp from wetness and strands of golden hair flattened themselves upon her forehead and cheeks. She smiled, and my resistance melted. Her blue eyes fixed upon my face. I one-eyed the other girls to distract myself from the intensity of her prettiness. The oldest one, Jannette, was my age, and she winked at me. I knew her, of course, and her younger sisters, but I had always dismissed them as just another family in town. How unaware we are of the future in our midst.

I sat down, and she brought her candlelit face right up to mine looking intently at my eye. I could see her every feature with utmost clarity. Her skin was soft with down and flushed pink from the cooling rain. Her wet lips were open and tantalizingly close. Her fresh breath caressed my cheek. Breathing the air she had just exhaled was overwhelming.

I admit that I was an innocent about love despite being in a tavern frequented by women who were forward in their attentions to men. I had not courted a girl and was barely pass the stage when I saw girls as creatures to be avoided.

I was sure she could hear my heart pounding as her face came closer to mine. Then she placed her fingertips lightly on my upper cheek pulling downward to examine my eye. Her cool, wet fingers on my fevered cheek instantly distracted me from my pain.

During her examination, she looked at me and smiled. I was bewitched. She sat bolt upright.

"It is a sty!" she said for all to hear. "Am I right, Father?" She looked to him for approval.

"Quite right, my dear. Now, what can you do for him?"

Returning her gaze to me, she said: "First, wash the eye thoroughly and place upon it something very warm. Then apply an ointment of Ragwort every night for five days."

"You have your solution, Mr. ..." the father said.

"Snedeker. Gerret Snedeker."

"...Mr. Snedeker. Given to you by the youngest and most precocious physician in all of New Netherlands: Elsje! Now onto the feast!"

I retreated into the back kitchen to help my mother keep the center table filled with food. The Nyssen family paid little attention to me when I refilled their tankards or walked past their table.

The rest of my evening revolved around her: how she was sitting, what she might be saying, how she interacted with her sisters. I longed to sit beside her, touch her hand with their cool fingers and see her lips smile again. But she did not glance my way or acknowledge me.

The time for them to leave came too soon. Mr. Nyssen went to my father's table to count the marks and pay his bill. The rest of the family put on their cloaks and prepared to enter the rainy night. As they were doing so, Elsje went to the center table and picked up something from the remains of the food. She walked to me.

"Place this in hot water and put it on your eye," she said as she brushed a loose strand of hair from her forehead.

Again her eyes pierced me with their directness and intensity. I held my breath.

"It will keep warm and soothe the pain."

She placed a single unshelled egg in my hand, twirled, and was off with her family. She left me to contemplate the gift and the girl with the healing touch. Elsje, the one with the sweet, fresh breath.

After that, I wanted to give to her everything that was beautiful.

Four

The Teunis home was at the north end of the colony, so I took walks in that direction. I made pretexts for my forays: to visit the market, to observe the unloading of a recently arrived vessel, to visit a friend. I hoped she'd be at the window or door, and I'd see her. I paused as I passed her house or hid behind a carriage or the trunk of a large oak tree across the street. From there, my heart would plead: "Come to the window! Give a smile to the sun! Breathe the same gentle breeze that has just passed by me!"

When I saw her, it was only for the briefest moments. Knowing I was near her, my heart quickened, and my spirit lifted. At night I would devise a way to free myself the next day.

Elsje and her father were rarely outside, and I learned the elder daughters did the work of the garden. But it was not neat and tidy like those of most Netherlanders. It was a neglected and weedy bramble punctuated by a few vegetables and the medicinal herbs for which the family was well known. The dozen or so apple and pear trees were unpruned, thick with suckers and dead branches. "They must have other priorities," I thought.

Later that winter, my blood emboldened by a warm winter sun, I left the street and entered their garden. Her two older sisters were gathering piles of leaves from around the trunks of fruit trees. I picked up a long and unwieldy branch from the ground and called to them, "Hallo, where would you like this?"

The two stood up and looked at me. The older one smiled broadly.

"That one," she said, "would be for firewood. See, there is the woodpile." She pointed to a shed roof attached to the house.

Balancing the branch over my head, I carried it to the woodpile. After trimming the branch to size with a pruning saw, I returned to the orchard and wordlessly gathered more branches. The two girls wore dark blue scarves tightly bound about their heads, several layers of blouses and soiled white aprons over their full skirts. They seemed amused at what I was doing.

"You are the boy from the tavern, aren't you? The one with the eye?"

"I am." They remembered me! "I'm Gerret."

"Jannette," said the taller one. "This is Mary." The other one curtsied to me.

"I've time today. I could remove the stump." I pointed to the remains of the apple tree whose broken branches I had been collecting. It was work that would take effort and time.

Jannette smiled and said, "I'd like that. I'd like that very much. I'll help you."

It was hard work and when the stump finally loosened I was satisfied. "Surely they will tell her about me," I thought.

S eizing an opportunity to see Elsje regularly, I feigned interest in my spiritual welfare and attended church services. Her family were faithful in their religious observances and sat in the front of the sanctuary beside other established and influential families. I sat in the back. One Sabbath day I delayed my exit until her family passed by.

"Well, Mr. Snedeker, the eye seems well healed." Mr. Nyssen recognized me.

"Yes, sir," I said. "Beg your pardon, sir," I said as I hurried to walk beside him. "I'd like to offer my services to work on your farm. I've an interest in learning how to do it and know you have no sons to do the hard work."

He appraised me up and down with his eyes. He was a gentle and welcoming man and his demeanor toward me was agreeable.

"And what might you expect in return for your offer?" New Amsterdam was a commercial settlement. Everything had a price.

"Ah, I expect no reward for the work. Simply the benefit of sharing the produce and learning the ways of the land. And, if I have the need, your attention to any illnesses I may have."

With a twinkle in his eye, he said, "Is that all...?" He knew my real reason. He had an interest in finding husbands for his six daughters. Certainly, I was not the only young man to bring himself to the attention of the family.

"Come by when you can, young man, and there will be work enough for you to do."

Before I tell you why I didn't go right away, let's you and I walk down to the wharf and see if ships are arriving. We'll sit on one of those benches or if it is too cold and windy we'll go back to our tavern.

Within days of this agreement, my life changed. It happened this way. My father used his fowling piece on Pearl Street to shoot a pheasant. Due to his poor marksmanship or his inebriation or both, his shot went awry and grazed a burly foreign sailor on the leg. My father, always aggressive, blamed the fellow for getting in the way of his target.

"You fat pig! Who told you to interfere in the business of the citizens of this colony? Go back to the whoring ways of sailors and get out of my way!"

Language like that is insulting enough to draw a hefty fine. The Portuguese sailor may not have understood what my father said, but the meaning was clear. He demanded an apology and payment for his pain. A scuffle ensued. My father was bruised and beaten but not cut by the blade the sailor used in his threats. Both were taken to the prison in the Fort to await a hearing before the Director General to whom the West India Company had given full authority over all affairs in New Netherlands.

My father rebelled against many of the Director's dictates. He said it wasn't in his blood to obey 'tyrants.' I'm embarrassed that the court records are full of charges and fines against him. Many people shared his sentiments and cheered his protests against the Director. But few condoned his outlandish behavior. He flaunted his notoriety by naming our tap *'The Wooden Horse'* a jab at a punishment he had received as a soldier when he was forced to straddle a wooden sawhorse with his ankles and wrists bound.

The Director was out of town when the episode happened, and my father languished in jail awaiting his return. I ran the tavern: buying and carrying the casks of ale, cleaning the tables, serving the patrons. Little time was left to dawdle in front of Elsje's house or to work on the Nyssen farm.

To my embarrassment, Dr. Nyssen was called to tend to my father's wounds. My father was indignant about how the Director General treated him. "That scoundrel has stolen away our freedoms!" he reportedly said. "He should be here in jail, not me! No hunting? What's he going to do next? Prohibit lovemaking to my wife?"

When my father finally came home after paying the two florin fine, he was a bitter man and did not hesitate to express his outrage about the Director. Patrons began staying away from the tavern to avoid him, so we put him in the back room to wash dishes or manage the accounts. Even then he was so angry at times that he threatened to take his musket and "find a target." On those occasions, my mother and I served him more drink to pacify him.

As the only son among many sisters, I was expected to take the mantle of the man of the house, to carry on the Snedeker name, to be the eventual provider and protector of the family. As my father's reputation sank, the burden of the family honor rested on me. I was determined to be as respectable as he was disrespectful. To be as honorable as he was dishonorable.

———◆———

Yes, yes. I'm getting to her story.

On sunny days women went to a small rippling brook beyond the wall to do their laundry. The water was swift and clear, perfect for cleaning clothes.

The old Lenape trail along the stream, named Maiden Lane, was where women socialized as they washed clothes. I was certain the Nyssen girls, whose home was nearby, would be there.

Once the laundry had been completed many women stopped on their way home at the Vly or Valley market that was on the flat area at the mouth of the stream. Vendors behind tables sold salted meats, dried fruits, preserves, and handwork. It was a convenient excuse for me to go there to purchase some item and walk up the stream to find Elsje.

The first time I saw her kneeling at the stream and placing wet clothes on tree branches, I walked past. Few men were in the area, and I was self-conscious about approaching her. The next time I paused on the trail just long enough to pretend I was interested in what they were doing or was in search of a particular person for whom I was delivering a message. When she looked up at me, I tipped my head and gave the slightest bow in her direction. She smiled knowing who I was.

One day I purchased a mincemeat pie and stood my ground above her waiting for her to glance my way. Her older sister, Jannette, noticed me and climbed the bank of the stream to me.

"I've brought a gift!" I said to her.

"Ah, and who might that be for?" She asked with a gleam in her eye.

"It is for your family," I said.

"To what do we owe the honor?"

"I have never made a proper thank you to your father or your sister for the attending to my sty."

Amused she threw back her head saying, "That was so long ago!"

"Please, take it," I said holding out the pie to her. "It is my pleasure to give it."

She wiped her wet hands on her apron, took the pie, and to my surprise took my hand and walked me toward her sisters.

"Look who has come to visit me!" Jannette shouted. "He brought me a pie!" She grabbed my elbow and drew me near so close that our hips and shoulders were touching. Her breast pushed against my arm. She winked at me.

I lingered with the girls as they admired the pie then returned to their work. When Elsje had filled a large basket with wet clothes, I lifted it for her and took it to the open space where she was to wring the wetness from them.

"Let me help you," I said as I lifted a bed sheet and started to twist it.

"Thank you," she said, "but that sheet is a job for two persons." She took one end and I the other and as we faced each other we squeezed out the water.

"The pie is actually for you," I said as the tightening sheet brought us closer together.

Her face sparkled with a smile.

"Well, anyone can eat it," I said. "But I intended it for you."

"Oh, you please me, Gerret."

"Then I'll bring you a pie every week!"

She laughed and covered her mouth with her hand. Her eyes twinkled.

"I like blueberry."

"Then that is what it will be: a blueberry pie for Elsje every week of the year."

When we had hung the clothes from the basket to dry on tree branches, I told her I needed to return to our family tavern. I watched as she skipped her way back to the stream and her sisters.

———

Of course, I couldn't bring a pie to her every week but, since it was spring, I did deliver something else.

One warm night I clipped a single tulip from our garden. Yes, you know what I'm going to tell you. We kept the old tradition. It was a tulip with pink stripes, a blush of blue near the stem and white feathered edges at the top. You know the one, the Admiral Sned.

The night conspired in my secret. A fog dampened my movements and concealed my presence. Not a soul was on the street for the watchman had shaken the rattle announcing the nightly curfew. I made my way to her house gliding like an owl silently through the woods. Down Pearl Street, left onto

De Heere Street, and along the elegant houses toward the Wall. An occasional light blinked through a window into the darkness. Even the water on the North River was still, and boats at wharfs kept their masts upright and unmoving. As tradition dictates, I laid the flower on her doorstep when no one was aware and with no note attached.

They would know who gave the flower. Every tulip cultivar, distinct in its color and shape and markings, revealed a signature. The Admiral Sned was our family tulip, developed decades ago by my great-grandfather. It would be clear that a Snedeker gave the flower.

Although it could have been for any of the girls in the family, she would know it was for her. That was all that mattered.

Several times that Spring my gifts graced her doorstep.

———

One Thursday in June when I was confident the Nyssen girls would be returning home by way of the Vly Market I was there at the likely time of their passing. Casually I walked along the tables with merchandise, my attention on the entrance to Maiden Lane. But I missed her arrival and Elsje came up behind me as I browsed a table of fresh spring berries. I was startled to hear her voice behind my shoulder.

"I love strawberries, Mr. Snedeker. Would you deliver them to my stoop as well?"

I didn't turn to face her. "Anything you order is my heart's desire," I said.

Fast as lightning she playfully slapped a bunch of garden greens on my back.

After hesitating a moment I said to the attendant, "Two handfuls of strawberries for the lady, please." I waited for her to hit me again with her greens. Instead, she teased me by drawing her finger down my back. I shivered. I can still feel the exact line of that touch.

With the strawberries in my basket, I turned to face her. "I will give you the berries but only after you agree to join me for a walk."

"What? Now?"

"I know a path familiar to you just up the way." I winked and nodded toward Maiden Lane. The warm spring sun was low in the sky, and the new green leaves on the trees shimmered from the rays of sunlight streaking from the canopy.

"But in the evening that path is a promenade for courting couples," she said.

"Yes ...?"

"People may get the wrong impression."

"Then let's go as acquaintances."

I lifted my elbow inviting her to join me.

After a moment of hesitation, she linked her wrist into the crook of my elbow. All my senses centered on the warm pressure where she touched me. I breathed deeply, exhaled and we started forth.

There are several things I remember about that walk. The silence between us is one of them. Oh, we talked but only about the weather, the leafing of the trees or the women washing at the stream.

Each time we passed others walking the other direction she slowed her pace and slinked behind me so that my body shielded her from the view of others. I took it as shyness, and I was proud to be the guardian of such a beautiful woman.

I'm still in love with the girl I knew that day. Everything was bright and full of promise. Since then there has been shadows and darkness. So much happened we could not prevent or control.

You will hear about these things. It is far better that you know them beforehand.

———◆———

There were days when my father was his old self: a jovial host mixing with the patrons, telling jokes, drinking beer. At times it seemed he was on the mend and had given up his rancor and his drink.

But there were days when he was morose, aggressive and secretive. At times he left home and we wouldn't see him for days and then he'd return dirty, unshaven and reeking of alcohol. A dog with his tail between his legs, apologetic and humble. We'd get angry with him and then forgive him when he promised to change his ways and never leave again. He'd sleep for more hours than a night, and we would not know which father would awake the next day.

When he was sober and capable of handling the tavern, I was relieved of the burden of managing it. On those rare occasions, I excused myself, to fulfill the offer I made to work the Nyssen farm. It was summer, and there was much to be done. I managed to be there about once a week, or if I was lucky two.

She came outside occasionally to gather herbs from the garden or to use the outhouse, and sometimes she greeted me, and we briefly chatted about mundane matters. Other times she single-mindedly did her business then returned inside without acknowledging me at all.

One day a large splinter penetrated deeply under my fingernail as I was wrestling with the trunk of a dead tree. I pulled the splinter out with my teeth but a small piece embedded itself near the quick. When my finger started to throb, I had a reason to fulfill the arrangement I had made with Dr. Nyssen. I knocked on the front door and to my delight, Elsje answered and warmly ushered me inside. I felt foolish asking for attention for a mere splinter knowing that much more serious ailments and wounds had preceded me.

"My father looks at everyone no matter who they are or what ails them," she said, "life threatening or not. Did you get that in our garden? Does it hurt?"

Sheepishly I nodded.

"Well, we definitely will do all we can. Before he sees you, let me get a washbasin for that hand." I was embarrassed knowing she would see my dirty fingernails.

We were alone in a small anteroom, most unusual for houses in New Amsterdam. It was only big enough for two benches facing each other with a narrow passageway between and doors on each end.

Within moments she returned carrying a small basin. She had draped a towel over her forearm. She sat down beside me placing the bowl between our hips. She reached for my hand, and I braced myself for her touch.

"Allow me," she said and with the gentlest of touches supported my palm upon hers before placing it in the bowl. As I looked up at her, our eyes met.

"Tell me if this hurts," she said. She took a corner of the towel, dampened it, and delicately stroked my finger. My cheeks reddened.

"Garret," she said still holding my hand. "I love the tulips. I'm putting the petals ..."

At that moment there was a loud knocking on the outside door reverberating in the tiny space we occupied. We both were startled. She stood up, dried her hands, and opened the door.

Standing there was an Indian dressed in Dutch pantaloons and a white collar askew over his naked neck and chest. He held his hand up to his cheek and blood was oozing through his fingers. Elsje unfazed by the blood signaled for him to sit opposite me. He said not a word and looked frightened and out of place.

Sitting down next to him, she reached for the bowl of water that she had just used and put it between them. She took his free hand in hers. Looking at him, she said, "My father looks at everyone no matter what ails them, life-threatening or not. We will do all we can for you. Does it hurt?"

She had such compassion, courage, and gentleness.

Her father joined us in the anteroom, told Elsje to wash the Indian's wound and apply pressure while he attended to me. After he had extracted the splint, he smeared Gladwin root mixed with verdigris and honey on my wound and sent me home with instructions to dip the finger in brandy several times a day.

"You do have spirits where you work, don't you?" he said with a smile on his face.

That night I couldn't sleep, wondering where she was placing the tulip petals and thinking about the way she said my name, "Gerret."

———————◆———————

"The fleshpots of Egypt are the tempters tools! The sugar you sprinkle over bread and pastry is a moral menace of frightening proportions!

Woe to you who succumb to the sweets the Devil puts before you to lead you away from the narrow path to heaven!" The minister preached on his favorite subject: the evils of sugar, spices, and sauces. In his black robe, shock of white hair, and imposing position in the high pulpit, he was a man who could terrify the strongest of men. He was the most powerful man in the settlement after the Director. The two of them dominated the church consistory and together decided all matters religious and civil.

Of course, you think differently of him. You know him in a way that none of the rest of us do. But you must know how we experienced him. He was honest, I'll admit that, and spoke his mind. No one could talk to the Mohawks as well as he could in their language, and he converted many of them to Christianity. He lived with them for a while, you know? Even wrote a scholarly book about how they live.

But with his congregation, he was like a wolf with fierce gray eyes looking for prey. If he found a wayward vulnerability in the beliefs or actions of a hapless parishioner, he attacked from the pulpit. And if that wasn't successful, he asked Stuyvesant to punish the offender. People wilted under the minister's authority and did what they could to avoid being the target of those steely eyes and scathing sermons.

When he preached, my eyes wandered to the Nyssen pew. Her mother and father sat with their daughters between them, and the girls passed their squirming baby brothers from one set of hands to another. Elsje sat upright, her head facing front. She rarely acknowledged me, but Jannette made a point of looking my way and flashing a fetching smile. I nodded back.

One Sunday following the service Pastor Megapolensis descended from the pulpit and went to the front pews to greet the faithful. At his side was his son, Samuel, who was my age, educated and well dressed. The two of them conversed with the Nyssen family who bowed respectfully and complimented the sermon. The Pastor moved on to greet others while Samuel remained. He looked at ease and made some comment to her. Elsje laughed and looked at him bright eyes.

He and I were different, and he was a formidable rival. He was witty, and I was quiet. He was educated, and I could only count numbers. He had every prospect of wealth and advancement, and I only knew how to tend a tavern. His father was a powerful man and my father ...

My heart fixed on her, and I resolved to pursue my suit of her. And when I faced obstacles like Samuel I would take courage from her words, "You please me, Gerret."

———◆———

Throughout summer I worked almost weekly at the Nyssen farm determined to give her reminders of me. The apple I picked she ate, a sign of my tending their orchard. Every squash and pumpkin I harvested, the fruit of the work I had done for her. I chopped and split wood for her to be warm. I repaired the chicken coops and fed the pigs so she could eat. I harvested seaweed to nourish the soil of her garden.

Her oldest sister, Jannette, often watched me work and chatted endlessly about whatever was on her mind.

"Don't you have work to do?" I asked her when I tired of her voice.

"Of course, but my sisters can handle it. Besides they are far better at housework than I. Except for Elsje, of course. I'd much rather be with you." She winked at me and tossed her head. I think she flirted with every man.

When I didn't respond she said, "You want Elsje, don't you."

I nodded.

"She's too interested in her silly ideas about becoming a doctor, Gerret. She's always going out with Father or working in the apothecary. You and I on the other hand ... why don't I meet you at your tavern some night?"

I laughed, "You don't ever give up do you?"

"Never!" she said. "What night will it be ...?"

"Any night, but only if you bring Elsje with you." They never came.

Not to be deterred, several times I knocked on their back door asking for Elsje and was told she wasn't there. In August I left the first ripe tomato of the season with Mary asking her to give it to Elsje, but I never heard if she received it. In my desperation, I approached Hannah, another sister, when she was pumping water from the well.

"Hannah, I'm always missing Elsje, and I don't know what to do to see her."

"Yes, I know," she said. "Even I don't see her much, and I'm close to her."

"Forgive my asking. Is she avoiding me?"

"She concentrates so much on working with Father that she forgets about everything and everybody else."

She filled her two buckets with water, and I offered to carry them to the house for her. The yoke she had planned to use we left at the pump.

"What can you suggest?" I asked.

"You could talk to Father, but he is gone even more than she is. You could invite her to do something with you then she'd at least have to respond. Write her a note and see what happens."

When we reached the back door, she said, "I'll speak to her when I get the chance. Be patient, Gerret, she's a little inexperienced about these things."

The Nyssens had a neighbor with whom I exchanged brief greetings. He was Tom Spicer and was tall and balding. I guessed he was older than me by more than a decade. He had a distinct English accent.

One day as I was picking beetles off potato leaves he approached and asked, "Why do you tend another man's garden? Are you indentured to old Mr. Nyssen or owe time to the Company?" No person actually owned land in Manhattan. All property was land granted and occupied at the pleasure of the Dutch West India Company.

I spoke candidly, "It all has to do with one of the daughters. I'm trying to impress her by doing the work."

"Ah, it must be the older one. She has teased and bewitched many a heart. I have my eye on her too."

"It's the middle one, Elsje."

"Ah, a pretty one she is. I could be keen on her as well." Over the next couple months, Tom gave me advice about cultivating, soil enrichment, pest control, and food storage. Our friendship deepened and with his help I made the farm produce abundantly that summer.

In August when the heat and humidity had drained us both of energy we shared a pipe as we sat on the ground.

"Gerret, have you made any progress with Elsje?"

"I don't know. She knows I'm here, but she's elusive, and we don't talk much. She waves to me sometimes, that's all."

"You are too timid! You've not given the courtship a chance, Gerret. Tell her you love her. Talk about your dreams. Offer something from your heart. It's like trapping a beaver ... you place before her attractive bait, bring her close. And snap! She'll be yours for the taking."

I didn't like the allusion to trapping and it was strange for a single man to give advice about wooing a wife.

"What bait do I have to offer?"

"Write her a letter. Any fool man can sweet-talk if he puts his mind to it. And I'll deliver it. I'm in the old man's good graces."

He saw my hesitation. "Ah, I see," he said realizing my deficiency. "Let me write it down. We'll find the right words and she'll be yours!"

"Let me think about it," I said.

"Have you noticed how odd they are becoming?" he asked changing the subject. "They stay inside much of the time."

I had noticed it. The two older daughters rarely came to the garden any-more. I thought they were leaving the work for me and was pleased with what I had accomplished. None of them seemed to leave the house except for necessary errands. They had no lack of patients and most of them seemed well pleased with the treatment they received. But the family itself was absent from the life of the settlement.

"Do you think there is trouble?"

"Known them for years but never figured them out..." he said shrugging his shoulders signaling that he was as much at a loss as I.

The next time I saw Tom, I asked him to write the letter. "Not one with fancy language but only a simple invitation. Ask her to meet me at the market before the Fort on Monday. Tell her I have something beautiful to show her."

———

I arrived at the market early in the day when carts laden with produce were arriving and animals to be sold were being herded from distant places. I wanted to be sure to be present whenever she came, whether it was early morning or mid-afternoon. The instant Elsje entered the marketplace east of the Fort I knew she was there. My senses had become attuned to her presence.

She wore a vermillion skirt with an embroidery of vines and flowers along the hem. Her blouse was white with billowy half-sleeves and had a serpentine pattern sewn along the front buttons. She had covered her head with a soft white bonnet. I could tell in an instant that she was not herself. Her clothing was rumpled and disordered, and her eyes darted from here to there.

"Gerret, I'm glad you invited me! I need to get away from home."

The busy market receded into the background, and it was just the two of us. "Away from home? Is everything all right?"

"It's just family life. I'm alright." It was apparent to me she wasn't.

"You can tell me, Elsje."

"I'm sorry, Garret, don't fret about me. I'm worried about everyone else ... my father, my sister, my mother, my brothers ... everyone wants me all the time!"

"We share that in common," I said. "What can I do, Elsje?"

"Your letter stated you wanted to show me something?"

"Yes! Something wonderful if you are up to it."

"Oh, exactly what I need! What is it?"

"It's not here. We'll have to walk to see it."

"Lead on, sir! I'm yours."

She took my elbow, and I led her up the street past her house and the Company Orchards planted on the shores of the North River.

When we reached the north end of New Amsterdam with the palisaded fence and armed guard at the hinged gate, she said, "I'm not supposed to go beyond the wall, my parents say it is too dangerous."

"Oh, nonsense," I replied, "There is nothing to fear and much to see. I've been there beyond counting."

We turned off the main road north onto the bouwerie lane and passed by several small farms and thick forests.

When we walked through a section of woods that was charred and smelled of smoke she said, "What a pity."

"The wilden did that," I said. "They call it bush-burning. The brush makes it difficult for them to hunt because walking on dried branches and leaves betrays them and frightens their game. So the wilden burn the brush. It also encloses game, so they are more easily taken."

"But these trees are so burned."

"It doesn't hurt them. These oaks and nut-woods are hard and resistant to quick fires."

"Gerret, how do you know this?"

"I ask a lot of questions. Sometimes I meet people who have answers." Then I added, "I knew Adriaen Vander Donck and you will never find a person smarter than him."

Everyone knew about him. He was the first lawyer in the New World and was granted land not far from where we were walking. His book and pamphlets about the wilden, the land, and beavers were very popular.

"You talked with him?" She was impressed.

"I met him on a hike and he and I became fast friends. I even stayed with him at Jonkheers, which is what people call his farm." I was hesitant to talk about Adriaens fierce opposition to Stuyvesant, his political views about the Company and his championing the rights of common people. I didn't know her opinion on these issues.

"I want to be like him," I said. "Educated and wise. He knew something about everything."

"But he was imprisoned and jailed for what he did," she said.

"And killed by the wilden on his own farm. You know he was cleared of all wrongdoing by the States General in the Netherlands?"

I thought it best to change the subject. "How about you, Elsje, whose footsteps do you want to follow?"

"My father, for sure," she said. "I'd like to be wise and educated like him and be a doctor. Of course, I'd have to dress like a man to do so." We both laughed. How refreshing to be with someone like me: always curious and wanting to learn more.

We followed the bouwerie lane two miles to the entrance to the Company Farm #1 now owned by Stuyvesant. A crushed shell walkway framed by low bushes led toward the wide and stately mansion at the top of an upward sloping lawn.

"Are we allowed to enter?" she asked as she gazed at the neat symmetry of the view spread out before us.

"We can't enter the house, of course," I responded, "but the farm and gardens have always been open to anyone."

Even so, we felt we were intruding as we walked beside the house and onto the veranda overlooking the farm fields. Before us were plots filled with vegetables and trees. Tall clumps of sunflowers added a counterpoint of red and yellow brilliance. The farm was a neatly arranged grid of crushed shell walkways between the various plots. A small army of slaves of all ages, the men with wide-brimmed straw hats and women with heads bundled in colorful cloth, worked the garden.

We walked the grid and admired the bounty of peppers, squash, and other vegetables. A field of maize waved tall stars of flowers above our heads. I was astounded by the lack of weeds and the neat trim of the gardens

"This could be our's," I said to her. "All of this. Well, maybe not this much. But I could make a farm like this for us."

"After we go to University, of course," she said smiling.

"Of course," I said.

We came to the peach orchard that was my intended destination. The trees were filled with ripe and fragrant fruit. We walked down one of the straight rows between the trees and found ourselves alone. I plucked a rosy peach and she widened her eyes at my audacity. I knelt before her and presented the peach saying, "For you, my dear!" With a smile tinged with the naughtiness of eating stolen fruit, she took a bite. The sticky juice dribbled down her chin and she leaned down towards me to protect her dress from the drops. The luscious tenderness of her face neared mine. I placed my hands on her cheeks and lightly brushed my lips on hers. Sensing no resistance I returned, kissed her and took into my mouth her full and sugary lower lip.

"Nothing could be sweeter!" I said whispered.

She closed her eyes and leaned into me, softening her body against mine. The smell of nectar bathed us in the afternoon breeze. We stood gently swaying her head against my chest and my arms encircling her. We spoke not a word not wanting to end our bliss.

I did not hear the cry. But she did. Of course, she would. A child in the distance screamed in pain ... a long repeated wail interspersed with gasping breaths. Disengaging from me and rubbing her sticky hands on her apron she raced away. I followed her out of the orchard and down the path toward the crying. Slaves were running as well and we converged upon the edge of a hayfield at the outer edge of the farm.

A boy of about twelve years of age was writhing on the ground his legs drawn tightly to his chest. Blood flowed from a wide gash on his left leg. Nearby a man stood stock still and trembling. He was holding a scythe apparently the instrument of the wound.

Without hesitating, Elsje called for someone to give her a head cloth. Kneeling down to the boy she took the cloth handed her and wrapped the leg tightly to stop the bleeding. As she did this, she asked where the mother or father was.

"He has none," was the reply. "He's an orphan."

Elsje wrapped herself around the boy cradling him within her arms. Her billowy dress getting soiled with blood and dirt. Calmly and gently she rocked and whispered to him. The bleeding stopped and boy quieted to moans and jerky breathing.

Looking at the crowd, Elsje said, "Tell the foreman this boy needs attention and help."

"All due respect, ma'am, he don't care. He's just a slave orphan. He don't mean nothing to anybody."

Turning to me she said, "Go to the house and get some brandy, Gerret. We need something to soothe him and kill the pain."

I obeyed and when I returned the care of the boy had been given over to one of the women. Elsje told her how to make a powder of the roots and seeds of Sumach and apply it to the wound. Then she instructed the woman to bring him to her house in New Amsterdam several days from now.

I was astonished by Elsje's forcefulness and competence in doctoring. At the same time, I was still intoxicated by the taste of her lips and warmth of her body.

"He is so young and helpless," she said. "How could they be so careless around children? And no one to go home to. Can you imagine, Gerret? He'll probably lose the leg. Then what will come of him? My father has done miracles for others. I've got to get him to look at the boy. At least we can relieve the pain. And if we have to we'll amputate the leg."

I hoped we'd spend the walk back together dreaming and planning our life together and the bounty of our farm. But Elsje's mind was focused only on the welfare of the boy.

"Gerret, would you make sure they bring him to me in a couple of days? If they can't, would you fetch him to me?"

"Of course," I promised.

It was a promise I couldn't keep.

———◆———

I returned home finding the tavern empty of patrons and my family in distress. Once again my father had drunk too much and he collapsed into delirium and violent trembling during which our patrons left in fear of evil spirits. By the time I arrived he was recovering in bed.

My mother was simmering in anger. "How could you!" she shouted. "You abandoned us to deal with him alone!"

I told them where I had been.

"You were sightseeing with a girl, seeking your own pleasure, while your family falls apart?"

In the aftermath, we kept my father away from the tavern hoping he wouldn't drink. We were wrong, of course. He had bottles of brandy hidden all over the house. He snuck from room to room imbibing or he slinked away to a tavern.

The burden of running *The Wooden Horse* again fell on me. Days passed without a chance to go to the bouwerie to fetch the injured boy. The first Sunday morning after my father's collapse, when the tavern was closed, I stayed at home with my sisters and mother trying to decide what to do with my father. The next Sunday I went to the bouwerie to get the boy and return with him to the Nyssen's home after they had returned from church.

I found the slave shanties behind a barrier of trees. An old woman sat on the wooden stoop of a tiny shack made of no more than sticks and straw. Her clothes and skin sagged, and her eyes had deep dark circles. Several children surrounded her and sidled close when I came near.

"He's dead," she said without expression in her voice. "Lost all his blood."

I was shocked. I sat beside her and told her how sorry I was. I raced back to St. Nicholas Church to tell Elsje. The angel on top of its square, stout steeple glared down at me as I crossed the open space within the Fort. A lone sentinel on the parapets looked askance at my passing.

The worship was in progress. I pushed open the heavy oak doors as quietly as I could. The floors squeaked beneath my feet, and the praying minister lifted his head to see who was disturbing the devotions. His steel gray eyes burned into me as I slid into a pew.

When he finished, and the worshipers rose to sing a psalm, I was the first one on my feet. She wasn't there! None of her family was there!

I remained until the end of the service and then returned to the tavern to serve customers who stopped by on their way home from church. It had been almost two weeks since she and I had been in the orchard and I had no way to communicate with Elsje.

More days past. When we had few patrons, I planned to close the tavern early and go to Elsje. But my mother demanded that we stay open. "We need every penny we can get," she said.

One Thursday morning about a month later as we held teacups to warm our hands against the early winter cold, I could contain myself no longer.

"I have to leave," I said simply. "I'm closing the tavern for a while." And with that, I locked the door to the tavern and walked briskly up De Heere Street.

It was a dry autumn. Tree leaves turned crispy brown and never showed their color. Roads were packed so hard withered leaves made scraping sounds with their pointed fingers as they skittered across the streets driven by the wind. Fields and gardens hardened, their soil cracked like webs made by drunken spiders. The high, cloudless dome of the sky hunched over the world trapping people, animals and land twisted with thirst. We all looked westward for rain.

The Nyssen farm was bone dry and in shambles. Bean plants twining up the stalks of maize had leaves laced with holes, their bean pods yellow with powdery mildew. Blackened apples rotted on the ground. Fruit on the squash had grown inedibly large. Dried weeds tangled themselves over the gardens having spent themselves choking the life out of all plantings. The tops of beets, turnips and carrots were cracked and blanched. Even the prized Nyssen herb garden lay listless and desiccated.

When Tom Spicer saw me, he called over the fence. "Where've you been? This place needed you."

"It's a long story," I replied. "The letter worked by the way. She met me at the market just as we asked her to do."

He nodded slowly. "She isn't here," he said.

"Oh?"

"None of them are here. They moved out."

"Moved?"

"Gone. They took their belongings and abandoned the house."

"Why? What happened?"

"Someone said they hadn't been paying their tenths to the Company. But that's true for many of us. I suspect it's more than that."

"Like what?"

"I don't know. I didn't ask and they didn't say. Kept to themselves those people. Never said much about their family business."

"Where did they go?"

"Long Island, I think. Not sure. Lot of land out there and more freedom from the Company."

"Did she ...?" I couldn't finish my sentence.

"No. Not a word. Sorry."

Mindlessly I harvested a few beets and apples then went to the Tavern, let myself in, then sat alone mulling over what to do next. Pieter, the tailor and old Van Doorn, knocked on the Tavern door demanding to know why it was locked. I opened the tavern, and my life resumed.

———◆———

You're wondering why I didn't go to Long Island to find her. I'm not sure I have an answer. I suppose so much time had elapsed that the urgency of telling her about the boy's death had lessened. The demands of the tavern were a convenient excuse, and I could have asked someone else to manage for a day, but I didn't. As winter descended and the days shortened, it became difficult to make a day trip to Long Island, and my excuse was the challenge of being away overnight.

Absent from the tavern, my father's drinking moderated but he sat at home a bitter and angry man. He blamed us for making a failure of his life. His language would be cause for arrest if he did so in the presence of the schout or sheriff. We tried to interest him in his old trade of shoemaking to help him feel useful but after a few half-hearted attempts he gave up. He missed the camaraderie of soldiers in the Tavern and took to retelling stories of his exploits as a cadet. He imagined most of it, but it made him feel proud and released him from of the prison into which he, and we, had placed him. Nevertheless, when the tavern was closed, my time was consumed caring for him and tending to our family now that I had assumed the mantle of being the man of the house.

As a way of increasing our business, I joined our customers playing games of nine pins on the bowling green that is enclosed by De Heere Street as it makes a circle in front of the fort. *The Wooden Horse,* which faced the lawn, became the center of tournaments and players came to compete from all parts of New Netherlands. We sold a lot of beer outside the tavern, and I was working more than ever. I became a decent bowler even on the frozen ground and specialized in spinning the ball.

Tom Spicer came to the tavern occasionally, and he continued to fuel my dream of owning a farm. It was during one of those conversations that the topic of the Nyssen property arose.

"The place is still empty," he said. "Shame to see it unused and deteriorating."

"What if I asked to have the place?" This thought had been growing in me for some time.

"I assume the Director wants to give land to someone," Tom said.

"You'd be my neighbor, and I could be your apprentice," I said with bright expectation.

Five

New Amsterdam was changing. Originally the Company was exclusively interested in creating a profitable trading post. But the pelt trade that fed their coffers had dwindled, and profits were falling. The settlement had grown, and now the Company had to administer a burgeoning town. They wanted every piece of property, like the Nyssen house, well cared for to promote civic well-being and to add to the marketable foodstuffs of the town.

Tom Spicer and I persuaded the Company to grant me the Nyssen property. We argued that I had proven myself the previous year by my care of the garden, and under Tom's tutelage I would be an ideal tenant. Stuyvesant, who decided the use and ownership of all land, was skeptical about a Snedeker having more property but relented in the absence of another option. He put conditions on his action. His first requirement was that I pay the tenths like everyone else. That, of course, I agreed to right away. And he required me to marry before moving into the house. "To prove your intentions to become a trustworthy and God-fearing burgher," he said.

I agreed, excited that I could have my own farm and in the process raise the status our family. The Directors' secretary, Cornelius van Tienhoven, drew up the documents, and I made a mark for my name.

First, I had to free myself from responsibilities at the tavern. A solution presented itself. My sister, Annette, was being courted by one of our cadet patrons, Lucus Elbertson, whose only skill was soldiering. He worked in the Fort one day in three so I invited him to apprentice himself to me so he could learn to be a tapster. He readily agreed and soon he was able to assume any responsibility I assigned him.

Lucus developed a close friendship with my father. They traded stories about soldiering, piracy and beaver trading, distracting my father from his alcoholic excesses. Lucus had unending patience with him, a quality long been spent in the rest of us. With the announcement of their marriage banns, Lucus moved out of the barracks and began living in our house on Pearl Street.

On a foggy morning in late April I went to Pecks Slip for the ferry to Long Island to fulfill the Director's second requirement. The rising sun lifting above the horizon was burning away the fog and promised a day of warmth and brightness. My spirits were high with the adventure of going to Long Island to propose to Elsje.

I knew the ferryman, of course, Pieter Lucasen, an outgoing, affable man who was a friend to everyone. He was a gossip and loved to know and trade juicy bits of information about others.

"Well, Master Snedeker, taking the trip finally!" he said when I handed him the toll of a short string of purple and white shells. Since I was a small child, I went to the ferry to watch boats navigate the straits and see the boats inch into the slip. I knew every one of the pilots, but Pieter was one of my favorites.

"What is the occasion?" he asked.

"I've an errand for the Nyssen family," I said. He was sure to know them.

"Of course," he replied. "Attractive girls in that family, eh?"

I smiled. "Do you know where I can find them?"

"Tell me your business and I'll tell you their whereabouts," he said trying to tease information from me. I was sure he would tell future passengers an embellished story about me.

"I've a proposal ..." I teased him back as I let the words hang in the air. His face lighted up in anticipation and speculation.

"Yes? ... and who might that proposal be for?"

"Oh, it's not who it is for, Pieter. It is what it is about." I enjoyed the suspense, and he the game of cat and mouse.

"Ah. It's business then. Let me guess: you've a bodily ailment to take to the doctor?"

"Look at me." I said, "Do I look like I need a physician?"

He examined me up and down as he let loose the lines from posts on the slip then stepped aft to grab the tiller and the main sheet. He asked me to use a pole to push us off from the dock.

As the wind filled the sails, he said, "So it is business, is it? A matter of trade perhaps? You're in need of Long Island barley or tobacco for the tap house?"

We entered the channel, and the water livened, the boat rocked, and I grabbed the gunwale. The thunderclaps of the flapping sail in the wind were deafening. I widened my feet for stability.

"Yes, you might say trade is the business," I shouted to him. An offer to marry is a trade of sorts. There was the matter of a dowry and the plan to use their old land as our home.

He wasn't satisfied. "You have to tell me more! I know exactly where the family is ..."

I relented to a point. "It is about the farm they used to have on the De Heere Street. I'm taking it on as my own."

The west wind moved us quickly, and we left behind a frothy wake. After docking at Fulton's Landing, Pieter stood in front of me barring my way off the boat.

"It's about one of the girls, isn't it?" He winked.

I smiled broadly. He had his answer.

"My lips are as tight as a clam!" he said relishing the conspiracy. I knew that clams had their shells open most of the time.

"Go south along the shoreline to the place they call Gowanus. The largest house. That's where they are."

———◆———

What can I tell you about the walk to Gowanus? I skirted forested hills and heights on my left and crossed expanses of salt marshes dotted with small shrubs. The long thin path I followed stretched into the distance and disappeared into the grasses. This was a new world for me. Manhattan was a young, vital town of 3,000 people or so, several markets, and houses lined up next to one another. There were always people on the streets, and the sound of the carpenter's hammer and the wheels of carts loaded with merchandise filled the day.

Long Island, on the other hand, was wild and open, lightly inhabited with small tobacco farms and an occasional mill on one of the many seaside streams. The roads were little more than Indian trails: one to Brooklyn that went eastward to the settlements of Midwout and New Amersfoort and another to Gowanus along the shoreline.

The few farmhouses I saw were temporary structures with loose plank siding, sagging rooflines and surrounded by wild grasses. I'm sure promises of new and secure houses were made to wives and children once the crops were established and profitable. One man waved as I passed by but otherwise I didn't encounter another person on my walk.

A cold spring wind whipped around me, and the choppy bay threw up sprays of water wetting my arms and cheeks. Gulls screeched noisily overhead as I disturbed their invisible nests. What had promised to be a warm spring day was turning chilly with a fierce wind, and I shivered beneath my light coat.

I recognized the house right away. Its size was astonishing especially on this desolate island. It had to be one of the finest homes in New Netherlands. The walls were made of imported brick and supported four chimneys, one at each end of the main house and two more visible on the lower additions at each end of the house. Large shutters framed the windows held in place by black hinges and S-shaped dogs. The three-story building had a tiled roof with a precise and colorful blue and white design. The plants around the foundations and the farm behind the house were typically Dutch: perfect and neat. Off to one side were two low buildings that looked like quarters for servants and field workers. This was the estate of a powerful and wealthy patroon.

I ascended onto the wide stoop and a short woman dressed in formal Dutch clothing responded when I pounded the pineapple knocker. She looked at me, curtsied, and spoke not a word.

"Good day," I said. "I may have the wrong house, but I am calling for the Nyssen family. Are they here?"

She looked at me blankly. Then with a gesture of her hand indicated that she couldn't understand me. Perhaps she was a recent arrival from Africa or the Islands.

I indicated that I would write a message if she could provide me a quill and paper. She invited me to enter and sit at the writing table by the front door. I smiled as I dipped a quill in ink and drew a tulip with the streaks and feathering of the Admiral Sned. If Elsje were here, she would know immediately who was calling. If she weren't, I was in for some embarrassing questions.

As I waited for the servant to deliver the message I looked at the room around me. The opulence was overwhelming. The walls were tiled with a dark marble and decorated with fine paintings. Over the fireplace was a landscape of a city in the Netherlands surrounded by a wide, fancy frame full of curlicues. The mantel, which was supported by filigreed pillars of stone, held tall golden candlesticks. They matched the broad chandelier of more than twenty candles that hung from the center of the room. A rich dark brown brocade cloth covered the table below. The seven chairs around the table had leather seats and backs held in place by golden tacks. The floor was white and black porcelain tile in a checkerboard pattern. A shaft of sunlight from a back window stretched across the room and highlighted the Delft bowl on the table that held a bouquet of colorful flowers.

A hearty male voice echoed down the hallway to what I presumed was the kitchen. "It must be Gerret Snedeker. Have you come to farm here too, young man?" It was the voice of Elsje's father. I couldn't see him as he approached and it was obvious he was moving slowly. There was a step and drag, a step and drag. Presently he appeared with Elsje at his side holding his arm. He was old, diminished, and thinner. His left arm was limp, and his left foot scraped the floor. Elsje gave me a brief and bright smile, but her attention was on her father.

His spirit was not diminished. "What a fine surprise to see you! Are you well?"

I assured him that I was. I winked at Elsje.

"Come, come. Let's sit and have tea. You can tell us what has happened in New Amsterdam since we left." I turned to sit in the dining room, but they slowly turned and shuffled back to the kitchen. I followed.

"What an elegant house you have," I said as we walked through the kitchen. "I was admiring the painting over the fireplace."

"Ah. That is one of my favorites," he replied. "Leyden, before the flood. Unique perspective wouldn't you say?"

Before I could answer, he continued, "It's not our house. This is the manor of Michiel Pauw. The land was granted to him way back in 1630 by their high mightinesses, the Lords States-General."

We came to the back door and negotiated the steps down to the open space behind the house. Elsje pointed to one of the two long low buildings that ran perpendicular to the manor.

"That one is where the slaves and servants live," she said nodding toward the left building. "We are in the other one."

We managed our way along a shell pathway like the one where she and I held hands at the Director's bouwerie. The building we entered once served as the stable for horses or cattle and had been converted to living quarters. The floor and walls were rough-hewn planks. The door through which we walked had wide-open cracks through which the wind blew after we closed it. The only light came from a fire in the shallow fireplace. Mrs. Nyssen sat in a rocking chair knitting from a dwindling ball of yarn on the floor. Three young children, two boys, and a girl were playing with a puppy who was snapping playfully with his teeth.

"I promised them a puppy when we moved here," Mr. Nyssen said as he eased himself down into the nicest chair in the room. "Only last week got around to finding one. I've been a little ... incapacitated you might say. They haven't named him yet. You know my wife, Phoebe? She's English."

"You always say that!" she exclaimed. "I'm as Dutch as you are, you old coot! How do you do Mr. Snedeker?" She spoke with a strong English accent.

Before I could answer Elsje said, "I'll get tea. Mother, do you want some?"

"You sit down with our guest, dear. I'll get the cups. It appears there might be business about you to be talked about!" She stood up and placed a hand on my shoulder. "Children, take the puppy outside, so he doesn't bother Mr. Snedeker."

Obediently they picked up the puppy and scampered away as the rest of us watched them. My drawing of the tulip was beside Elsje's chair.

"Well, Mr. Snedeker, we're in need of a man like you." He was taking a pipe out of a basket next to his chair and was packing it with tobacco. "You want to smoke?"

"Glad to, thanks. What is it you need?" I reached over to the long white clay pipe he was handing to me.

"We've bought land over in Amersfoort, about three miles east near Jamaica Bay. Going to grow tobacco. Here," he said handing me a capped jar filled with dried leaves.

"I know what you are thinking! How can I farm in this condition? I can still be a physician and have an apothecary and ...," he paused, "... I have five unmarried daughters." He left his sentence hanging and looked over to Elsje, who focused on her knitting without looking up. The tulip drawing was now on her lap.

Mrs. Nyssen rescued me from responding to her husband. She entered with four kiln-fired cups; handles laced around her fingers. She also balanced in her hands a cup of tea leaves. We watched as she took a pot that was hanging over the fire and poured steaming water into our cups.

"There," she said as she took another chair and then leaned over to Elsje. "Thank you, dear, you are so good to do the knitting! Now, what brings you out here, Mr. Snedeker?"

I concentrated on putting tobacco in my pipe then slowly lighting it with a burning stick from the fireplace. My mind was racing trying to find a way to work the Nyssen's new farm in Amersfoort while at the same time fulfilling my contract with the Director about the property in Manhattan. If I tried to get out of my contract I was sure the Director would call me a weasel and blackball me from any future in the settlement. Damn, I hated that man!

"Are you okay?" Mrs. Nyssen said. I had been staring blankly at her since she asked her question.

"Oh, yes, I'm fine," I said, recovering. Instead of answering her question, I turned to Elsje's father, "Why tobacco?"

Mr. Nyssen explained that tobacco grown in the sandy soil of Long Island brings in double the value of Virginia or New Amstel tobacco. He told me about the need to top the plants when they are flowering and how to dry them in barns.

"It will take a couple of years, at least. Clear the land, build the barns, plant the crop. But Michiel has offered to let us live here in this splendid place until we are ready to move to Amersfoort." He smiled at me. "And he will supply all our food as well. The good Lord has blessed us with a grateful patron!"

The conversation turned to other things while we drank our tea and smoked our pipes. Elsje didn't speak. Finally, Mr. Nyssen stood up and said, "Wife, take me out back, and we'll leave these two to visit."

After they had gone, I looked at Elsje, who was concentrating on her needles.

"Seeing you heals me," I said.

She smiled broadly without looking up.

Then I asked, "Did your family move here just because your father wanted to farm tobacco?"

"The reasons are many," she murmered.

She stopped her knitting and looked at me with sad eyes.

"I like my father's plan for a farm out here, and nothing would please me more than seeing you, Gerret. I've kept petals from the tulips you put on our stoop in my Bible. They remind me of you at my every devotional. Our time in the orchard I keep close to my heart."

"As do I," I said.

"But I am not ready for marriage. My place is with my father. He carries heavy burdens. You can see how it has affected his health. I take care of him and help with the few patients we have. Thank the Lord for the patronage of the Pauws!"

"But we could marry, and I could live on the farm in Amersfoort. That way you could be with me." To hell with Stuyvesant, she was all that mattered.

"I cannot be a good wife or companion while my father is like this. I have to be at his side. My mother looks after my brothers and sisters, this little house, and, my, what a struggle it is for her to keep us in warm clothes in this drafty place! Even at night, I tend to father. He needs me, Gerret. Please understand. Can you be patient with me? Perhaps later ...?"

I told her about the contract I had made with the Director. I would give it up for her I said. When she heard I was obligated to marry right away, she shook her head, and a tear ran down her cheek. When the next tear fell, I couldn't stand it any longer. I stood beside her and held her head against my chest. I stroked her hair. Her hands stayed in her lap.

We embraced in silence for a very long time.

———————

When Tom and I opened the front door to the house on De Heere Street, a rush of wind escaped that smelled of wet ashes and dead mouse. The two facing benches in the small entry room were still there, and the door to the interior was open.

We entered the main living area. Our footfalls echoed on the wooden floor. Spanning a window an old spider web sagged under the weight of the accumulated dust. The rooms were empty except for a few pieces of furniture: a table with a broken leg, a dresser nailed to the wall, a chair whose rush seating worn to shreds.

"What am I to do with all this space, Tom? I've no money to buy furniture. And what use do I have for three fireplaces?"

"You'll fill it, Gerret, You're just starting, and everyone begins with nothing. Let's go upstairs."

It felt like we were intruding on someone else's private space.

Upstairs it was obvious which was the girls room. Several wooden bed frames were built into the flower-painted wall and had straw mattresses. It was the first time I had seen Elsje's window from the inside. The glass was broken and jagged. I peered through the door while Tom inspected the room.

"Come here," he said while leaning over one of the beds. I inched into the room. There was a sachet on the mattress. He picked it up, massaged it, and put to his nose. "Smell this."

"It's hers." I said, "She likes lavender." I glanced around the room imagining her living in this space.

The stairs creaked as I descended and I put my feet on the edges to keep them silent. As I made the turn in the stairs, I smelled lavender again as though she had just preceded me. There was so much in this house that reminded me of her. I unlatched the back door and went outside.

I was astonished by what I saw. The garden and the farm were not as I had last seen them. Vegetable plants were dark green and in neat rows. The herbs were weeded and separated from each other. At the far end pruned pear trees were laden with blossoms. Chickens pecked at the ground near a newly constructed coop. I expected I would be starting from scratch, yet before me was a fully functioning farm.

"I thought I'd surprise you," Tom said behind me.

"This must have been a lot of work."

"True," he said. "You deserve it. The Lord has brought you through a rough time. I wanted this to be your land of milk and honey. Your new start."

"Thank you!" I said. "Together we'll make it work."

We went back to Tom's house and drank beer deep into the night celebrating our friendship and my new start. We didn't speak of my sadness about Elsje.

———————◆———————

One bright day in early October a ship named 'The Baker's Cow' arrived in the harbor and I went down to watch the unloading of its cargo. While I was there, the Company factor announced there were women on board who could be met the next day in front of the Stadt Houis. This happened with regularity. The Company recruited women in Europe to be brides for the single men in the settlement. Choosing one of them would be a quick way to fulfill my obligation to Stuyvesant.

When I first saw them, they were clutched in a tight circle. I wondered how to introduce myself. I found the captain of the ship who was taking with a couple of sailors.

"Excuse me," I said as I pointed to the clutch of women standing in a circle. "Are those women brought here as brides?"

"That they are," the captain said.

"You know them best, Captain. Which one would you recommend?"

"Ah, well, the two smaller ones are timid and not very smart. But they work hard. Either one of them would keep a good home for you. Now, see the older one, the woman in all those layers of clothing? She was fined for selling herself in Amsterdam and now says she wants to leave it all behind. But she seems to know everything about cooking and household work. Can't beat that for a wife, experienced in bed and the kitchen! The big one, wide in all places, talks non-stop. She'd be a handful but if you want to fill your house she'd do it in more ways than one." He laughed.

"The last two were married and lost their husbands. The one with the white bonnet would provide you all the company you want in bed." He winked. "She tempted many of my sailors into her sleeping place at night. The other one is quiet and retiring, and I know little about her."

I couldn't imagine my life with any one of them.

The three men looked at me waiting.

"What's the name of the talkative one?" I finally said. Perhaps if she didn't prattle on too much, she would be good company after a long day on the farm. I'd find a way to love her and make a life with her.

"Wilhelmina Fockens, from one of those poor, isolated farms in Drenthe. I think she was so bored for company that she went to Utrecht to find friends and she hasn't stopped talking since. I'm afraid she has no dowry. Do you want me to bring her over?"

That is how I met my wife.

Six

At the end of a winter day three years later I arrived home in the dark of the early evening exhausted from pruning trees and gathering sticks. Wilhelmina was adding spices to a kettle hung from an iron bracket that she had swiveled away from the fire. A moist, warm aroma of lamb stew filled the house. I looked at her with admiration. She kept our family together, raised our children, and comforted me at night. We were reliable partners.

Nevertheless, Elsje was a shadow on the walls of my life. When I was outside, I saw her face in the window. When a breeze crossed my path, it was her touch that tussled my hair. When the floorboards creaked, it was from the fall of her footstep. On one a cold winter day I came home and sat on the bench near the front door and Elsje took my cold hands into hers. On nights when Wilhelmina left our bed to nurse our baby, it was Elsje's head that lay down on the pillow next to me.

Several times I heard laughter while I was harvesting pears or apples. When I turned, I thought I saw one of her sisters running from me through the orchard. Even the doctor entered the side door of the house in his black cloak. I lived with two families.

One evening as I was putting our first daughter, Griet, to sleep, she said she had a new friend.

"Who is she?" I asked.

"Alice," Griet said. I was taken aback. Alice is the English name for Elsje. "She's older than me," my daughter said. "But she knows everything."

"Where did you meet her?"

"She goes to bed with me. She tells me stories."

"What kind of stories?"

"Oh, about all the people she meets. She's a doctor, and she helps people."

"Where did she come upon the name of Alice?" I asked Wilhelmina.

"I have no idea. She claims you told her the name."

"I did no such thing! It wouldn't be right." My wife knew of my early interest in Elsje Nyssen.

"Have you imagined yourself with her?"

"No! That is past. Certainly, I remember her, but she is gone. Our family is my life now."

"I think I've heard a voice," she said under her breath.

"What?"

"Whispering. Sometimes in the morning just as I'm awakening. Sometimes in the dark of night. I usually can't make out what is being said."

"How could that be?"

"Maybe it was just my imagination. I was laying beside you, and you hadn't yet awakened. The voice came from the doorway."

Tom Spicer told me once that when the place was vacant before I moved in, that he heard noises in the house. Not just the expected creaking of an old house, more like the moans of the sick or cries of pain of the injured. He thought maybe the doctor's patients were crying for him to return.

We lived with a mystery.

———◆———

When Wilhelmina was with child again, it did not go well. She was ill to her stomach and took to bed most days. That left me with all the household chores. I would have hired help or bought a slave, but those were well beyond my means. I did what had to be done with little rest or sleep.

I loved my three children, Griet, Jan, and Christian, but my work on the farm and in the tavern limited my time with them. Like most families, they were their mother's children more than mine, and they lived in her domain.

Wilhelmina's skin paled, and her cheeks hollowed as the child grew within her. Her feet swelled, and she walked little. She used her chamberpot in bed.

The night the baby was born Wilhelmina was in labor for 30 hours, far longer than her previous childbirths. Her wet hair stuck to her face in long strands, and her body was limp even during her contractions. I waited in the kitchen, unable to see into the birthing room. The midwife frequently visited, keeping me informed of my wife's progress. The children stayed next door with Tom.

As the night wore on the midwife came to me less frequently. When she did, she had nothing new to say, and I could hear the growing concern in her voice. She was exhausted and frustrated.

Just before morning, I was allowed into the room to bring my wife encouragement and tea. I looked at her for a long time. I was so accustomed to her talking that I had retreated into quietness when we were together. Now she was too tired to talk, and I was at a loss for words.

"How are the children?" she asked.

"They're fine. They are with Tom."

"Take good care of them."

"Of course, we'll both take care of them." But that is not what she meant, and I knew it.

In the window, a bouquet of flowers was drooping. I sat on the side of the bed holding her hand. "How short it all can be," I thought. "She's had a hard life and was so pleased to have a husband and children and her own home. She has filled my life with talk, and laughter and children. Everything I needed. We never had a deep passionate love, but we were sure we'd survive whatever came our way."

I massaged her knuckles with my thumb as she drifted into sleep.

"You deserved better," I said aloud knowing that she probably wouldn't hear me. I wished I had loved her more and given her more joy.

Afterward, a tiny sliver of a moon led me to the orchard. At a secluded spot between the trees where the long grass grows and ripe apples drop, I tore up the turf with my hands; then dug her grave with a shovel I had brought with me. But it was a grave for more than Wilhelmina. It was for a life we had cobbled together from the traumas of our pasts.

Two days later with my children surrounding me, we walked in procession to the orchard where we buried Wilhelmina and the stillborn baby to whom I had given the name Abraham.

In the days immediately following Wilhelmina's death, my family talked about what was to happen next especially with the children.

My mother stated the obvious: "I hate to admit it, but I don't think they should stay with us. Your father just isn't well enough." My father was bitter and unpredictable. Children were not safe in his presence. Christian was one-year-old, Jan was two and Griet was not yet five.

"Gerret," my Mother said, "could we send them to Wilhelmina's family in Drenthe?"

"They're my children," I said, "how could I part with them and not see them again? Wilhelmina never wanted to talk much about what she experienced when she grew up, but I suspect that whatever happened was not good."

My oldest sister Annette and her husband, Lucus, were silent. It pained her not to offer, but they ran the tavern and lived with my mother and father in the Pearl Street house.

"Well, there is only one obvious solution," my sister Christina said. "They will come and live with us ... but only until you get back on your feet, Gerret."

"But you and Jochem are just married," my mother said. "Are you sure you are ready for three young ones right away?" Jochem was a recent arrival from Gouda, and was just getting his own cheese business started. His life with Christina was a whirlwind of travel, adventure, and gaiety in taverns.

"We have to settle down sometime," Christina said. "I'm sure we'll have our own children soon and besides, what else are we going to do with Gerret's children?" Jochem looked at her skeptically but nodded his assent.

I loved young Griet's company, and the two boys brought me laughter and playfulness after long days on the farm. But I agreed with my family. They needed to be cherished and raised by a steady woman's hand. It was obvious I could not do that, and Christina was the best solution. She and Jochem lived a short walk away from my home, and I'd see the children whenever I wanted.

Occasionally I went down to the wharf and looked at the newly arrived single women thinking that I might find among them a new wife. But the women were not appealing and no other options presented themselves. Dutifully I kept up the farm, visited my children when I could, and tolerated living alone in the big house.

"Why are we doing this?" Tom asked me one day as he was pruning pear trees in his orchard and I was resting on my shovel.

"What do you mean?"

"Look at us! Two men living alone trying to eke out a living out from this stingy soil. This is no place to make a profit on a farm!"

"But I just started. Perhaps if we enrich the soil with more manure and seaweed?"

"I've been doing that for years and look where it has gotten me. We have to make a change."

He was right. Life wasn't better than it was before I married. I had a house and a voice in the affairs of the settlement. But being a burgher was not what it once was. In the past, only the richest and wealthiest citizens were burghers and with it came power and reputation. But recently anyone could buy that status. One didn't even have to own land.

"But we've worked so hard here," I said.

"People are moving to where the growing is much better: settlements on the North River all the way to Beverwyck, out on Long Island, and I've heard New Jersey soil is excellent. What do you think your father did when he left home and came here? Thousands have started over and so can we."

My ears picked up when he mentioned Long Island. I had worked hard to keep from thinking about who lived there. Nevertheless, the thrill of the possibility reached down to my toes.

I picked up my shovel and turned over wilted summer tomato plants and fall leaves mixing them with cow manure and kitchen compost.

"But, Tom," I said a few minutes later, "how would we even get new land? What would we do with what we have here? And what about my obligation to Stuyvesant?"

He let me stew in my questions as he carried his branches to a growing pile of wood to be burned later.

I untied onions that hung on the fence to dry and placed them in a box for cold storage wondering where I would plant them next year.

When twilight descended, the quarter moon was bright enough for me to make my way next door. Tom sat by a dwindling fire with his pipe. A fragrant trail of tobacco smoke permeated the room. I sat down on the hearth facing him.

"So?" he said.

I had no idea how to answer him. I had obligations and a good life in New Amsterdam, and so many reasons why leaving was the right thing to do.

O n an early September day when the sky was crystal blue and the air was humid, a messenger boy came up De Heere Street summoning me to appear immediately at *The Wooden Horse*. I no longer went to the tavern regularly, so I was sure it was a catastrophe involving my father. I left quickly.

The roads were in turmoil. A squadron of English ships had perched themselves in the harbor surrounding New Amsterdam with the apparent intention of taking possession of our settlement. The Dutch and English had been at war on and off for decades, and we were always uneasy about how close the English colonies were to us. We built the Wall at the north end of Manhattan and kept cadets and armaments in the Fort to defend ourselves against them. In recent years the English had become more aggressive by infringing on our trading routes and by claiming land in Connecticut and Long Island. But a sudden attack we didn't expect.

People were trading rumors:

"The New Englanders are mustering at Wall Street and are streaming through the guardhouse!"

"The English in town have stashed away muskets and cutlasses and are going to massacre us!"

"They can never be trusted, those English. They have staked out houses to sack and loot!"

"We'll lose everything. We've got to save our women and children!"

Of course, there was nowhere to go. We were trapped on the tip of an island. Most people migrated to the wharfs to observe whatever was going to happen.

One thing seemed true: Director Stuyvesant and the English captain of the squadron, a young man named Richard Nichols, had exchanged letters. Everyone wondered what was in them.

When I arrived, I was told Stuyvesant was preparing to meet Governor Winthrop of the Connecticut Colony in our tavern.

"Here? Why here?" I asked Lucus, who had made the taproom larger and more respectable since he had been in charge.

"It is close to the Fort, I guess," he said. "The tap at the Stadt Houis is being used by the magistrates doing who knows what."

"But why Winthrop? What's he to do with the English ships?"

"He is the ranking English official in the New World. That's all I know. Help me move these tables, Gerret. We need to make more room."

A crowd gathered outside looking for the men to arrive. The two knew each other, of course. Their friendly relationship had weathered well the wars between the Dutch and the English.

We removed the chairs and tables and put them outside near the vegetable garden. We left the large serving table in place and put some fruit, nuts, and cheeses on it for the two men and their assistants. Stuyvesant arrived with a grim, determined look and Winthrop ceremoniously carried a letter in his hand. People in the crowd shouted questions at them, in English and Dutch, trying to find out what their business was. But the men refused to answer.

The crowd surged into the tavern and tried to overhear the conversation between the two men. When Stuyvesant read the letter from the English, he stood up and faced the crowd.

Loudly he said: "I utterly refuse these terms! We are obliged to defend what is ours!" With that, he took the letter, tore it to pieces and threw the fragments on the table. He stomped out of the tavern with a thump-thump from his peg leg and went across the street to the Fort. Governor Winthrop, left alone at the table silently left the tavern.

The crowd erupted. "What did that letter say," they demanded? But, of course, it was unreadable.

Nicasius de Sille, a regular at our tavern, shouted: "Move aside! Move aside! I'll read the letter!" He sat down and began to piece the letter back together. Men swarmed the table shouting instructions about which piece fit with the others. Once Nicasius repaired the letter, he stood on top of the table to be seen and heard and read the letter to the hushed crowd.

"...*All people shall still continue free denizens and enjoy their lands, houses, goods, ships ...*" Nicasius read, and the crowd gasped at the generous terms being offered by the English.

" ... *The Dutch here shall enjoy the liberty of their consciences in Divine Worship ...*" shouts of agreement. No Puritan purge was to happen here.

The terms were extraordinary. We were to be freed from the tyranny of Stuyvesant and the Company and protected by the laws of the English. Everything else would stay the same. No wonder Stuyvesant tore up the letter.

When the terms were known, everyone smelled freedom and abandoned the Company and the Director. He was persuaded to capitulate by Rev. Megapolensis and his son, Samuel, as the three of them stood on the ramparts of the fort looking out at the English ships. Stuyvesant had manipulated us for the last time.

One sentence of the Twenty-Three Articles of Capitulation, as that letter came to be known, seemed directed to me. "*If any inhabitant has a mind to remove himself he shall have a year and six weeks from this day to remove himself, wife, children, servants, goods, and to dispose of his lands here.*"

I was released from my obligations to Stuyvesant and the Company. I found Tom near the gardens behind the Stadt Houis, and we started making plans in earnest to leave Manhattan.

Part III
Elsje

Seven

The Atlantic Ocean
Aboard the *Princess Amelia*
Eight Years After the Storm

Thank you for welcoming to this table an unmarried woman traveling alone on her first voyage beyond New Netherlands. Our time has passed so quickly because of the stories each of you have told. My story will have no heroic ship-of-the-line adventures, no high finance intrigues, no explorations into hostile unchartered lands, no daring escapes from religious wars like your stories. I'm a simple Dutch woman who lived my whole life in a Company trading post.

I will answer your question, Captain, about why am I taking this voyage. I'm a doctor of physic and patients share with me private matters, secrets if you will, but none as shocking as the one I will tell you. I've lived my life assuming something happened when in fact it had not. This trip is to satisfy my curiosity and reclaim loves that were lost for more years than I can remember. No, more than lost: stolen from me and covered up with secrets and lies! I am twenty-seven years of age, and I must find out if anything remains for me from what was taken from me.

Eight

New Amsterdam
Eleven Years Before the Storm

When the schoolmaster read from the Holy Book before the sermon: "Suffer the little children to come unto me," I could see my father embracing his ill young patients. It was my father who healed the lame man at the well and the woman who bled all those years. Just as Jesus was besieged by crowds and retreated to a lonely place, so he and I would go to the shore or walk the woods to escape and be by ourselves. Nothing has been finer than those days with him.

"I want to be a physician just like you, Father!" I pronounced when I was young.

My Father laughed and patted me on the head.

"I'm serious!"

"Of course, you are, Pumpkin. But little girls have very important work to do at home when they become women."

Not to be deterred I asked, "How did you become a physician?"

"I apprenticed myself to a ship's surgeon and learned from books."

"I can do that! I can read, and you will teach me to be a doctor." As far as I was concerned, the matter was settled. I would be exactly like my father.

When I was twelve, I accompanied him as he went from a sick house, to a ship to treat sailors, and to the market to buy plants for his apothecary. While my sisters spun cloth, cooked and watched my infant brothers, I learned about unguents, liniments, plasters, and decoctions. They chatted about doll's dresses while I comforted a woman whose newborn baby had died. They dressed up in costumes while I helped my father understand the accented words of a Swede whose musket had backfired and destroyed half his face. While they formed a girls club and kept secrets, I met people from around the world and learned about the correct phases of the moon to harvest herbs.

"Mother!" I said with confident directness. "I need a skull cap and long black robe."

"To look like your father?"

I nodded.

"But you look pretty in your dresses and shawls. Why cover up in a robe? You can help your father just as you are!"

I refused to back down. "I need it!"

"Perhaps you should make it yourself," she said. "Every girl should know how to sew."

She was right, but I didn't like spending my days inside with cloth, needle, and loom. I had three older sisters who made our clothes and the materials we sold. When my father said I had a temporary obsession, and it would pass, my mother relented and let me go with him dressed as a miniature doctor.

Of course, my sisters found it amusing and tormented me.

"You think you are better than us, don't you!"

"No one will marry you, and you'll become an old witch!"

"You act like a boy! No one wants to be your friend."

The more they teased me, the more determined I became. I turned the other cheek and put on a brave and impassive face to their insults. I missed my childhood by being so adult, responsible and unwilling to play with my sisters. I regret that now.

———◆———

I call my father a physician and so did everyone else, but he was not what most people assume a physician to be. He didn't go to a university to learn doctoring, he practiced far more than the bleeding, blistering, and purging that were the primary tools of the trade, and he was open-minded to all other treatments. Typically sailors need doctors when their ship's barber has bled them or butchered them almost to death. Settlers are desperate for help when their remedies and potions have failed them. Every housewife had healing knowledge passed down from the generations of women before her. Every household garden had medicinal herbs. Physicians were the last resort after the home remedies had failed.

Of course, he believed in balancing humours by bleeding or purging patients who needed those treatments. But my father honored and used any treatment that worked for his patients. He learned from them their passed down wisdom about healthy regimens and healing practices. He applied that knowledge wherever he could. In the Netherlands or any other place in Europe, he would have been a pariah and never allowed to enter the physicians guild. But people in New Netherlands were far more tolerant and admired my father's pragmatism. They needed what he could do because everyone was far from home and separated from the wisdom of their extended family. In fact, they consulted him on every kind of ailment. They were not likely to go to a usual physician who would immediately bleed or blister or purge their patients. I adored him.

As you know, New Amsterdam is a trading town where people from all nations and colonies come to make money. The Brazilians were my favorites. They laughed easily and played on the floor with me. The French-speaking Huguenots pronounced their O's and U's in such funny way that I corrected them as a schoolmaster might; then giggled when they continued to get it wrong. The English entered stiff and sour, and I'd mirror their faces until they smiled. The Islanders wore headscarves and long dresses printed in bright reds and yellows. I unabashedly asked the women to share their scarves for a splash of color to my black gown. I was an expert in capturing the attention of adults.

One night my father spoke of the people he had seen that day. He turned to me and said, "Pumpkin, promise me something."

"Anything, Father," I said.

"Be kind and take care of everyone no matter who they are or where they come from."

"Of course, Father," I said readily. It is a promise I found devilishly hard to keep.

Some of my father's patients paid him an annual fee in pelts or sewan, or they bartered what they could. Silver spoons or porcelain plates were frequent payments as were valued pieces of jewelry or a rabbit or pheasant. During dinner, my father would show the family what had been given to him that day and say, "Well, what shall we do with this?"

I was keen on a baby stuffed alligator. A Spanish sailor with yellow skin and angry, open wounds gave it to my father when he treated his scurvy with citrus extract. The alligator was two hands long with a wide-open mouth and sharp teeth. The glass eyeballs were painted yellow with black slits. Of course, we wanted to play with it and threaten each other with its jaws. But the alligator went on a high shelf far out of our reach. "It will break too easily," my mother said.

A primary source of our income was from spinning and weaving done by my sisters. When we reached our fifth birthdays, a new spinning wheel was brought inside our home. Mine went unused and was taken apart over the years for spare parts. The sounds of treadles, twirling spools, rattling loom and talking women filled that half of the house. It was a world unto itself, and I had little part in it. I spent my days in the apothecary on the other side of the house, or I was away from home in sickrooms.

Well, that is not entirely true. Our home contained books on arithmetic, architecture, surgery, fortifications, and hydraulics and I devoured them all. I learned English so I could read "The Complete Herbal" by Nicholas Culpepper, which to this day I still carry with me. I loved "Batavische Arcadia," the most popular book of the day, and I dreamt about nymphs and shepherds and romantic far away places. And, of course, we were required to memorize the Catechism and the Holy Scriptures.

The Company hired schoolmasters for the children of the settlement. One of them, Mr. Oosterman, held competitions for us to learn the Catechism. Two students stood before the others, and he asked one of the catechismal questions. The first student to recite the correct answer would face the next student with the next question until one was left standing.

One day the question was: "What do you believe concerning, 'the forgiveness of sins'?"

I was beside Samuel, Pastor Megapolensis' son, and we raced through the answer speaking at the same time:

"I believe that God,
because of Christ's satisfaction,
will no longer remember any of my sins or my sinful nature
which I need to struggle against all my life.
"Rather, by grace God grants me the righteousness of Christ
to free me forever from judgment."

"You recited it wrong!" Samuel said to me. He was exasperating. How could he know what I said when he was speaking so fast?

"You left out, '*which I need to struggle against all my life.*' That's why you finished first!" he shouted. "I won!"

Usually, he and I were the final students in the competition. His memory was phenomenal, but he was full of pride and not keen on a girl beating him. I wanted best him and put him in his place. We pushed each other to excel in our lessons.

Despite our competition we were playmates. One Sabbath afternoon, when we were ten years old, he and I were together behind our home.

"The Pastor goes first," he said when we lined up our rocks painted as people.

"Not so," I countered. A bug had died, and we were marching its funeral procession of painted rocks to a cemetery. It was a torturous route around tree trunks and over gullies. "The dead are the most important," I said as I carefully put a dead beetle at the head of the line of rocks, "and they should be in the place of honor."

"That is ridiculous! How can a dead bug know the way to the cemetery?"

"Because I'm moving it and I know the way." And move the procession we did, one rock at a time, step by step, to the small cemetery we had marked with stick crosses.

Perhaps I should have listened to my sisters when they teased me about my 'love' of Samuel. But that wasn't true. He wasn't my favorite person by far, but he was a playmate who took me away from my sister's silly games.

They were jealous, and we grew farther apart. They had their world, and I mine.

I must tell you about Samuel's father, Rev. Megapolensis, who was pastor of St. Nicholas Church longer than any of us can remember or, for that matter, wanted. He came to New Amsterdam from Beverwyck to be our minister yet his enduring interest was converting pagan wilden to the true faith. To them, he showed compassion and patience. But he targeted his own 'wayward and perverse' congregation, as he called us, with stinging accusations and damning threats.

I suppose he held us to a very high standard and such preaching kept in check the wayward impulses of people. Yet God put light and goodness in us as well. Why didn't the Preacher speak of those things and lift up our works of grace and charity? He treated us as though we lived in profound darkness and he drove the fear of God into us.

Some of his targets were obvious: drunks, villains, law-breakers, and thieves. We had our share of them and, yes, they needed to be brought back to the narrow way. Their actions were evidence of their wrong beliefs. "Repent," the minister said, "show the world that you hold the true faith of the elect." But nobody changed because of his words. He never understood that compassion and love motivate us far more than fear.

Once he discovered that my father consulted the medical practices of the wilden, Brazilians and slaves from Haiti he became an object lesson from the pulpit.

"Teunis Nyssen," the preacher proclaimed while pointing directly at my father, "beware of succumbing to the Devil's temptations!"

On another occasion, he said, "The Evil One is leading you astray, physician, and corrupting your faith. Your mortal soul is in danger!"

His attacks on my father were out of proportion to what he meted out on others who deserved it far more than he.

"Papa, why does he say those things about you?" I asked him more than once.

His reply was always the same, "We should never question what the preacher says from the pulpit for he speaks the word of God."

"But, Papa, you are helping people. Can't he see that?"

"Of course he can, Pumpkin. He worries that our faith and belief in God are corrupted by our patients who aren't Dutch Reformed."

"What's wrong with our patients? All we are doing is helping their bodies."

"The minister wants us to have a pure faith that God saves us not by what we do but by what we believe. He is trying to protect us so we will go to heaven."

"Yes, but, he frightens me."

"He frightens me too, Pumpkin. Let me tell you a secret. People often say and do things because of what has happened to them in the past and not because of what is going on right now. Do you understand what I'm saying."

"I don't know, Papa."

"Do you remember a couple of days ago that you were so mad at your sisters for teasing you that you said things that weren't very nice?"

"Yes, but they deserved it."

"That may be, but you were so angry that words came out of your mouth that you would never say at any other time."

I was silent.

"You love your sisters, don't you?"

"Sometimes."

"Well, your anger about what they did, got in the way of your love for them. That is what I'm saying about the minister."

I didn't understand his wisdom for a long, long time.

Our family continued to attend church no matter what the preacher said from the pulpit. "Our reputation depends on it," my father said. So we sat in silence, and he did not defend himself. I admired his humility and integrity, but I knew it ate away at him. Sometimes after those sermons, he would wink at me and say, "Remember the secret I told you about why he is saying these things?"

His patients kept coming to him despite what they heard in church. "I do whatever works for you," he said to them. "What does the preacher know about such things?" They loved him for his courage and his attention to their needs.

For a while I wanted the Church to appoint me as a zieckentrooster to read the Holy Scriptures and sermons to the sick. That would have been powerful healing: our treatments and medicines and the soothing and correcting Word of God! But it was not to be. I simply couldn't read that man's sermons to anyone.

———

My oldest sister's weakness was the dashing cadets at the Fort, who came from exotic places like Russia, and Constantinople, and Goa. They were on duty only one day in three, so they often had the run of the colony. Jannette sought them out at taverns, the wharf and the playing fields inside the fort. Often she walked the streets of town arm in arm with several soldiers at a time. Her bodice, frilly petticoats and bloomers she flashed playfully at the men. At home, she barely maintained her quota of the sewing and spinning, and she was often out late at night after the rattle watch announced the curfew.

Jannette and I had little in common. I thought one thing, and she the opposite. For example, she claimed I was ingratiating myself to our father by trying to be like him. Jannette claimed I did it to get a bigger dowry than she and thus a more suitable husband. Nothing could have been further from the truth!

Mary, the next oldest of my four older sisters, liked the church, quickly memorized the Catechism, read sermons, and engaged in endless discussions about theology. The church appointed her assistant to the sexton, and she spent hours cleaning floors, polishing pews, and obsessing about dust and dirt in the holy places.

Of course, she did not approve of my black robe and my doing men's work.

"It is contrary to the order God has established, Elsje. Men do men things. And women belong in the home," she said.

She was, of course, a strict rule keeper. During our childhood the Company laws became more numerous and onerous. There were good ones, of course, such as the ban on hunting south of the wall and in the streets of New Amsterdam. My father and I had seen many victims of careless hunters stalking their prey directly in front of our houses.

But there were other laws that I still don't understand. Tell me why a physician has to report to the Director-General the names and wounds of all of his patients? What was he going to do with that information? Some of our patients refused to have their ailments treated because their names would be reported and perhaps used to their disadvantage.

The Director imposed precise and strict limits on working hours and applied them across the settlement. That might be common in your countries, but for the Dutch commercial needs come first before anything else. Many people resented him getting in the way of business. He even banned doctoring on the Sabbath no matter how serious an injury or illness. My father chafed under the rules and usually ignored them.

Mary was aghast and pestered him for days afterward to confess and amend his ways. "It is embarrassing, Father! What will people think of you? Of us?"

He would smile and say something like, "You are right. I need to amend my ways." But he did not hesitate to do what he thought right when a patient was in need.

I was closest to Hannah, who was a year older than me. We shared the same temperament and became allies for each other in our sisterly squabbles and jealousies with the others. Hannah and I confided our secrets and dreams to each other.

My mother had a similar personality: quiet, dutiful, worrisome and not engaged in the world outside our home. She so absorbed herself in housework, that a full day would pass without speaking a word to anyone. She was a fear-filled woman and worried that my father couldn't sustain us with his doctoring. She never understood the wisdom of being paid in yearly amounts.

"What if one of them dies or leaves town? What will we do then?"

"My dear, this town is growing rapidly. There will always be new patients."

At the end of the day when my father showed her what he had earned, it never was enough to overcome her fears of the poorhouse. When father was unable to pay the required tithes to the Company, she had nightmares of soldiers evicting us from our house.

She badgered my father endlessly about the condition of the farm.

"Husband, you haven't tended to the farm for weeks and look at it! It is a disgrace that you allow it to be in such condition. Mangled trees and weeds everywhere! No crops being planted or harvested. How could you let that happen? Our families have been here almost thirty years, and we have reputations to keep up. And all of us to feed! And where will the dowries for our daughters come from?"

"Because of your negligence," she would continue, "your daughters have to work themselves to the bone spinning and then have to tend the garden. I won't accept this! We'll no longer be respectable burghers in town because of you. We're heading to the poorhouse!"

My father remained silent during her tirades. The storm would pass and later he would bring her posies or a small gift. She would forgive him only to return to her ranting another day.

Our household joy was our twin baby brothers, Denys and Jan, who were born years after the rest of us. I was ten when they entered the world. Oh, how delightful it was to hear their giggles and see their antics and tricks!

I regret that I missed so much of their childhood. I lost so much that I can never recover.

Nine

Tonight I want to skip five years over my childhood and tell you about Gerret Snedeker. Even though he and I were different in every way, I was attracted to Gerret. He couldn't read or write. He stumbled over the Catechism, and he was not interested in medicine or religion.

But he was a man of integrity and decency and was curious about everything. I learned more from him than from all the books I read. He was devoted to his family. He respected my dream of being a doctor.

Of course, I knew he was courting me. The tulips he put on our stoop flattered me. But, my, I was young! I wasn't ready for that kind of attention and didn't know how to respond to it. I avoided him even though he worked on our farm. I peeked inconspicuously out the back window when he was near, but I dared not go near him for I didn't know what to say in his presence.

I wish I had been older when all that happened. I would have welcomed his courtship, and I'd know how to be wooed. That is the way of life, isn't it? We can't choose the timing of events only hope that when they come we have the wisdom and skills to handle them. With Gerret I had neither.

We spent a day at the Directors bouwerie. It was the most romantic time we were together. We walked among the peach trees ... I leaned into him ... we embraced... we had our first kiss.

But we were interrupted when one of the Director's slaves, a young boy working near us, was injured. I treated the boy, but he died a couple of days later. I was afraid I'd be blamed for the loss of the Director's property thus adding another reason for the Director and the Minister to disparage my family.

Gerret wanted me but after that kiss and the boy .... I was convinced I was involved with things that were beyond me. I wasn't ready for men and the places to which they could take me. When my father started having strokes, I was the one to watch over him and help him recover. Courtship seemed frivolous in the face of the serious work of medicine and caring for him.

Gerret was married you know. How could I blame him? I told him that my father, because of his health, had to come first but could he wait for me. Life is short, and he needed to make his way, find his helpmate and have his family. Wilhelmina was her name. A new immigrant wet from crossing the sea.

How does the saying go? "As you have brewed, so you must drink?" I refused him when he needed me and ever since I have had a bitter taste in my mouth.

———

Just as I was fretting over what happened at the Directors bouwerie, my sister Jannette made an announcement at our family schmervond, the social time around the fire before supper. I remember what she was wearing. Instead of her usual tight corset and open bodice framed with frilly lace, she wore one of my Father's high collared shirts that hung loosely around her.

"He's very kind to me, Father, and he will take care of me." She talked to my Father, who was softer and more accepting than my mother.

"But, Jannie, I've never met him, and I don't know anything about his family. We must get acquainted before I give my approval."

"His family is from Zeeland," she said knowing that someone from the Netherlands would be preferable to any other. Then a little sheepishly she said, "He's a sailor."

"Does he intend on staying here and providing for you?" my Father asked.

Her silence was answer enough for that question. Then she said, "I'm planning on going with him wherever he goes."

Wives and girlfriends didn't join merchant sailors at sea! Apparently, she was too infatuated with him to think clearly.

My mother could not keep quiet any longer: "How can you do this to us? How can you trust a man like that? You will leave us, and we'll have no one to replace your spinning and weaving. On top of that, we'll have to find a dowry for you. We can't afford that. It will ruin us. Is that what you want?"

"I have to marry him, mother."

"You have to?"

"I carry his child."

My mother exhaled then shook her head while my father turned his back and stared at the wall. Jannette's circumstance was not that unusual. We Netherlanders may not condone such relations before marriage, but we are a tolerant people when it comes to private matters between a man and a woman.

In the ensuing days, Jannette refused to talk, and my mother walked around with pursed lips. In her simmering anger, she noisily banged pots and violently weaved her shuttle. My father and I kept busy seeing patients and preparing medicines for the apothecary.

One day he and I were crossing the great canal and smelling the bad odor that always arose from it at low tide. He spoke to me.

"I'm worried that your sister will ask you to purge her for an untimely birth."

That possibility had never crossed my mind. I knew of midwives who were accused with witchcraft for doing such a thing. But there were no laws about it.

"Culpepper says that after the baby quickens, it is murder to do so, Father."

"Ah, I see you have been reading. And what do you think, my pumpkin?"

I had never been faced with such a question before.

"I would only do what is right, Father. We should do all we can to keep the mother and child alive."

"Good," he said, "but she might go to a midwife. Some do not hesitate to purge the child for money. And God forbid that she go to an English barber! Butchers every one of them. Do you think you could talk to her and find out what she is thinking?"

Jannette was open with me. She did not want the child. All she wanted to do was be with the father. When I pressed her about who would care for the child, she turned to me and said, "You can have her, Elsje! You love children. It will be an instant family for you and you wouldn't have to bother with courtship which you seem so averse to doing."

"You mock me!" I said.

"No, I mean it. The child can be yours or Hannah's. I'll never give her to Mary; the church shouldn't get their clutches on this baby!"

At least I discovered that she was planning on giving birth. When I reported the conversation to my father he said, "Well, we will see what we will do."

———

Our family had challenges. My Father couldn't pay our tithes to the Company. The Minister continued warning my Father about consorting with the heathen which was ironic because Pastor Megapolensis was an ardent missionary to the wilden. New laws limited the work of physicians and when and how they could practice. I was in danger because of the boy at the Directors bouwerie. And we faced the consequences of Jannette's condition. Living in New Amsterdam became less and less tolerable.

One night Jannette and I overheard a conversation between my parents.

"Good wife," my father said, with a slight slur to his voice, "we must do what our forefathers did: start a new life elsewhere."

"Leave? Abandon your patients and what both our families have built up for so long?"

"It's all slipping through our fingers. Life is too hard and too much for this old body of mine."

She knew it was true. "But where would we go?"

"There are new settlements on Long Island: Bruecklen, Amersfort, Midwout, Gowanus. We could go there."

"What about your patients? How can you leave them? They are our income."

"Long Island is not that far away. I could travel to see them. I'll keep them while I find new patients."

"Tuenis! There are no people over there!"

"But the population is growing. And there are no physicians there. I could treat everyone free of the Director's restraints and mandates."

"How can you say that! The West India Company controls everything even on Long Island. We'd be as beholden to the Director there as much as here."

"Ah, not so. The Company gives Long Island land to farmers free and clear. Sure we'd still have to give a tithe to the Company, which we should do as citizens. But people there choose their leaders so we would make our own laws. Ones that would be fair and helpful."

"But it is unsafe. No soldiers to protect us from the Indians or pirates. No laws or schout to keep order."

"We'd elect a schout and pay him. The Canarsie Indians are much more peaceful than other Mohawks. They are fishermen and farmers and get along well with others. Each settlement has a stockade fence where families can retreat if there is any danger. Some houses are within the palisade and farmers go out to their farms during the day."

"Farms! Don't tell me you are thinking of farming. You can't even keep the one we have here. What makes you think things will be any better there?"

"Could it get any worse than here, Phoebe? We can't stay here. I have a plan."

"Oh, it is already settled, is it? And what exactly is your plan that you've not consulted me about?"

"Do you remember Michiel Pauw who almost lost his leg from an infection? He followed my regime of adders tongue, oil, and balsam and fully recovered. He is so grateful that he offered us board at his home in Gowanus as long as we need."

"And what does he expect in return?"

"Nothing. Except, of course, I'll be the physician for him, his servants, and slaves."

"He has servants and slaves?"

"He is a wealthy man. I know it is a distance from New Amsterdam, but it's a perfect solution. We'd live with him until I get my medical practice and an apothecary going. I'll trade our land here for a plot on the Island. We'll start a farm and a medicinal garden while we are living with him and eventually we can build a home. Doesn't that sound like a perfect solution?"

My mother's resistance was melting. "And how could you possibly do all this in your condition?"

"I hear there are bachelor farmers on Long Island. We have daughters to marry ..." he left the sentence unfinished.

———◆———

The move to Long Island happened slowly. My father finished his yearly contracts so that by the time we moved he had only a few patients in Manhattan.

It was not easy. Our income plummeted, and we scrimped on every expense. We sold belongings and furnishings and kept the essentials. As Jannette's condition became evident, she did not leave the house. We knew tongues would wag if the public saw her. They might even shave her and flog her in front of the Stadt House for being with child before marriage. Her intended husband was absent, and I never met him.

I cared for Jannette. Of course, that meant I was not with my father as much as before, but he kept me informed about his patients and the course and progress of his treatments.

Jannette's pregnancy was not easy. Her morning sickness was severe from the start, so I gave her raspberry juice boiled into a syrup. It helped a little but several times a day I had to empty the brass bucket beside her bed as well as her chamberpot.

As her time to deliver approached, her complaints increased. "Elsje, my back hurts. Would you rub it?" or "Look at my feet! They are so swollen and ugly. Would you massage them, Elsje?" or "Isn't there something you can give me to make me feel better?"

I gave her a tea of feverfew flowers, cordials of quince, cinnamon and cloves, and infusions of the roots of Solomon's Seal. Anything to stay her vomiting. My sisters and mother helped occasionally, but I considered this experience part of my training to be a doctor. I learned all I could about pregnancy and childbirth.

I was so involved with Jannette that it felt like I was having the baby. My back and feet were sore. I was nauseous from the buckets of vomit and her chamberpot. I was looking forward to the baby far more than my she was.

"I'm too sick to make the move to Long Island," Jannette pronounced more than once. "It's boring there." But when it was time to go, our family left our house early in the morning when few people were on the streets. I supported Jannette as best I could as she waddled her way to the ferry and then on the long walk to Gowanus. We were slow, of course, and our family went on ahead to prepare our lodging while we made our way as best we could.

At one rest stop, I asked her, "What are you going to name the baby?"

"I don't care." She replied.

"After all this you don't care? A child needs a name! What are we going to call her when she is baptized?" I was certain it was a girl.

"Baptized!" she said with a snort. "It is a way for the church to own him and make demands on his life. That damned minister is not going to have my baby!"

I'd heard enough from her about the church, so I let the topic of baptism pass. We continued our slow and halting walk.

Frequently she needed to lay down on reeds to relieve her back. I made a sling out of my scarf to support her belly, but she said, "This scarf is chafing my neck and giving me a headache!"

In Gowanus, we were not given the expected living quarters inside the Pauw's home. Instead, we were taken to the servant's shed behind the house. It looked like a home for chickens. My mother grumbled and was mortified about living next to household help. But the rooms were adequate and the servants pleasant and hospitable. We rarely saw the Pauws.

Our new home was a series of separate rooms each with a door to the outside. There were five rooms: three for bedrooms, one our kitchen and living area, and the fifth for a spinning and weaving workroom. Patients saw my father in his bedroom which was also the apothecary.

The manor was as close to a patroonship as there was on Long Island. Michiel Pauw had 160 morgans of land and was trying to make Gowanus like the Van Rensselaer or Van Cortlandt holdings. He was recruiting 50 families to create a village with market, church, and courthouse and we were one of the recruits. My father was appointed the director of surgeons and physicians, although there were no other doctors, and to my astonishment, I was appointed midwife.

Before we had two nights in our new home, Jannette said to me, "I'm thinking of giving the baby to the orphan master."

The care of orphans and urchins was the responsibility of the orphan master who was appointed by the Company. He hired them out for work or sometimes sold them as slaves or indentured servants. He may have been their protector, but it was not a pleasant life.

I was shocked. "But he is ours, Jannette! Surely you don't want your baby to live an orphan's life."

Apparently, she had said all she was going to say about the matter.

———

Our arrival coincided with a portent: a whale beached itself on Coney Island. The seaweed draped curiosity attracted people from all over New Netherlands, who were transported by canoe to the Island by enterprising Lenape Indians.

Some of you at this table are not Netherlanders, and you may not know we believe that portents have meaning. The Almighty directs everything that happens and these omens are messages from the Divine. A minister would tell us what God's was saying in the whale and what we were to do in response. But there was no preacher on the Island so the conversation was lively about it's meaning and what it might portend for the future.

"It's an ill omen," some said. "The sea is sick and has vomited forth the whale as the sign that a flood is going to happen." That possibility was on everyone's mind after the All Saint's flood of 1570 in Holland when many thousands drowned.

Others were convinced that it was a warning, "The loose morals of New Amsterdam will bring God's judgment upon us all! We must change our ways."

"It is the sign of Jonah. We must convert more Jews and heathens."

In quiet and hushed conversations some said it was a sign that Director Stuyvesant's tyrannical ways were condemned by the Almighty, and He had doomed New Amsterdam as punishment.

Our family went to see the beached whale several times, and we met other inquisitive neighbors. A small settlement of shacks was erected to shield people from the sun. When the wind changed, and the stench of the rotting carcass was overwhelming, the shacks were moved upwind. One man and his wife set up a kitchen and sold coney stew and bread. To this day that rabbit stew remains the most delicious and savory food I have ever tasted. My father circulated among the spectators introducing himself as a doctor of physic and apothecary.

Less than a month after we arrived in Gowanus, Jannette went into her travails. "I can't do this!" she cried, "It's too much. I can't bear to go on!"

To calm her I gave her tablets of powdered raspberry leaves, and when she begged for something else, I gave her laudanum and soon she was silent to the world. Her stomach contracted on its own, but she was unable to to push. I did the work of the delivery assisted by my mother, and when the birth came, I pushed the baby out into the world. I gathered her into my arms cuddling her as my own. I cleaned her, put a bow in her wispy hair, and instantly fell in love with her.

When Jannette revived, I gave her breast to the baby and my disinterested sister looked out the window where clouds, brilliant from the setting sun, were shining with yellow and red colors. Other dark and threatening clouds obscured the sunset with twisting and tortured billows. The two kinds of clouds were moving in opposite directions as they sometimes do near the seashore.

The baby suckled for milk, but Jannette was dry. I gave her the usual remedy of Viper's Bugloss in wine, but she was never able to nurse.

In New Amsterdam, there were many wet nurses we could have hired. Under normal circumstances, we would have found a woman who was healthy, conscientious, well behaved, observant, and sober.   But on Long Island, the only wet nurse was a young, flighty, temperamental slave girl from Africa whose hair was a dirty red.   Such a nurse guarantees the child would have a fiery and uncontrollable personality. But she was our only option. My mother, aghast at this arrangement, could offer no other solution.

Jannette, relieved not to order her life around the feeding schedule of the baby, returned to spinning at home and longing for the male companion-ship she'd had on the streets and taverns of New Amsterdam. I embraced her daughter as though she was my own.

After the baby was born a bright star blazed across the early night sky leaving a brilliant trail that lasted several minutes. We knew it was a sign concerning the child.

"She will shine like that star!" I said, trying to generate some interest in Jannette about the child's future.

But she said, "She'll be like our family falling downward and burning out."

When the remnants of the falling star were discovered near Bruckelen and put on display, my sisters speculated that the dead and disfigured rock did not bode well for the baby's prospects.

"It has nothing to do with anything," I said to them. However, I worried about the baby's future.

Ten

Please forgive me for taking so many nights to tell my story! Lord willing I'll be finished by the time our journey is over!

We stayed at the Pauw's house for less than a year then moved to our farm in Amersfoort. The wilden cleared the forest on our land many years before we arrived, so we were able immediately to plant a garden and farm. With the considerable help of slaves from the Pauws, we constructed a modest house of timbers and planking built with the generous help of our new neighbors and soon the farm returned an income.

Most of my father's strokes were minor and didn't affect him for long: a blurry mind for a few days and weakness in his left hand and foot. But the succession of strokes left him with a halting walk and twisted weak hands. I cared for him, determined to produce for him the miracles I had seen him perform for his patients.

Bleeding was the treatment of choice, of course. I bled him from his neck to remove the bad blood that was damaging his brain and from his leg to discharge the poisons that were withering his limbs. I followed a strict regimen when the alignment of the planets and moon allowed it. I made an herbal drink of dried spinach and pureed carrots to produce blood and balance the humours in his body. To address his convulsions and swimming in the head, I had him take a strict regimen of Lily of the Valley flowers distilled in wine twice a day.

In my desperation to find a cure I experimented with new treatments. I spoke to Indians, Islanders from the Caribbean, sailors from Java and healers from Africa, all had suggestions that we tried. I ground roots, brewed leaves, extracted juice from seeds, shaved the bark of trees, pulverized minerals, all to make new potions and salves. Some made him nauseous or light-headed or break out in hives. Others had no effect whatsoever. Nothing halted his decline, but we learned to live with his limitations.

As more people moved to Long Island, my father and I gained a reputation and patients sought out the withered old doctor and the young woman healer. His bodily weaknesses made him mystical in their eyes, and I supposedly had magical powers attributed to old female healers.

The round trip to New Amsterdam took so much time for Sunday worshippers that a new church was built in Midwout, the largest settlement on Long Island. It was the first public building on the Island and we were interested in its construction. My sister Mary, delighted to be a part of a newly formed church, watched the construction unfold. It was a 45-minute walk from our house. One day I went with her and Hannah, and we all wondered why a wall was erected inside the building that sealed off the top arm of the cruciform structure.

"Isn't that where the chancel is supposed to be?" I questioned my sisters. They had no answers, so we approached a man whom we'd frequently seen at the site. He introduced himself as Jan Stryker, a recent resident of Midwout.

"That section is where the minister and his family will be living," he said. "We've decided to build the church first, and eventually a home for the pastor. But this is all we can afford now."

"But it is such a tiny space for a family to live in!" Hannah said.

"Yes, well, that is what it will be."

"Who decided this?" Mary said. "The minister should be honored with more than a single room inside the church!" She was often on her high horse about the importance of religion and piety in the lives of colonists.

"If you must know," Jan Stryker said, "I did along with the other two men the Director appointed to oversee the construction."

"We want to complain about this injustice!" Mary said.

I backed away from her. How could she be telling this man about how to build a church?

"You have the right to do that," he said. "Who might I say will be filing it?"

"Our whole family!" Mary said with authority although she had no place to say that. "Our father is Teunis Nyssen, the physician."

I cringed. Father would be appalled that they would file a complaint in his name.

"I will tell the other two of your intentions," he said turning back to his work.

"And who might they be?" Mary asked.

"The minister from New Amsterdam, Pastor Megapolensis, for one."

Of course. The minister inserted himself and his opinions in everything. We couldn't escape the long reach of his tentacles.

"And Gerret Snedeker. He was granted forty morgans of land over here and has already built a house in Midwout."

Hannah and I glanced at each other. She knew what I was thinking and spoke, "We knew him and his family in Manhattan." I had, of course, shared with Hannah everything I knew about Gerret and his family. "He's with his family I assume?"

"That I wouldn't know. I've just worked with him on this project."

———◆———

A pale and corpulent man approached us on a hot summer day as we watched the shingles being nailed onto the roof of the new church. He had a broad smile on his face, and he waddled as he walked from the excess weight he carried on his body.

"Hello," he said panting from his exertions. "I'm Rev. Polhemus, and I have the pleasure of meeting ...?"

We introduced ourselves then chatted briefly about the construction. My sisters were awed at meeting the new minister and, wanting to make a positive impression on him, kept silent about their criticisms of the constructions.

Mary asked him, "Where is your family? I heard that you have children?"

"Ah, such a tale! I trust that they are safe in the Fatherland. I came here on a separate ship from Itamarca in Brazil to start my service. They went to Amsterdam to visit family and to take a complaint to the Company. Hopefully, they will arrive in a few months."

"You came alone?"

"Yes, but that is not the half of it. It was quite an adventure for me! As we passed Tortuga, we were accosted by Spanish pirates who emptied our ship's cargo of sugar and brazil wood. Our best seamen abandoned us and joined the pirates who had offered them full shares of their takings and equal voice on the ship. I was left behind, and we passengers sailed the ship by ourselves! Imagine a minister of the Word of God cooking meals and climbing rigging! By the good graces of God, blessed be His Holy Name, a French frigate found us when we were dead in the wind. They offered sailors to manage our ship and delivered us to New Amsterdam. Lord forbid that that happen to my family!"

The new minister liked to talk! Especially about himself. I knew my sister's ears were itching to hear about the complaint taken to the Company and about the Pastor's children.

"My son Theodorus is about your ages," he said. "He is the oldest. I have four daughters and a baby boy. I'm embarrassed by this but Catherine, my wife, is demanding that the Company give her the unpaid wages owed for my service in Brazil. I'm just a humble servant of the Lord, and I don't mind living a life of sacrifice. My wife is of a different mind."

"They will find a welcome here, Pastor," Hannah said.

When she arrived months later, Catherine Polhemus was not pleased by her new home: a walled-off room in the church building. Immediately she complained to Rev. Megapolensis, who investigated the matter and found out that someone had removed planking intended for the church and then sold it for a profit. The accused person was Jan Snedeker who was one of the three on the building committee. I knew that Jan Snedeker, had a reputation for disregarding the laws he didn't agree with, and now he continued that unruliness on Long Island. I was sure Gerret would have no part in such thing and be mortified by the accusation against his father.

Our family attended divine worship as soon as Pastor Polhemus started services. Not surprisingly Gerret's family was never there. Of the three thousand or so settlers on the Island, only a few were faithful attenders at Church. Nevertheless, my hopes were raised that he might be living on Long Island or visit his family here, and I might see him.

Was it foolish to have those hopes? What was I expecting? He was married and probably had children. But I felt a fluttering inside at the hearing of his name. The heart has its reasons of which reason knows nothing.

After the church building had been completed Pastor Polhemus launched a crusade to ensure to baptize all the children of the Island. He visited every house and asked about the condition of the souls that lived there. Many parents had never had their baby baptized because there had been no church or minister on the Island.

It was during this crusade that he discovered that Jannette's baby was not baptized. Polhemus admonished us and reported the fact to Rev. Megapolensis to whom all Dutch Reformed ministers in New Netherland were accountable.

Megapolensis used this information to renew his attacks on our family. He and Pastor Polhemus occasionally traded pulpits, but now it became more frequent. Our family attended and once again we had to sit through his sermons. On other weeks Polhemus picked up on where those tirades left off and began to warn his parishioners about the dangers our medical practices.

One evening I confronted Jannette.
"You must name the baby," I said. "She's over a year old, and it can't go on like this forever!"

We called her 'the baby' or 'the little one', and all of us longed to call her by name.

"I know, I know," she said.

"It's not about the baptism," I said. "We can continue to avoid that if you insist. We could call her 'Jannetje.' It makes sense to call your daughter that."

"Not that name. It makes me feel like she's just a little me and that she belongs to me."

"Jannette, she is yours! You can never escape that."

"Stop pressuring me, Elsje!"

"But you are her mother! You can't neglect her forever."

"Of course, I can. Watch me. I won't be her mother." She was about to walk out the door when she spun around and shouted at me.

"You want her to have a name! All right, here it is. I name her 'Alice' after you. And you can have her. She is your child. You worry about her. I'm done!"

She stomped over to the small dresser that contained her belongings, opened the bottom drawer and fished about her clothing. She pulled out a small object and came to me. Pulling my arm up, she thrust into my hand a tarnished silver hairpin with the seal of Holland attached to it.

"Take this," she said to me. "Use it for her. Sell it or make it her dowry, whatever you want. It's the only thing I have from her father. Now you have it all. I'm leaving."

We never saw her again.

Eleven

In the spring of the year when farmers go out to plant, I put on my outdoor clogs and went out to garden. The rain-soaked soil smelled of earthworms and composted cow and horse manure and caked onto my shoes. In the place reserved for vegetables, I saw the tender stalk of a single risking tulip. The rising sun glinted off the marbles of dew on the dark green leaves and the flower bud on top blushed with the redness it was to become.

It was extraordinarily beautiful, and as I lifted my face and felt the warmth of the sun, I realized how many blessings I had in my life. I exhaled a 'thank you' to God. As I looked back at the flower bud, I knew I had to share the flower with someone. But who could it be? Where was a lover who adored me and admired my maidenhood? A man to plant new life within me? Preoccupied with Alice and doctoring, I had neglected the needs of my own heart and body.

I dreamed that night that I was walking arm in arm with Gerret, and he was whispering in my ear. My body tingled from his closeness and my heart pounded. His beard brushed upon my cheek. I smelled ripe peaches in the air. I melted into him.

The dream did not fade in the morning. His image stayed with me, and I saw his eyes in the eyes of patients that day. I heard his voice in their voices. My mind turned to him again and again.

But he was married! He couldn't be my lover and protector! I had to forget him and dislodge him from my heart if I was to find another.

The audacity of the plan that formed that evening filled me with dread and excitement. In the morning I would pluck the flower bud in the garden and deliver it to the stoop of Gerret's house. It would be my farewell gift to him. He had given me tulips and my gift would cancel any debt I owed him. I know girls don't give flowers to men. But if I could be a physician then surely I could reverse this custom one time!

When the road to Midwout was dark and empty, I began my mission. I would speak to no one nor leave a note with the flower. I would place it on the stoop in the early morning wrapped in a wet cloth to keep it fresh. He did not need to know who gave the gift, but for me, it would mark the end of our relationship and the beginning of my freedom to seek someone else.

When I reached the Snedeker house after dawn had broken, it was silent, and no one was visible. I approached the house walking along a copse of trees into which it nestled. The straw roof was askew, and its walls were uneven planks with gaps to the inside. I guessed that Gerret and his father were working the tobacco fields in the distance, and the women of the family were busy already at their looms and spinning wheels.

My heart raced when I placed the tulip on the large flat stone that served as the stoop. A good sign I thought. My heart could still feel passion. Someday I would share that with someone else.

At least, so I thought.

———

Market day was on Saturday in Amersfoort. Farmers, bakers, cheese makers, musicians, coopers, brewers were there every week. Mary and my mother bought our food while Hannah and I set up our stall to sell our potions, salves, medicinal herbs and concoctions as well as yarn and cloth we had made.

What attracted people to what we had to sell was four-year-old Alice. She assumed it was her responsibility to charm and attract every passerby with her bright blue eyes and magnetic smile. She had a remarkable memory and spoke the names of our regular customers as soon as she saw them in the distance. Of course, nobody could resist her.

"What a beautiful daughter you have!" strangers said. Naturally, I wouldn't correct them.

"You look exactly like your mother." And she did. Her hair was wispy flaxen but lighter than mine. She had the same slender build, turned up nose, and bright blue eyes.

People familiar with us knew that Jannette was Alice's mother but were sensitive enough not to mention it or ask about my sister. A curtain was drawn over Alice's past, and we all conspired to make her life as normal as possible without her natural mother.

She used all her charms on my father. When she was very young, she toddled to his chair at mealtime and, with adoring eyes, repeatedly said, "Ooooopa!" until he could stand it no more and let her crawl into his lap. She cuddled in and looked at the rest of us with a victorious smile as though to say, "He's mine anytime I want him!" And as she grew her attentions towards him never ceased.

They were the loves of my life. But I wasn't the only one in love. Hannah and Theodorus Polhemus had a fast courtship and with my father's blessing, they announced their banns and a wedding was scheduled.

Pastor Megapolensis was invited by Rev. Polhemus to officiate and preach at the wedding. Reverend Polhemus wanted only to be the proud father of the groom. The wedding went well but during Megapolensis' sermon, he said, "Woe to you, physicians and practitioners of the healing arts, you hypocrites! You pay your tenths to the church and show yourselves in worship. But you have fermented pagan concoctions, practiced witchcraft and wicken ceremonies and fed them to the faithful."

We refused to let the sermon spoil the occasion. Hannah was splendid in her white silk dress, perfumed gloves, and Chinese fan decorated with long-tailed birds with colorful feathers. We dallied over her hair, braiding it into an intricate crosshatch pattern laced with colorful ribbons. She carried a basket filled with a green garland and flowers. Little Alice had a basket for Theodorus filled with the traditional lace collar and cuffs and decorated pipe that he would wear and use at the festivities the next couple of days. Fortunately, no one said a word about Alice not being baptized.

The following Sunday Rev. Megapolensis preached again. My father insisted that we sit through the sermon. "Our reputations depend on it," he said. As I sat in our pew, I fought to keep at bay the rebellion in my heart.

This time, his topic was Jonah and the whale. "Foreboding tidings have come to this Island. God beached the great fish on these shores to warn sinners to forsake their ways just as he summoned the whale to swallow and rebuke Jonah when he ran away from the Lord's commands. Some have fled God's ways. Do not be deceived! The Lord's judgments cannot be avoided no matter how far you stray or how distant you are from the Church. Sure as the sun rises and sets, the houses of the unrepentant will be visited by the wrath of God and calamity will be certain."

Many people remembered those warnings when the events that were to come happened.

———

After services that Sunday our family was still talking about the wedding. Hannah had returned home for supper as her new husband was on a hunting trip somewhere near the Fresh River.

"Father," Hannah said as she sat on a stool near the fire dipping bread into a bowl of cornmeal soup, "thank you for being so generous about the wedding. It was exactly the day I dreamed it would be."

He was sitting at a small table he used as a desk no longer able to hold his plates or bowls steady as he ate. We didn't sit at a table for meals but in our favorite chairs or stools or wherever we felt comfortable. "Of course, my love. We've made a good match for you and you deserve it. Every daughter of mine will have exactly what she wants for her wedding day."

I smiled reveling in my imagined day until I thought of the service itself. "Only I don't want to have Pastor Megapolensis preach or officiate at mine," I said. "He shouldn't have said those things at the wedding nor in today's sermon."

"How can you say that, Elsje?" It was Mary, of course, and I wasn't surprised in the least that she responded quickly to what I said. "He warned us of the dangers of not obeying God. Don't you think that is always appropriate? At a wedding we want a couple to look forward to blessings and not troubles that would come if they don't follow God's ways."

I sighed. Mary and I were frequently at odds, and these conversations always ended up with her feeling divinely justified, and I saddened by the distance between us.

Hannah, often the peacemaker, said, "Of course you don't have to have Rev. Megapolensis, Elsje. I'm sure Theodorus' father would be glad to do it, and you can be married right here in the new church."

I had to respond to Mary, "I agree that a minister has the freedom to preach what he thinks God calls him to say. But don't you see, Mary, how it is affecting Father?"

We all looked at him. "You are both right," he said, "he has the freedom to preach and Elsje, we have the freedom to choose where you are married and who performs the ceremony."

"But, Father," I said, "it isn't right what he says about you. I can tell it upsets you. Surely that's not good for you."

"And, Pumpkin, I have the freedom not to agree with him."

"And ignore him," I said.

"Yes, I suppose you are right. I don't have to do as he says."

"Don't you see?" Mary was getting agitated. "It will be even worse for you, for all of us, if you ignore his instructions. It's disobeying God. Don't misunderstand me, Father. I love you and want what is best for you. But the consequences of ignoring God's Word are far more severe than a few uncomfortable moments listening to sermons."

My mother, always uncomfortable with conflict, tried to break the rising tension. "Can I serve anyone more soup? Hannah, would you take the bread and offer more to your father?"

"Listen, girls," my father said as he broke off a chunk of bread. "I do my best to please and serve God and at the same time to treat and care for my patients in the best way I know how. It can be a delicate balance sometimes, but I think I've done well."

"It's not only about obeying God, Father," I said. "It is about how that minister treats you and talks about you in front of everyone. It's ruining your health."

"This is too much," Mary said. "The minister is not deliberately trying to ruin Father's health. He says the same things about other people at every Lord's Day service. All of us go astray, and the minister should point that out whenever he can. It is part of the call and responsibility of a preacher. You should have heard him talk to the VanDyke boy a few weeks ago when I was at St. Nicholas Church. Lashed him mightily after the third time he was caught sending notes in worship to his friend, Nels. He's always reprimanding someone."

"She's right," my father said around bread in his mouth. "Over the years I've seen just about every church member getting a correction from the pulpit. We should be thankful that we have ministers who care enough do that for all of our benefits." I looked at my father skeptically thinking that he was only saying this for our benefit.

Encouraged by what Father said, Mary continued, "Elsje, you're oversensitive, that's all."

"Oversensitive? You don't understand do you? Rev. Megapolensis has had a private war against Father ever since his son Johan died. He blames Father and hasn't forgiven him, even if there is nothing for which to be forgiven. I know. I was there."

"That was so long ago," my mother said. "Flushed out of the canal years ago and forgotten by everyone."

"Not him," I asserted.

———◆———

Mary also found a husband: Hieronymus Rapalie, who was born into one of the wealthiest families in New Amsterdam. Hieronymus did not have to work and spent his time hunting, living with the Indians, and sampling the weekly markets around New Netherlands. He was jovial and inquisitive, and when he came to the Amersfoort market, he was drawn to Alice and in the process met Mary. To our delight, they settled on our farm after they were married. He built a large brick house with an imported tile roof next to our humble home. They filled it with imported paintings, expensive drapery, rugs, and furniture. He had his servants and slaves work our farm, and they made it productive and profitable.

I had a lot more patients as the towns on Long Island grew. I say, 'my patients' because my father's apoplexy continued to take a toll on him and I visited patients on my own that could not come to our home. Once again the variety of our patients resembled the streets of New Amsterdam with many skin colors and dresses and languages.

"Never deny anyone treatment, Elsje," my father once again advised, "no matter who they are or where they call home. The good Lord has given us our skills and our medicines and He cares for everyone. We should too."

"We are already doing that, Father, and I'm not about to do anything other than that."

One day I received a letter from the Botanical Gardens in Leyden requesting that I send them native plants from the New World that they would catalog and grow in their extensive collection. It was an honor because Leyden was the premier university in the world for doctors, botanists, and lawyers. I immediately set about collecting and preparing what I was to send and after that on a regular basis I took potted plants to the Ferry Tavern where I delivered them to the factor who arranged for their shipment to Leyden.

On those trips, I developed a friendship with the wife of the ferrymen, Miriam Lucasen. She had a way of saying, 'How are you' that made you want to bare your soul and tell her your secrets. The two of us sat in her tavern or on the dock and chatted endlessly often so late into the night that I slept the night in the inn above the taproom.

Late one afternoon when the tavern was empty, and we had comforted ourselves with a couple of pints of beer she said to me: "How do you feel about what Pastor Polhemus is saying about you from the pulpit? His words are not kind."

"He doesn't hold back much, does he? He's under the thumb of Megapolensis, and I suspect they preach the same sermons. I think a lot of people have heard these things so often that they no longer listen or care."

"But he is a powerful man, Elsje, and he says things like 'witchcraft' and 'evil spells' and 'signs of the devil.' I'm worried for you."

"I know you're worried, but we're not like the English on that matter. Dutch never try witches and never will. I don't think anything will come of it. "

"I wish I could be so sure," Miriam said.

———

On a steamy Monday afternoon as storm clouds rumbled on the western horizon, our family was paid an extraordinary visit. The knocker on our front door banged suddenly, and its noise reverberated through the house. Alice darted to the window to see who was there.

"It's three men, Oma!" she said to my mother who was stirring a pot of boiling beans at the fireplace.

I suspected that they had come for emergency medical treatment.

"Well invite them in, Alice, before they melt from the rain," my mother said.

She and I went to the door and opened the upper half. The men stood under the roof of the stoop and were shaking water off their clothes.

"Beg your pardon, Mam," one of them said looking at me, "better we stay outside under the porch and not muddy your floor. We are seeking Theodorus Polhemus. He wasn't at his home in Brooklyn, and we were told he might be here."

I was about to answer him to tell him that indeed Theodorus was here when one of the other men spoke.

"Elsje!" The tallest one said as he removed his rain gear, "It's me, Samuel. Samuel Megapolensis. Surely you remember me?"

I was astonished. Instead of the stick thin boy with whom I had played as a little girl there stood before me a regal looking man with well-tended long hair and a lacy jabot bunched up under his white starched collar and tied in a bow.

"I've been away a long time and just got back," he said, his voice competing with the roar of the rain on the roof. "I was in Leyden studying for the ministry. I'm ordained now. And, thanks to your inspiration, I'm also a physician." I recognized the smile he put on when he beat me in our childhood spelling competitions.

The sleeves of my blouse were wet under my arms from the humid heat of the summer, and my white apron was bloody from a patient who sliced his leg as he split wood. The bonnet I should have been wearing in the company of men was suspended from an iron hook beside the cooking pots. My naked hair was damp and limp. Couldn't this meeting have taken place somewhere else and at some other time?

I was about to stammer out a reply when one of the other men said, "And I'm your old neighbor from New Amsterdam, Tom Spicer." Immediately I recognized him despite his bushy beard.

He paused waiting for me to register who he was. "We're here for Theodorus. We have a proposal for him but wanted to talk to your father first."

The third man I didn't recognize. He was stroking a black crow feather on his hat and peered beyond us into the house as though searching for something.

"I'll fetch him," my mother said. "We've just started schmervond." She turned as though to go then spun around and said: "Where are my manners? On second thought why don't you men shake off your wetness and join us? You can get dry around the fire."

My father, my sister Hannah and her husband Theodorus, and my baby brothers sat around the hearth. They all stood up when the men entered except my father whose frailty made it difficult for him to do so. The clouds darkened outside leaving us lit by the flickering fire that cast dancing shadows of the people in the room.

All three men sat together on a kitchen bench. Alice delightedly offered them doughnuts saying, "Oma just made these. The ones with icing on top are my favorites." They each took a doughnut and Alice's eyes widened as she hoped there would be one left for her.

"Beer gentlemen?" Theodorus asked. They nodded and were handed tankards overflowing with foam.

"We all live on Long Island," Samuel said. "Tom in Midwout. And Joost," he nodded to his companion, "and I live in Brueckelen. We are Schepens appointed to the citizens council."

The conversation turned to the growing threat of pirates and robbers on the Island and the uncertain actions of the Indians.

"Obviously, with all these dangers we need a schout on the Island," Tom said. "Someone to investigate crimes and bring to justice those who endanger our families."

The men looked at my twenty-year-old brother-in-law, Theodorus, who was using a poker to arrange wood in the fire. "We'd like to appoint you as Schout, Theodorus," Tom said.

"Me? Why me?" he said turning from the fire. The log he was tending rolled out onto the hearth, and he stabbed the poker in front of it. "I don't know anything about the work of a schout! I've never even been a cadet."

"Look at it this way, Theodorus. You know all the towns on the Island and many of the citizens. You have a solid reputation and are respected because you are your father's son."

He balked. "Gentlemen, I'm honored by your proposal. But I'm needed here ... my wife is with child, the farm needs my supervision, and to be truthful, my spirit is not inclined toward laws and rules. I prefer being a free man."

"But you would be free!" Tom interjected. "You would have complete freedom to decide how to do this job and to travel wherever you wished."

"Ah, yes," he replied, "but I'm afraid people would see me as the enemy. They want freedom and wouldn't be pleased that I'd be inquiring into their actions and intentions and then taking them to justice. That doesn't sound like something I'm called to do."

The conversation paused, and Alice bounced into the adult circle and asked our visitors, "Would you like to see my hideout? It's right here."

Without receiving an answer, she went over to the fireplace and opened a stout wooden door to reveal a newly built, brick, beehive warming oven. A rectangular cubbyhole underneath meant to hold kindling was stuffed with toys.

"See?" Alice said. She demonstrated how she was just the right size to fit inside. She peeked out at us with a broad smile on her face a blanket in hand. Her mother's silver hairpin with the seal of Holland upon it dangled precariously from a few strands of her thin blond hair.

The men were charmed, and Samuel said, "I wish I could come inside and visit you!"

"We've never had a fire in it since we built it," my mother said. "She has taken exclusive possession of it, and I've put off baking in it until she outgrows it."

Alice giggled and said, "I'm allowed to have my tea inside too!"

As she pretended to drink from a tiny cup, we returned to our conversation.

Samuel's voice lowered to a more serious tone, "It is children like Alice that we need to protect, Theodorus. Surely you want to be a part of that for your little ones especially since you have a new one coming."

Tom spoke, "As Schout, you'd be respected and could keep everyone safe. You are the perfect candidate."

Theodorus was trapped, and he knew it. If he said, 'no' he would disappoint his father who would relish the new power of his son and disappoint his wife's family who would benefit from his protection as Schout.

Wisely Theodorus chose not to answer their request until several days later when he declined. Instead, Evert Duyckingh, the old former schout of New Amsterdam, was appointed because there was no one else who agreed to do it.

The men drank their beer, and we chatted about other matters. Samuel took the last doughnut and gave it to Alice in her cubbyhole. My heart fluttered as he winked at me afterward.

I walked the men out to the porch. A long band of bright sunlight peeked under dark clouds in the western sky. We said our goodbyes and Samuel asked if he could visit me again. "Not on any official business," he said. "Just to catch up on our friendship." I agreed.

Tom Spicer lingered after the other two had left.

"You know, of course, that Gerret lives in Midwout?"

"I do," I said.

"We farm together, and I know for a fact that he would welcome seeing you again. He is too shy to approach you, and I thought that maybe ... since neither of you is married..."

"He isn't with his wife and family?" I looked at Tom confused.

"Oh, no. It's just the two of us. He has his place, and I mine adjacent to one another."

"What happened ...?"

"His wife died in childbirth. Tragic. His sister cares for his children at the tavern."

I wondered if he ever discovered the tulip I delivered, and if he did what he made of it.

Part IV
Gerret and Elsje

Twelve

The Day of the Storm
Gerret

I paid little attention to the swirling wind as I rode my horse to the East River ferry. When I arrived, I could see the rolling waves and wind blown whitecaps on the East River. I looked forward to the excitement of the crossing.

I had several errands. I would visit my sister and children at the *"Blue Cow"* which was the new name my brother-in-law Lucus gave the old tavern. I planned to go to the Company farm where grafts for apple and pear trees were being sold to add them to the rootstock I had been growing. I would then meet with Governor Nichols, who had replaced Stuyvesant. The English were keen on giving land grants to increase the population of the settlement. I would ask Nichols how I could obtain more land on Long Island.

But the ferry was not running. Pieter Lucasen said that the crossing was too dangerous, and until further notice, everyone who wanted to go to New York were invited stay in his tavern. There was perhaps a dozen of us who sheltered the night while the tempest raged outside.

The taproom had a barrel organ played by a man who had a deep singing voice. He was a boisterous entertainer and as the storm threw winds and agitated the seas we sang and danced keeping our spirits high. Miriam, Pieter's wife who ran the tavern, was a lively, buxom woman who had us clap our hands to the music and dance with her. Beer flowed, and the entertainments went on deep into the night. We were having so much fun that we were unaware of the havoc all around us.

The next morning dawned clear and windless with a bright blue sky. I imagined that the town of New York would be newly washed and inviting. I looked forward to returning to the food stalls, wharf markets, and bustle of people from all over the world.

The ferry ride started ominously. Pieter asked us to help clean up the branches and flotsam jammed around the pilings of the wharf. We bailed the boat of water and debris. Up and down the shoreline, the storm had uprooted trees and denuded others.

When we arrived at Peck's Landing, the city was not glittering and inviting. Rubble and wreckage covered the streets: broken glass, splintered shutters, stray clothing, and trash. Old stately trees that once were solidly in place lay corpselike across streets and fields their arms raised to the sky in supplication. Everyone was engaged in the cleanup, suspending their normal life. The sound of axes and two-handed saws echoed down every street. Huge piles of debris grew in front of houses and businesses.

I made my way along Pearl Street astonished by the destruction the tempest had inflicted along the shore. The sea wall had collapsed in many places, and the surge of the tide had washed away both houses and streets. I scrambled over trees and crossed canyons carved into the muddy roads. The once beautiful avenues and houses on both sides of the canal had ugly and raw wounds as though mangled by a sea monster. Destroyed and flooded outhouses spilled their stench and brown ooze. Boats perched land and looked like dead whales beside tangled flotsam. The lower bridges across the canal on Broad Street were washed away, so I walked northward along the canal to the Beaver Street Bridge, which was undamaged. Then I headed straight toward the bowling green to the *Blue Cow* hoping my family was unscathed by the storm.

The tavern was inland several blocks and uphill from the shore, but it did not fare well. The thirty-year-old building made with rough planking, coarse seashell mortar, and a thatch roof of waterweed and Hazelwood sticks sustained damage. Large swaths of the roof were gone leaving yawning holes open to the inside. My childhood home had been violated and dismantled.

To my relief my children, parents, sisters Annette and Christina, and Annette's husband Lucus were unharmed. They huddled during the tempest in the driest corner of the house drinking beer and singing hymns to ward off their fear and invoke God's protection. When I arrived, Lucus, was out looking for waterweed to put a temporary repair on the roof and Annette was pushing water out of the house with a broom. My mother was cleaning the wet fireplace. My father was lost to the world due to his heavy drinking during the night.

"It was amazing," my son Jan said to me. "It was like we were under water and there was noise everywhere. You should have been here, Father!"

He was right. I fully trusted Christina and Jochem to watch and raise them. But what was I doing out on Long Island singing and dancing to a barrel organ while they were experiencing the storm?

My daughter Griet seemed unperturbed that her home and surroundings were so altered. She had found her doll carriage and was navigating it around the wet debris.

"And how are you, darling?" I asked her as I swept her up into my arms. She wriggled trying to get down, and she reached for her doll. She apparently didn't want my comfort. I put her down and ran away.

Assured that everyone had survived, I set off up Broadway to the Company farm to see the grafts I hoped to buy. Across the street from the farm was the old Nyssen place. An enormous tree branch had pierced the roof and stood upright like the mast of a schooner. It's mangled leaves ripped and dying. On the front stoop, where patients used to wait for Elsje and her father, a lone woman stood her shoulders drooping and her hand against the side of her face. She looked entirely undone.

As much as I wanted to avoid the house and the memories it had for me, I couldn't pass by the woman. She was so lost and helpless. When I approached, she shuffled to me, her head facing the ground. Without hesitation, I surrounded her skinny, limp body in my arms. I walked her inside.

Her young son, delighted by the strange phenomenon of a thick tree branch in his living room, was trying to climb upon it. The mother seemed to have no strength to do anything about her circumstance.

"Where is your husband?" I asked her.

"I have no husband," she said. "He died."

"Have you no menfolk to help you? Or family?"

She answered by shaking her head 'no' as she continued to look at the floor. I was at a loss about what to do for her when I heard the eerie and familiar creaking of the house.

"Is someone upstairs?" I asked the woman thinking that the house was unsafe and no one should be upstairs. She shook her head again.

I looked upstairs and saw something moving on the sidewall. A chill went up my spine. It was probably the shadow of a leaf or bird projected by the sun through the pierced opening of the roof.

When I turned back to the woman, she had her head in her hands in despair.

"I'll find someone to help you with the tree and the roof," I said knowing full well that I could not enter that house again.

On my way down Broadway, I spoke to neighbors whose homes were less damaged: "There's a woman in the old Nyssen place that lives alone and desperately needs help." When they agreed to help, my conscience was comforted.

I did not complete my errands. The Company farm did not sell anything that day nor would they for a long time to come. They sent their slaves to repair the houses of the Company officials and clean up uprooted and damaged trees. Governor Nichols, consumed in the business of finding shelter for homeless citizens, had no time to meet with me about land in Flatbush.

After helping Lucus repair the tavern, and assuring myself that my family would recover, I went to the wharf and turned my face toward the East River. Above me, the gallows from the Dutch days still stood with its rope and noose swinging. Black crows cawed at each other vying for spots on the crossbeam.

On the ferry, people only talked about the terrible toll the storm had taken on New Netherlands. As I was disembarking, Pieter spoke to me.

"Miriam wants a word you." I did not know her well, and I presumed she wanted to talk to me about an article of clothing I had left in the tavern or some other matter. I found Miriam with her arms around a couple shaken by their storm-related tragedy.

When she saw me, she disengaged from them and took me to a darkened corner of the room. She absentmindedly twisted a dishtowel with her hands.

"Something has happened in Flatlands. I hear the road there is nearly impassable," she said. Flatlands was the name the English gave to Amersfoort. "Someone even said that the storm destroyed houses and that people were dead. I thought you would want to know."

"There is destruction everywhere," I replied wondering why she thought this observation was worthy of summoning me. "It was quite a storm."

"Yes," she said then continued so that no one else could hear, "Elsje Nyssen lives in Amersfoort."

She had my full attention.

"She's a friend and has told me about you," she said under her breath. "I promised not to share this with anyone, but she confessed to me her affection for you."

I stared at her as I drew up a chair. I was so intent on what she had just said that didn't even think to offer her a seat as I sat down.

"I'm worried about her," she said still wringing her dishtowel. "There are far too many people I need to care for here but perhaps you ... " She paused.

Instantly I stood up.

"Thank you!" I headed for the stables.

The door to my horse's stall creaked as I opened it.

The two-hour trip from the ferry to Amersfoort took me nine days. The roads were impassable, so I returned to the inn, stabled my horse and set off walking to Flatbush. I climbed over massive trees and branches and made long detours through woods. Several times I got lost and had to backtrack. Small streams that normally were easy to cross were unfordable raging rivers.

I encountered few people on the road. Most of the farmers and residents were repairing their houses and tending to what was left of their crops. The coming winter did not bode well for them. The fall barley, flattened to the ground, was starting to rot. The tobacco crop had been harvested, and the leaves hung to dry in barns. But even that was rotting because the barn planking and roofs were torn away and water drenched the leaves.

Despite my urgency to find Elsje I did not have the heart to pass by homesteads where families faced tragedies and losses. I helped shore up a barn and briefly lent a hand to a man repairing his roof. I lent a hand to a man replanking a bridge that I had to cross. Each person had a sorrowful story about his or her experience in the storm, and I listened to their woes.

I had no trouble locating the Nyssen home. An older man with a face lined with many years of wrinkles from the sun and whose sorrow filled eyes were evidence of a long life of troubles, gave me the directions. He said to me, "It's a black thing that happened."

"In New Amsterdam, the damage is everywhere. Everyone was affected one way or another."

"If you are going to the Nyssen house prepare yourself, young man."

"What do you mean?"

Shaking his head, he let out a long breath saying, "Blackness. Destruction. Death. Beware the place is cursed."

He gave no more information and my steps quickened toward Amersfoort. When I saw the tall narrow house made of imported brick, I was relieved. It appeared undamaged by the storm.

A house servant answered the door after I used the heavy brass knocker.

"Good day," I said. "I'm looking for Elsje Nyssen. Is she receiving visitors?"

"No, sir," the servant said.

"I thought this was the house of the physician Tuenis Nyssen and that his daughter lived here."

"Oh, no, sir. Miss. Elsje was living here for a while. This is the home of Hieronyomus Rapalie and his wife, Mary."

"Would that be Mary Nyssen, Tuenis' daughter?"

"Yes, sir. She would know where Miss. Elsje is. Would you like me to announce you? And whom would I say is calling?"

"Please let Mrs. Rapalie know that Gerret Snedeker is here and that I very much would like to talk to her."

He left me standing on the stoop outside. The day was turning colder, and a raw wind snaked its way onto the porch and bit my face and hands. Brown leaves raced in circles and threw themselves dead at my feet. I was in the same clothes I wore two weeks ago when I left for Manhattan. I had not bathed, and the stubble on my face was rough and unkempt.

Mary did not look well when she came to the door. Her eyes were sunken, and she walked as though dragging a heavy weight. Her voice was weighted and without spirit.

"Oh, Gerret. Isn't it awful?" she was shaking her head in apparent disbelief. "You're looking for Elsje?"

Mary's lively personality was gone. Her voice was slow and subdued. She invited me inside, and we sat on a wooden bench near the front door where people changed into their house clogs.

"She survived. Did you know that?" she asked me in a quiet voice.

"I know nothing. What did she survive? What happened, Mary?"

She didn't speak, then stood up and led me to a side window.

"Look. There," she said pointing out the window.

The carcass of a huge tree lay across the wreckage of a house. Little was recognizable other than the outline of the stone basement and the remains of a fireplace. A few chairs, a cupboard and a spinning wheel from the house had been rescued and lay scattered in the field.

"That is where Elsje and my parents lived. The tempest and fire took it all."

I stared at the appalling scene in front of us.

"Oh, Mary, I'm sorry. What about ... ?"

"Gone. All dead. Except for Elsje. And Hannah. She is with Theodorus' family in Brooklyn." She said downcast.

"Your father and mother? And your little brothers?"

She turned to sit back down on the bench.

I stood at the window not knowing what to say.

Finally, Mary spoke. "Elsje stayed here the night after it happened. But she couldn't be close to the ... the old house." She paused as she suppressed a sob. "The day after the fire Hannah came and took her to Brooklyn."

Brooklyn! I had passed right by her on my way from the ferry to Amersfoort.

Mary continued, "We've lost everybody: father and mother, the boys, Alice."

"Everything?" I was appalled. "Who is Alice?" I asked.

"Her daughter," she replied.

"She has a daughter?"

"Well, she's Jannette's daughter, but Eljse is ... was mothering her."

Mary looked as though she couldn't handle any more questions.

"Can I find Elsje in Brooklyn?"

"I think so. If she isn't with my sister, she would know."

I put a hand on Mary's shoulder. "I'm so very sorry," I said.

As I turned to leave a man dressed in a full frock, a shirt with lace, and tall boots entered the room.

"Hieronymus Rapalie," he said to me taking my hand. "You are a friend of the family I presume? Hermann, my manservant, told me you were here."

I introduced myself.

"Looks like you've been helping with the cleanup. Lord what a terrible storm! Terrible. We are all feeling devastated by what happened. You should stay here and clean yourself up. Matter of fact, why don't you remain here for supper and the night. You look worn out!"

He was right. My bones were tired, and I needed a change of clothes. Whenever I found Elsje, I wanted to be rested and ready for her. Surely she would need me at my best.

Thirteen

Immediately After the Storm
Elsje

"I know death," I had said to myself. "I am prepared for death no matter how it happens." I had seen children pass in their mother's arms, and young ladies in the prime of youth die in childbirth, and the strongest of men whimper as they closed their eyes for the last time.

But this was different. Emptiness swallowed me. I would never see my parents, my younger brothers or Alice again, nor hear their voices nor touch their skin. At Hannah's house, where I was taken after the fire, I was so distraught that I was incapable of understanding what others were saying and unable to say more than a word or two. My world was the tiny space I occupied. It was like being locked in the deep, dark hold of a ship without light or human contact.

I have practically no memories of the tempest. I can see myself sitting with my mother beside my father's bed watching the window tarp rip open by a rush of wind. A wind that whipped up my life, wrenched it from its foundations, and erased everything. I've tried to recall more details when people have asked, but all I can say is that it is a black hole that I peer into but see nothing.

What I do remember was being obsessed with looking out the window of Hannah's house at what was once my home. I tried to imagine what it must have been like for my parents and the children as the tree fell upon them. I dreaded those images, but I kept bringing them to mind so that I could be with my family in their final moments. I lived a strange dance of lying in my bed in a daze, then moving to the window and experiencing the visions, then being so tired I had to go to bed again.

I didn't cry. I know that sounds strange. I had sudden gasps for breath when my throat clenched. And unstoppable tremors when I felt I would never get warm again. Occasionally I had conversations with Hannah and Mary, but each of us was in our separate world. The companionship and ease we once had with one another were absent.

I recalled more than once in those days the slave boy from the Director's farm who died from his injuries. I had not saved him. I failed him, and now I failed my family. Surely there was something I could have done to get them out of the house. Why had I been so selfish by sleeping in the safety of the basement right in the middle of a storm? Why didn't I try harder to rescue them from the fire?

Grief consumed me, so much so I was unaware that death cards had been delivered to friends and neighbors announcing the funeral. It was held at the cemetery of the Flatbush Dutch Reformed Church, the only church on Long Island, about two miles from where my home had been. The attendance was small, and only a few of our patients came. I assumed people had tragedies to manage or had difficulty navigating the road to Amersfoort. My father deserved better.

At the cemetery, I saw how small our family had become. Within a single grave, the remains of my family were laid. As the graveyard attendant shoveled dirt over them, I watched as one twisted, dry, brown leaf blown by the wind found its final refuge among the ones I loved. In moments it was crushed by a shovelful of dirt.

In the absence of Jannette, my older sister Hannah was the one to speak at the gravesite. But she was overcome with tears. Mary, the next oldest was so reluctant that I did the speaking. My throat choked as I gave the names:

"Tuenis Nyssen, born in Bunnick in Utrecht.
Phoebe Seals his wife.
Denys and Jan, their twin sons.
Alice, daughter of Jannette Nyssen."

The two-yard long, black, crepe weepers attached to our bonnets and hats angrily snapped and contorted in the wind. Mine blew into my face as I was speaking and I pushed it aside with my hand. The distraction helped me get through the few words I spoke.

As we were leaving the cemetery, a man who had been standing beside the church watching the committal approached me. I recognized him as Cornelius Van der Block, one of my yearly patients, whose sickly young son I had treated months before.

"Beg your pardon, Dr. Nyssen. May I speak with you a moment?" He said to me.

I walked him aside so that the others could not hear our conversation.

"It's my son," he said. "He has taken deathly ill, and we don't know what to do. I'm sorry to bother you at this time but could you see him?"

I wasn't keen on returning to Hannah and Theodorus' house and facing the hubbub of their parlor and talking about what had happened.

"Of course," I said as I removed my weeper.

I found the boy listless and vomiting blood. He had had a severe cough and was wheezing.

"It is the foul air," I said, "released by the storm. We must purge him first." We forced the young boy to drink a large glass of salt water then I gagged him with my fingers, and he expelled the contents of his stomach. "He must be removed from this place but only when the moon has waxed fully. It will be safer that way. Burn his clothes and bedding right away." We carried the limp boy to a closed closet where the foul air may not have penetrated.

"Bring a pot of boiling water," I ordered the father, "and if you have some dried mint or thyme throw that on top."

I stayed with the boy through the night helping him breathe the minted steam. At morning light I could tell there was no hope. Blood continued to flow from his mouth, and his coughs were weak and ineffective.

When the sun shone through the kitchen window, Cornelius and his wife cradled the dying child as we drank tea. I comforted them and urged them to move their farmhouse further away from the river.

"I'm sorry about your loss," Cornelius said to me and we sympathized with one another. Sometime during the night the millstone of grief that had weighted me down had been lifted as I tended to the boy.

When I informed Hannah that I had to get away from Amersfoort, she agreed and suggested that we all go to Brooklyn.

"They've set up a shelter there for the homeless, and I'm sure some are wounded that need you, Elsje. We could go there, and it will distract your mind."

Little did I know that the shelter was the home of Samuel Megapolensis. I didn't want to face him in my condition. I had not cared for my hair, my clothes were borrowed from Hannah, and my face was puffy and drawn. Before long, I was so focused on the needs of patients in his house that he could have been Willam of Orange, and I would not have noticed.

Once we were there, I shared a bedroom with Hannah, Theodorus, and their daughters. But I could not sleep at night. My body ached from work, and I was restless. My mind raced from thought to thought: my family, the tempest, my loss, the impossibility of my life without my father and Alice, and the dreadful consequences of my neglect.

One morning as I slowly descended to the lower floor Samuel stopped me on the stairs and said, "You can't go on like this, Elsje. You must get more rest! Let me take care of you. Take this laudanum. It will calm you down and give you relief so you can sleep. Now you go back upstairs and don't come down until you've truly slept."

That is how it started.

Fourteen

The Days After the Storm
Gerret

I was shocked when I found the house in Brooklyn where Elsje was supposed to be. The symbol on the gable of the house announced it was a Megapolensis property: three crosses on top of a rock and emblazoned with preaching tabs and the letter "M." It was a large house three or four stories high and wider than most homes even in New Amsterdam. Why would Elsje go there of all places?

Before I approached the house, I needed to know more, so I wandered up the main road looking for someone to talk to. I had not gone far when a young girl of about twelve years of age came skipping toward me. I recognized her as one of the young daughters of Johannes Polhemus, the minister at the church in Midwout where I lived.

She carried a stick and was rolling a hoop while skipping at the same time.

"What a talented young girl you are!" I said to her.

She giggled. "I can do it going uphill also," she said proudly. "You want to see me?"

There were no hills in sight. "Some other time," I said. "You are Maragrietje, right?"

"No," she said in a tone that indicated I was obviously wrong. "That's my sister. I'm Elizabeth."

"Do you remember me? I'm Mr. Snedeker. I live in Midwout just like you."

"We don't live there now. We live here. See?" She pointed to the house with the Megapolensis symbol upon it.

"Why are you living here?"

"We're helping lots of people who don't have homes anymore. From the storm. I bring people water and biscuits."

"And who lives with you there, Elizabeth?" I asked her.

"My Father and Mother and my sisters. We all stay in one room. And my uncle Theodorus and Hannah. The minister lives here too. He has the big bedroom in the front. See? It's that window there." She pointed.

"Doesn't someone named Elsje live there too?"

"Oh, yes. That's my aunt. She's a doctor."

Elsje was staying in a Megapolensis house! I could never imagine her doing so.

Elizabeth took me to the house, and we walked in without knocking. The front parlor and the dining room floors were covered with bed mats. Adults and children sat in the rooms appearing drawn and stunned. Untended chamber pots filled the house with an unpleasant smell.

In one corner I saw Reverend Polhemus praying over a patient. When he saw me, he arose, Bible in hand, and walked over to me.

"Have you come to help?" he asked. "There is so much to do."

"Well ... yes. I can help." Of that, I wasn't so sure. I was never comfortable in the presence of distraught and wounded people.

"And I've come to find the doctor. Do you know where she is?"

"Thank you for coming. You can start by emptying those chamber pots. Rinse them in the pot of lye and water outside. It will keep the odor down."

"And the doctor?" I asked.

"She is not here. She left yesterday. Many people need her help especially on the shore where the storm damage was the worst. She is probably down there, Gravesend maybe. She might return today or tomorrow or several days hence. There's much you can do around here while you wait for her."

At that point, I felt obligated to clean the chamber pots. On one of my trips carrying them to an outside cesspool, I saw a tall man conversing with a couple of servant girls. I recognized him instantly even though I hadn't seen him in many years. Samuel Megapolensis was dressed in the long cassock of a clergyman. I felt the familiar rush of jealousy of years ago when he entertained Elsje with his humor and good looks.

I tried to put the pieces of the puzzle together. Whose house was this, Reverend Megapolensis' or his son Samuel's? Why did he turn his beautiful home into a shelter? How could Elsje allow herself to be taken in by any clergyman, especially a Megapolensis, after what she had experienced from their hands? How could she be caring for patients after what had happened to her?

I continued my unpleasant chore. When I crossed the path of one of the servant girls to whom Samuel had been talking, I stopped her.

"Can you tell me who you were talking to?"

"Yes, sir. That's the master of the house."

"He is a clergyman I presume?"

"Yes, sir. And a physician."

A physician too! His black cassock could be for either a clergyman or a physician.

When I finished with the chamber pots, I found Elizabeth and asked her to tell her father that I had an errand to do. I set off for Gravesend to find Elsje as quickly as possible.

The Kings Road out of Brooklyn splits after the small settlement of Boswijck that the English call Bedford. I followed the south road that goes past Midwout toward Gravesend. The road was a narrow path but cleared of storm damage. Carcasses of dead trees were piled along the edge of the path.

The clear sky that late afternoon was accompanied by a deepening cold that would be the first freeze of the season. At nightfall, I made it to my house in Midwout finding it cold and dark intending to sleep the night there and set off as early as I could in the morning. In the distance, a warm glow of light come from Tom Spicer's small house. Under normal circumstances, I would have joined him for a stein of beer. But my mind was addled and confused by the revelations of the day. I needed time to sift through my questions and plan my approach to Elsje. I curled under my down comforter and pulled a pillow over my head.

I was awake the whole night thinking about what was to come.

———◆———

The destruction from the storm increased as I approached Gravesend. The tall grasses of the marshes were flattened and in their place flotsam and jetsam were pushed up against the sandy shores. In one inlet a dozen fishing skiffs heaped against one another their masts a tangled pile looking like discarded sticks and branches. Most of the houses were severely damaged so as to be unlivable. The storm seemed to have unleashed the worst of its fury on the South shoreline.

The square, wooden palisade that surrounded Gravesend had collapsed. In the central yard, amid fallen trees, was an undamaged meetinghouse. The survivors of the storm had gathered there, so I headed in that direction.

The meetinghouse was a shelter for those made homeless by the storm. The pews, once filled with the religious fervor of the Anabaptists and the silence of Quakers, now were home to the distressed and injured. The room smelled of unwashed people despite the open windows.

I stood at the narrow front door and peered inside. In a moment I saw Elsje. She was dressed in the modest, black dress of one who is grieving. Tendrils of wet blond hair unbound by her braids and bonnet draped over her face. Her eyes were bleary and sunken.

I observed her from a distance admiring her. She moved from person to person doing less doctoring than supporting people who seemed stunned and lost. She whispered gently to them, held their hands, and often gave them a hug. Eventually, she headed for the door. When she saw me, her eyes widened, and she cupped her hands over her mouth and nose. She burst out crying. I went to her and she collapsed in my arms.

Slowly and gently I guided her outside. Three men occupying a bench on the front stoop yielded their places. We sat down. Side by side, her head cradled in my chest, I let her emotions run their course until they ebbed away.

I comforted her with whispers: "All will be well." "You are no longer alone."

Finally, she disentangled herself from me and took my kerchief to dry her wet face. She looked uno at me and said one word, "Gerret." Then she snuggled into me again. I poured my body around her.

"I know what happened," I said. "You need to get away from all this."

She looked up at me her eyes glistening.

"I'm needed here," she said.

"Yes, you are," I conceded.

She remained silent as though trying to grasp an idea that eluded her.

"You are going to drown here, Elsje. You must care for yourself. I'll help you."

I held her head tightly to my chest to protect her from the cold gusty wind. We fit together as though made for each other.

Eventually, she calmed and said, "I must go back inside."

I said, "No, you need rest. Where are you staying?"

"In there," she said meaning with the patients in the meetinghouse.

"Not tonight. I'll find us a place where you can get some sleep."

And I did. Men had erected makeshift tents around the meetinghouse for the displaced persons that wandered aimlessly through town. I obtained one of those, and that is how Elsje and I spent our first night together our bodies clasped tightly to ward off the harsh world outside.

She did not sleep well and startled awake several times trembling. I calmed her until she relaxed. As we lay there with her body curled within mine, I thought to myself: "This is what God has called me to do. To care for this extraordinary woman."

In the morning as she turned to go back to the meetinghouse and her patient I said, "How can I help you?"

"Stay beside me," she said. "I have much for you to do. And," she paused, "don't leave me."

As we walked into the tumult of the meetinghouse hospital, I felt entirely incapable of giving the comfort and solace people needed. Staying beside her was not going to be easy. But I was inspired and encouraged to do so once I saw how well she calmed her patients and how competent she was.

———

There were times though when the strain she was enduring showed through. I was with her when a man told her, "My family has suffered so much that I'm going to put a torch to the house to drive away the sickness and the memories." It was a common practice that people followed with reluctance.

Elsje didn't respond to him normally. She stared into the air as though she was all by herself. A few silent moments passed, and the man and I looked at each other surprised by Elsje's distance from us.

"Elsje?" I whispered to her.

She still was in her reverie, so I placed my hand on her forearm. That seemed to awaken her.

"I'm ... I'm sorry," she said. "Take chamomile tea with mint twice at least twice a day. That should help."

Gently I said to her, "We were talking about burning this man's house."

"Oh," she said nodding her head, "the house." I could see that her mind was still somewhere else. Then, without excusing herself, she walked rapidly toward the back corner of the room where she turned her back to everyone and put her hands on her face.

I came up close behind her and whispered into her ear, "Are you all right?"

"I can't think ... I don't remember what I'm doing." She let out a long breath and leaned backward into me. I could feel her body shaking.

"Shhh," I said to her. "You're not alone. I'm with you."

Fifteen

Elsje

I arrived in Gravesend with no instruments or medicines, so I improvised. Gerret helped by finding what I needed. He was my constant companion and fetched buckets of water, emptied chamber pots, or found rags to use as bandages.

Amid the damage and death, a saving grace was uncovered. Among the shelves of goods stored in the basement were medicines, recently unloaded from a ship from the Netherlands, and I used every one of them. But people often misused what I gave them or found ways to steal medicines from the meetinghouse during those chaotic days. The suffering that resulted from that abuse was a terrible price to pay in addition to the other mounting losses.

As inevitable as the grave follows death so did disease follow the storm. Brooklyn was visited by a pestilence, and I was afraid it was the plague that had recently ravished London. But instead, it was cholera, infections, consumption and stomach ailments. Dead animals rotted in the streams and rivers, and foul humours arose from the waters bringing illness. Houses were boarded up and sealed against the intrusion of the deadly airs.

The muddy pathways to the burying grounds were worn deep by the wheels of the undertakers' wagon. In towns like Gravesend communal burying pits were dug to accommodate the bodies discovered among the ruins of houses. One Sabbath day in Brooklyn the sad news of the uncovering of twenty bodies the night before caused the bell to ring all day and the funeral biers to make repeated trips to Finsbury Field near Cripplegate.

People turned to me for advice as I was the only doctor in Gravesend. I told them to kill stray animals, isolate themselves from their sick neighbors, stay away from foul water, and spread lime where the dead had laid.

During the day I could keep thoughts of my family and our destroyed house at bay. But at night despite my exhaustion, I couldn't sleep. My usual remedy for sleeplessness was a syrup of poppy flowers, but it wasn't working so I took laudanum to calm myself. It dulled my senses and dampened the storms inside me.

I pushed myself forward to deal with one patient at a time and lost track of the days in Gravesend.

After ten days or so Gerret said to me, "I'm taking you to my farm. We need to take care of your health."

"But, Gerret, people need me!" I said imagining what would happen if these people had no doctor.

"Yes, but you won't be able to help anybody if you continue like this. You are coming with me!"

I had no energy to resist him.

Gerret found an abandoned wagon for our trip to Midwout. "I just commandeered it," he said. "There is green mold on the bed and the wheels squeak from lack of use so I don't think it will be missed." He put a wool blanket on the cracked black leather seat to shield us from the cotton stuffing that was still soaking from the storm. In two hours we arrived at his small cabin whose front stoop was on the Amersfoort Road.

Gerret brushed aside the branches and leaves that had been tossed by the storm onto the porch. He opened the crude plank door then helped me down from the wagon. I was groggy from the ride from Gravesend and he guided me inside the dark, shuttered, single room cabin whose peacefulness and musty smell enveloped me with a welcome stillness.

"It's not much," he announced. "I've been living here alone. You lie down on the bed while I open up." He motioned toward the bed in the back corner of the room. I placed my satchel of belongings on the bed and watched as it sank into the down comforter.

"Ohh," I sighed as I snuggled in next to the satchel. "It is soft compared to the ground in Gravesend!" I bunched up the comforter to support my head, curled my body into a ball and closed my eyes.

When I awoke, moving dust in the air was bright with morning sun-beams, and I shielded my eyes from the direct sunlight. Gerret sat at the table slicing food with a knife and looked up when I stirred.

"You must be hungry," he said. "I'm fixing rabbit stew."

His mention of food made me realize that my stomach ached.

"When did we last eat?" I asked groggily.

"Well, I ate last night. Your last meal was yesterday morning."

"Yesterday?"

"You've slept since yesterday morning," he said with a smile. "Except, of course, when you went to the outhouse. I gave you a little broth then."

I looked at him quizzically.

"I didn't think you'd remember. Your eyes were at half-mast, and you said not a word."

I stretched and sat up wiggling my toes. I could tell the plank floor be-neath me hadn't been polished or cleaned with sand in months.

"What would you like to eat with the stew?" he asked.

"Strawberries!" I teased him knowing full well they were out of season.

"Love to give them to you," he laughed. "But even Willem of Orange himself couldn't get strawberries this time of year."

"Then stew it will be," I replied.

"How about a peach first?" He fetched a rosy pink orb from a bowl and handed it to me as I sat on the bed. I bit into it. Nectar dripped down my forearm. I leaned over to let the drips fall on the floor instead of the bed.

"Sorry," I said to him looking at the wet and now sticky floor.

He laughed. "It doesn't matter. Someday it will be tile covered and then I'll expect you to be a paragon of cleanliness and propriety."

"Ah, so you think I'm slovenly!" I said feigning offense at what he had said.

"My dear, Elsje, how sweet you tasted when we were in the Director's peach orchard years ago. Remember?"

"I do," I confessed looking at him. Our conversation paused while we remembered both the good and the bad of that day.

"Come," he said unable to look into my eyes any longer, "have some fresh milk. While you were sleeping, I went to Tom's farm. We share a cow that produces enough milk for both of us."

While he spread out the logs and embers and added bits of rabbit to the stew, I sat on the bed drinking sweet milk. I looked around the cabin.

Everything was made for a house larger than the current single room. The thick ceiling beams of dark wood were stout enough to support an upper floor that did not yet exist. The fireplace was as wide as the room and if filled with blazing wood would overheat the room like a blacksmith's furnace. Three of the walls were wainscoted on the lower half and plastered above. It seemed odd that a bachelor farmer would care about such luxury. The fourth wall was stacked, rough timber giving the house an unfinished look.

Gerret noticed me looking at the wall and said, "When I have a family again I'll build the rest of the house out that direction."

As I stared at the wall, a growling hollowness grew in my stomach. We'd both lost families. He must feel the same emptiness I felt.

He gave me a bowl of stew. I thought of my family that no longer existed. My eyes were wetting. "I'm no longer hungry. Sorry, Gerret."

"You've got to be hungry."

He knelt down beside me on the bed and put his arm around my shoulders trying to comfort me.

"Come," he said cheerily. "Let's go for a walk. Maybe that will bring back your appetite. It's a beautiful day and I'll show you around the farm."

When I stood up a sharp pain raced up my leg and I immediately sat down again. He looked at me quizzically.

"I cut my foot. I don't exactly remember when." I had paid little attention to it. I took off the cloth that I had wrapped around my foot days before. It was caked in dried blood and the wound was infected and oozing. "I'm not a very good patient," I confessed. "I don't do for myself what I tell my patients to do. I knew it was throbbing and I've tried to ignore it."

Gerret didn't look at the wound.

"Do you have brandy, Gerret? I think I'm going to need it."

"Of course, but what are you going to do?"

"You are going to cauterize this wound, Gerret, and I'm going to try not to be a baby about it. That's why I need the brandy and on this empty stomach I should be feeling dreamy fast."

Gerret panicked.

"It's all right," I comforted him, "I've done this before and I'll tell you exactly what to do. Now, find something that is flat and made of iron and I'll start on the brandy."

"I can't do that! Especially to you."

"It will only get worse if you don't. And, yes, Gerret, you can do this."

After Gerret had found an iron knife he heated it in the fire then knelt down before me and looked so piteous that my heart melted. He picked up my foot and cradled it gently on his thigh.

"Close your eyes, Gerret, and I'll guide the iron to the right place."

He did what he had to do and when I complemented him he smiled sheepishly and said, "Please don't ask me to do that again!"

The pain in my foot was excruciating and Gerret covered my wound with bear fat.

A day later when I was able to walk gingerly he showed me around his house and farm.

"Why don't you have a cellar?"

"I don't need one. Tom and I share his. When I need something I take the short walk to his house. It's only a few minutes there and back."

"But, Gerret, won't you eventually need a cellar? Surely your family won't want to trudge all the way to Tom's house."

He paused, "I don't like cellars. I'd just as soon never be in one again."

We walked in silence along the edge of the woods. What he said baffled me. Cellars were in every Dutch home even in the lowlands where water was constantly seeping in. Everything was kept in the cellar: salted beef and pork, firkins of fish, butter and lard. Sausages and cheeses were hung from the ceiling and we had bins for the summer harvest of potatoes, turnips, apples and pears. The cellar was where we saved wood ashes from the fireplaces to make soap. How could a house be without a cellar?

My silence apparently prompted him to say, "Do you know anything about the Tugthuis in Amsterdam?"

"You mean the big prison there? I know it exists, that's all."

"There is a cellar in that prison called the drowning cell. To get prisoners to confess they chain them to the wall or to a chair in this cell. They slowly fill the cellar with water so that it rises up the prisoner's body and threatens to drown him. All the while the schout or jailers urge him to confess his sins. If he does, the flow of water is stopped."

"That's a savage way to treat people! This can't be true."

"I haven't met anyone who has actually seen it but it's like the hangman's noose at the wharf in New Amsterdam. The drowning chair and the gallows are supposed to remind us what happens when one goes astray of the law or the Church."

"How do you know about the drowning room?"

His eyes looked down at our feet walking the grassy path toward the apple orchard where tiny trees had been planted. When he answered his voice was low and slow.

"My parents threatened to put me in a drowning cell in our cellar in New Amsterdam."

I stopped walking and stared at him.

"It was mostly me," he said. "I was the only boy so they were more determined about me than my sisters. They thought I was lazy and disobedient so they kept a small chair in our cellar and said they would tie me to it and let water in through the window."

"Did they ever do it?" My quiet voice matched his.

"No, but I never put it past them. All they needed to do was to remind me of the Tuighuis or threaten to take me to the cellar. The idea so frightened me I did whatever they asked of me."

"Oh, Gerret!" I took his hand in mine.

"I try not to think about it and not go in any cellar, even Tom's. But, of course, it can't be avoided."

Sixteen

Gerret

My heart leaps remembering those ten days in my cabin: the sun shone brighter, the fall leaves were more colorful, the breezes softer and Elsje more beautiful than ever. We walked hand in hand, and I told her my plans to clear the forest to plant rows of tobacco that would dry in barns I would build nearby. We watched the swallows swooping across the sky and the Nighthawks darting back and forth eating gnats and mosquitoes for their evening meal. We looked over the grassy fields that lay golden before us as the setting sun danced with the shadows of the trees.

"I love your smell in the comforter!" she said once when we retired for the night. She wrapped her arms and legs around me as though we were the only two people in the world. She yielded herself to me with soft but desperate urgency as though she had a vast emptiness to fill. Our fingers and bodies intertwined and her blue eyes pierced me with passion.

Often she awoke at night with moans that gathered into screams, and I knew the past horrors had found had their way back.

"It was Alice," she said once, "calling my name from under the rubble of the house. I ran to save her, but my feet were stuck in mud, and I couldn't move. I couldn't reach her in time."

"I wish I had met her," I said.

"Oh, Gerret, ... you would have loved her. Everybody did." And she told me about her 'daughter' amid pauses and tears.

She whispered after one of the dreams, "Something evil was looking for me because I was the only one left. It was trying to get me, but there was no place to hide."

"I'll be your hiding place," I offered.

After the night terrors, she occasionally took laudanum to calm herself down and help her sleep. On those nights she slept soundly into the mornings as I pumped water, prepared breakfast, or fetched eggs. Every part of her was beautiful: her hair in a mist on her pillow, her delicate hand and fingers exposed to the air, the curves of her body under the quilt.

I thought it inevitable that we would stay together, that this was to be our home and our life. One day without much forethought I asked, "When do you think we should publish the marriage banns?"

She looked at me without answering.

"Elsje, God destined us to live as husband and wife. These days have been proof of that. Surely you must have thought about marriage?"

She shook her head. "No, it's not that. I mean ... yes, since I was a child I dreamed about getting married. I always imagined the moment I would tell my father that I had found someone like you to love and protect me. He would be overwhelmed, with delight and we would hug each other, and he would look at me with tears in his eyes..."

She reached out to me. As I stepped toward her, the rough wooden kitchen bench she was sitting on creaked just as the floorboards under my feet groaned. The sounds grated against each other like two violins out of tune.

"I do love you, Gerret. These days have rekindled my spirit. I owe everything to you. But I can't abandon my work, especially with Father gone. People need what I do for them. It is what I must do. It is what God has given me to do. I want to be with you, but I can't be a farmer's wife."

"We can find a way for you to be a doctor and we can be together. Tell me what you want and I'll do it."

"My heart wants you, Gerret, but right now it is somewhere else. I can't give you the love you deserve. If we are to marry, I want to think about you and you alone, but my heart beats for my father and mother and Alice. It can't stop it moving in their direction. I can't give my heart to you until it is free until I am free. And it isn't now ... it's burning for them."

"Let me be your heart's doctor," I said.

She laid her head on my chest. "I wish it were that easy," she said. "I wish there was a poultice I could put on my heart to take away this sadness. They can't be forgotten. And life can't go on as though nothing happened... as though they never existed."

"Shhh," I said as I stroked her hair. "I will wait for you."

Later in the day to distract her I showed her a small instrument about five inches long and two inches wide.

"You'd be interested in this," I said. "It is an occhiolino. It makes tiny objects attached to this little screw look much larger than they are."

She turned it over in her hand and said, "Show me."

"Put the flat back side against your cheek so your eye looks through that tiny hole with the lens inside. Hold it up to the sun shining in the window. What do you see?"

"Just a big screw," she said.

"Ah, but that is not a big screw. It's the tiny screw on the other side."

She turned the instrument over and gaped at the screw. "But it is so small!"

"I know," I said. "Now look at this." I removed the screw and placed the instrument over a bowl of stagnant water that was lit by a beam of sunlight. "You may have to move it back and forth to focus it."

As she did so, her mouth opened wide. "Bugs are swimming in there! I see wiggling things and grains of sand!"

"I've made drawings. Look." I showed her my sketches. "These move in circles, these have tiny hairs like centipedes and these have tails that propel them."

"Where did you get this?" she said wide-eyed looking at the instrument.

"Adriaen Vander Donck gave it to me. He called it a microscope. It was first made in Holland a few years ago by glass makers. People are discovering new worlds we have never seen before but have been there all the time!"

She looked again through the lens into the water. "Your drawings are so accurate, Gerret."

She smiled at me and brushed her hair from her face. "I would like to have known Adriaen."

"He showed me how little I know. I'm going to remedy that and one day I'll be like him: traveling, learning about everything, teaching myself how to draw, maybe inventing something new. He called me his apprentice. Imagine that! A tapper and a farmer trained by the smartest man in New Netherlands. It is so sad he was killed by the wilden."

We experimented looking at other objects through the occhiolino.

"What dream do you have for your future, Elsje? What do you want to make sure you do someday?"

"I want to be a respected doctor and accepted into the Amsterdam Guild of Physicians."

"If you weren't a woman I've no doubt you could do that."

"I want to try," she said.

"But, Elsje, what do you want for yourself? Something that is just for you?"

She thought for a moment. "I would like to go to the Botanical Gardens in Leyden and see the plants they have collected and find out what they've done with the herbs and bulbs I've sent them." There was a faraway look in her eyes.

"We'll do it! I'd love to see it too. What else?"

"I want to be present at one of Dr. Tulp's dissections."

"Dr. Tulp?"

"He is the most famous physician in Amsterdam. Every year he performs a public dissection of the body of a convicted and hanged criminal. Hundreds attend the public theater at New Market Square where he does it. He is an old man now, and I'd like to be there for one of the dissections before he's gone."

"He does it in public? Isn't there a lot of blood?" The thought both repulsed and intrigued me.

"Oh, it is a city-wide event. Ministers say prayers for the body beforehand. Dr. Tulp explains what he removes from the corpse, and afterward, there is a feast. I could mingle with the best physicians in the world."

When we talked about such things she was the excited girl I met years ago.

She avoided tending the fire, of course, and at night she made sure I banked the glowing logs and embers. "Just to be safe," she said, and I knew what she meant.

Late one afternoon as the heat of the day built into threatening clouds and thunder rumbled in the distance she announced she was going outside.

"I'll go with you," I offered. But she wanted to be by herself.

"Then come back before the storm hits," I said.

But she didn't. Before long the house was pelted with rain and shook from sudden and penetrating thunder. I saw her in the open field where I planned to grow tobacco. Her arms were outstretched, and she was looking up to the dark and roiling sky. Lightening flashed and made her white clothes brilliant.

"What are you doing?" I demanded when I reached her.

"Leave me, Gerret. I have to do this."

"You have to get out of the rain! It is dangerous here."

"No, leave me alone. It's my time." She did not take her eyes off the heavens.

"Elsje, you've got to come with me."

She did not respond and stood there imploring the lightning to strike her.

"Take me," she shouted. "Take me as well."

Afterward, she and I sat at the kitchen table holding hands and bowing our heads.

Another storm inside her had passed.

Seventeen

Elsje

The day after the thunderstorm Gerret proposed that I return to doctoring: "If you don't get busy you're going to go crazy," he said.

He was right. With nothing to do little things bothered me. Every time I passed a large Delft pot that held kindling wood for the fire, I felt anxious. One day Gerret's leg brushed it, and it tipped over.

"Gerret, why can't you be more careful! You are so clumsy, and that pot can hurt someone if it broke. Take it somewhere else and don't drop it."

"But, sweetheart, it is only a pot. It's been there a long time, and nothing has happened. It's not going to break itself and seek a leg to cut."

"Just get rid of it, Gerret. It's horrid to use a pot that way. I don't ever want to see it again."

He stared at me and after a few moments said, "Elsje, this isn't like you. Why are you so upset by such a trivial thing?"

As he was talking, I was rubbing the red scab over the wound on my foot and a sudden flash of memory came to me. I saw myself racing out of the storm-damaged house and crushing a pot with my foot as I was carrying a spinning wheel. I hadn't remembered that before.

"I'm sorry, Gerret. It's just that ... I know now how I cut my foot. That pot triggered my memory." And I told him what I had just remembered.

———

G erret refurbished a farm wagon he found in Gravesend and made it into a portable doctor's office and apothecary.

"This way you'll be able to doctor when and where you want," he explained. "And if we need to come back here we can."

"How many shelves do you need for the medicines?" he asked. "Should we keep the bleeding knives and buckets here or here?"

It was an odd combination: sturdy, rough farm wagon below and a fancy carriage above. The outside walls he painted shiny black upon which Tom Spicer printed a circle of bold yellow letters: *"Elsje Teunis Nyssen. Physician-Midwife-Apothecary"*. In the center of the circle was a tulip painted the colors of an Admiral Sned. Garret proudly attached fancy lanterns he had salvaged from a carriage destroyed in the storm.

The thought of seeing patients and returning to making medicines energized me.

"I'll try it out," I said. "But I'm not up to driving the wagon, caring for the horses, or cooking on my own."

"Count on me for that," he replied. "We'll be together, and you'll do the doctoring. Those are the things that matter."

Within days we launched forth to visit my yearly patients in Flatbush.

We traveled a circuit from Brooklyn to Gowanus, New Utrecht, Gravesend, Midwout, Heemstede, Maspeth and back to Brooklyn. I insisted that we avoid Amersfoort. I couldn't bear to see our destroyed house or to visit the gravesite again. Although my wealthier patients occasionally offered lodging, we usually camped beside the road, slept in the wagon, and cooked outside.

I know some of you around this table listening to my story will disapprove that I shared Gerret's bed. I don't regret it nor feel guilty about it. I am long past the point of judging what people do when they are grieving or distressed. People do what they must do to survive. I needed the comfort that Gerret could give, and I took it. I wouldn't have survived without him. Being with him at night was one of the luxuries I allowed myself.

We Dutch are different from most of you in this ... we have no issue with courting couples staying the night together. "Queesting" we call it, though we often separate the lovers with a bundling board down the length of the bed. Our wagon did not have a bundling board for I needed his touch and the consolation of his warmth.

One day we took the ferry to the city of New York. I wanted to see several of my father's former patients who had asked that I attend to them. And Gerret went to visit his parents and children.

While we were, there I said to Gerret, "I think I'll go to worship tomorrow at St. Nicholas."

"I'm surprised. You'd do that!"

"I know some good people there from years ago. And, besides, it might do me some good."

"Isn't Rev. Megapolensis still there?"

"Yes." The preacher had remained after the English took over Manhattan but he was no longer the only minister in town. New churches had been started: Lutheran, Romanist, Presbyterian and Quaker Meetinghouses. They were banned during the time of Stuyvesant.

Gerret did not join me. Later on, the rough ferry ride back to Long Island when we were bracing ourselves at the railing looking toward Devil's Gate he asked me about the sermon.

"He spoke about the sins for which the Lord sends pestilence or floods or destruction as punishment. I've heard it before, but it makes more sense now."

Gerret didn't respond.

I went on. "He talked about how Jonah refused God's command to go to Ninevah and had to face the consequences of a storm and the great fish. The preacher said the tempest that destroyed our homes and killed people was exactly like what Jonah had to face. Until we repent and change our ways, we will continue to experience the wrath of God."

"And that makes more sense to you now?" We both lurched as the ferry tilted from a high wave.

"Well, yes. Maybe it is my fault my family died. I fled the house instead of trying to save them. I didn't go to church, ran away from God, and I certainly wasn't obeying what the Church said about using pagan medicine and baptizing Alice. I told you about the beached whale on Coney Island, didn't I? I'm sure it was a warning to me from God, and I didn't listen."

"Elsje, You didn't cause what happened." His voice was rising to talk over the wind and sound of the waves. "There are storms every year that uproot trees, and there are accidents that cause houses to collapse. They happen for no particular reason. You are a virtuous person, full of compassion just like Jesus was. God has blessed you with great healing powers. There is no reason God would discipline you."

"That may be, but I don't want to provoke the wrath of God. If it wasn't punishment then perhaps God made the tree fall on the house to teach me."

He shook his head in disbelief.

"Oh, Gerret," I continued, "why can't I be both a God-fearing Christian and a good physician?"

"That is exactly what you are. You've done far more good for people than anyone I know."

"Oh, Gerret, I don't know! I have this dread that if I don't do something that I'm going to make it happen again. Someone else will be swallowed by a flood or disease or fire because of me. I couldn't live with myself if that happened."

At that moment the bow of the ferry submerged for an instant and water splashed our faces and wet our feet. We faced forward anticipating the next spray lost in our thoughts.

———◆———

It was a challenge to find the medicines and supplies I needed. Everything my father and I had accumulated was destroyed in the tempest: instruments, salves, herbs, minerals and our journals. Often I sent Gerret across the East River to purchase bandages, or a surgical knife, or mixtures of teas and herbs and minerals at the shops along the wharf or from ships that arrived at the docks.

I was often paid for my doctoring with lodging or a meal or such things as bags of barley, or honey, or tobacco most of which were of no use to us. We bartered them for the things we needed, but with little money, we lived day by day, trusting the good Lord to provide for us.

Help came from a unexpected person: Samuel Megapolensis. His home, where I had stayed briefly after the tempest, was in the style of the Pauw mansion in Gowanus: made of brick and tile, imported furniture, brocaded curtains made in the Black Forest of Germany, a kitchen with two fireplaces, several bedrooms on three stories, and servant quarters.

Samuel was a gentleman of leisure and despite his education in Leyden medical schools and seminaries, he only dabbled in those professions. It was evident that his father was wealthy, but how a preacher could come by such wealth was beyond my knowing. Perhaps his family in the Netherlands supported him or maybe he had hidden business interests. At Rev. Polhemus' invitation Samuel occasionally preached at the fledgling Flatbush Reformed Church that had just built their sanctuary in the middle of the highway to Fulton's Landing. But that was the only work I ever saw him do.

Samuel spoke to me after worship on the second Sunday of Advent. Yes, I was now attending divine services at the Flatbush Church when I could.

"Elsje, I hear good reports about you! How are you getting along?"

I thanked him for his compliment. I told him about the shortages of medical supplies.

"The Church and I would like to do something about that," he said. "After all, we walk in the footsteps of the Great Physician! Come to my house for supper and we'll talk about it."

"I'm with Gerret Snedeker. Can he join us? He accompanies me. As my assistant. He has a farm in Midwout."

"Well, good for him. I knew he was traveling with you. Of course, he can join us if you insist. But I have a proposition for you and want to talk about what you are doing to become so ... famous!" His smile was charming. I looked forward to talking to someone who had knowledge about doctoring.

It was two months after the tempest and Samuel's house was clean and tidy now that the storm survivors had left. Our meal was a feast. His servants attended our every wish and served our food on fine porcelain with silver utensils and poured us new glasses of wine for every course. It was just the three of us at the table, and we caught up on each of our lives and discussed the changes the English were making. After dinner, we retired around the hearth and talked about new medical practices he had learned in Leyden.

"I am more and more convinced that disease is not an imbalance of humours. It is a product of distinct irritating and invading entities that exist as parasites in the body." He was lecturing us. "Bloodletting doesn't solve anything but instead weakens the patient's constitution. You should be using more mercury, Elsje, just as Paracelsus advocated a hundred years ago."

"But where am I to get mercury? I have trouble finding even laudanum!"

"Now that's what my first proposition is about," Samuel said sitting forward. The padded leather seat was well worn, and the carved wooden armrests were smooth. My eyes were drawn to the legs of the chair that ended in ornately carved talons clutching balls.

"Let me be your agent in finding the medicines you want. I have contacts in New York and the Netherlands and can obtain anything you might need including mercury."

"But how could we purchase these from you? We don't have money."

"I know that can be a problem. I have another idea that might help. It includes you, Mr. Snedeker."

Finally, he was to be a part of the conversation.

"The Church here in Brooklyn has begun a new work of charity. We rent cows to people of meager means. The renters get half of the milk for their use and all of the offspring of the cows. In return, the Church receives the other half of the milk as rent. The milk is sold, and the money is available for holy work. I propose that we use the Church's income from the cows to buy your medical supplies. What do you think?"

Gerret spoke after being silent most of the evening. "And I'd be expected to care for the cows that you 'rent' to Elsje?"

"Exactly, Mr. Snedeker. I understand you are a farmer, and this would get you back to your land that you have neglected. It's a quick way for you to get restarted and make a quick profit."

Gerret looked skeptical. I knew his intention was to grow tobacco and fruit trees and not be a dairy farmer. Then it dawned on me that Samuel might be trying to find a way to separate us

"But who would help you, Elsje?" Gerret said apparently feeling the same fear about our being apart. "You can't be by yourself with the carriage and your patients. I'm very glad to help. No, I want to help."

"Here is what I suggest, Elsje," Samuel interrupted. "You can't continue forever doctoring out of a farm wagon. Why don't you set up small rooms in a couple of towns where your patients can come to you? Perhaps have one here in Brooklyn and another in Gowanus or even Gravesend. That way you'd have proper places to do your surgeries, see your patients and keep your supplies."

All these ideas swirled in my head, and I couldn't think straight. It would be very helpful to have a guaranteed source of medicines, but Gerret and I had settled into a comfortable pattern of life. Despite having two men willing and able to help me who I wanted was my father. He would know what to do.

"Samuel, this is too much for me right now," I said. "I need time to think it through." Then I asked him as a courtesy, "What can I do for you?"

"Ah, I have something very specific in mind. The deacons of the church have a new undertaking. When the English took control of New York, they ended the work of the orphan master. The Church has assumed the care of urchins and abandoned children and three of us, Rev. Polhemus, my father and I, are making special provisions for promising and talented children. We find them good Christian homes where they can grow to become honorable and stalwart church members and respectable citizens. For us, it is a matter of saving their souls."

"Here is where you can help, Elsje. You enter the homes of many families, and you are present when mothers or fathers leave this world or are unable to care for their children for one reason or another. You can help us save these children from descending into perverse and unChristian lives."

I was still looking at the talons of his chair.

"I assume I would identify children and bring them to the Church?"

"Yes. You find them, and the Deacons will get them. The consistory has taken notice of your noble and Godly works, Elsje. Perhaps all this will be sufficient to restore your soul and atone for your previous neglect of the Church admonitions and your transgressions."

In that, I knew he was wrong. There was nothing I could do to make amends for what I had done to my parents, and sisters and brothers, or Alice.

When the evening ended Samuel invited us to stay the night. It was a welcome offer as we were drowsy from food, wine, and conversation. He escorted Gerret and me upstairs to different rooms.

The house, built in the manner of the Dutch, was narrow in width but deep with long hallways running to the rear of the house. Our bedrooms were up a steep and narrow staircase. Mine was in the front and after I said goodnight to the two men I paused in my doorway and looked down the dimly lit hallway. At the far end of the hallway emerging from the darkness, I saw a small girl in a blue dress and white bonnet. She looked directly at me, said not a word, and in an instant disappeared.

My heart pounded in my chest. I was certain it was Alice! I covered my mouth and tears came to my eyes. I wanted to race down the hall and find her and embrace her, but I knew she wouldn't be there. Trembling with fear and confusion, I turned into my bedroom.

"My world is tilting," I said to myself. I grasped the post of the bed and collapsed upon the feather mattress. Then I reached for a spoon and the bottle of laudanum that I kept with me at all times.

That wasn't the only time I saw Alice.

I visited an old couple in their small house. He frequently fell and complained of dizzy spells. And she had a rash on her skin that itched terribly. Fortunately, they had a pond adjacent to their land where water lilies grew. I was able to distil the few remaining flowers into a salve for her skin, and for him I had in the wagon a decoction of lavender, horehound, fennel and asparagus root flavored with cinnamon which I told him to drink twice a day. When I finished with their instructions, they apologized for not having a meal for me as they had not been able to tend their garden or find game to eat. They were exceptionally poor, and I didn't want to impose on them and eat any of their meager rations. "While I've been here," I said, "Gerret has been oystering and hoping that he might get a duck or trade some wampum for a fish from the Indians. We'll manage, and I'm sure we'll have something for supper."

After saying goodbye to them, I went outside to wait beside the wagon which was parked on the road directly in front of the couple's house. As Gerret was not there, I strolled down the road keeping our wagon in my sight. I came across the ruins of a small cabin built many years ago. The foundation stones were still there and marked the outline of the house, but there was little evidence of roof or walls.

In the far corner of the foundation was a small girl and as I approached, I could see it was Alice. She was sitting upright, in a nest of branches and leaves and had a blanket over her lap.

"Alice, what are you doing here? Aren't you supposed to be ..." I didn't know how to finish my sentence.

"Waiting for you," she said.

"Oh, Alice, I've missed you so." I went over to her and encircled her with my arms.

"Where were you?" she asked me.

My breath stopped. "I've been with you all along," I murmured into her ear.

"I needed you," she said.

"Oh, Alice, I'm so sorry."

"It hurt."

I pulled her closer not knowing what I could say to make it better. The warmth of her body turned cold, and she started fading out of my embrace.

"Alice, wait. Don't leave." My arms now were hugging air. "Alice, please! I didn't mean it. I wanted so very much to be with you. I love you."

But she was gone, leaving me in a pile of leaves in the corner of a ruined house. A rock dove cooed mournfully in the woods behind me.

Later Garret returned to the wagon and reported, "You won't believe it. I came across a dozen or so Lenape on the shore who were smoking oysters, and they just gave me all these." He showed me a cloth bag filled with blackened oysters. "And, look," he said, "and a fried sturgeon. We are going to eat well tonight!"

"What's wrong," he asked when I didn't share his enthusiasm. "Didn't it go well with the old man and woman?"

"No, they'll be all right. It's nothing," I said, "I must be over tired."

After that, I applied an ointment of cowslip flowers to my wrists every day to remedy false apparitions and nightmares. But Alice continued to appear. Each time my world tipped more steeply, and I was closer to falling off the edge of sanity.

Eighteen

Gerret

Elsje and I continued our vagabond life going from village to village, farm to farm, patient to patient. We talked about Samuel Megapolensis' offers but delayed responding to him. Both of us felt that something didn't feel right about what he proposed and that we wanted to stay together.

One Sunday after she had returned from church services she started packing her doctor's bag. "Elsje, doesn't the Church teach that the Sabbath is a day of rest? Can't you leave off from doctoring for one day?"

"I can't stop," she said. Her eyes now had dark circles under them. "I'm not sure I want to. What would I do?"

"We could settle down and have your patients come to the farm. We could have a life with children. Host our friends, smoke our pipes and tell stories around the hearth. We could stroll together like we did on Maiden Lane. Grow old together. I miss what we had when we were in the orchard."

"I miss that too, Gerret. But I'm scared. What if I became too close to you and I lost you too? I couldn't manage that. I can't risk that. I'm just not ready."

"Can we at least talk about our future?"

"I can't right now. Mrs. Van Doorn is about to have a baby, and I need to be with her."

"We need to be together, Elsje! You are always working. And you don't ride next to me on the wagon anymore you stay in the back making your medicines. Do you want to be alone?"

"Of course, I do. I'll think about it, and we'll discuss it. I know I need to change." She fumbled with the buttons on her cloak preparing to leave. I offered to help.

"Let me be, Gerret. I can manage myself."

Where had the youthful, exuberant, and passionate girl I had known gone?

We stared at each other in silence. Then she said, "The Van Doorn baby could come at any minute." And she was gone.

I haven't forgotten the exact day: the fourteenth of December, 1666. The previous week had been rainy, and we stayed in our carriage at night rather than impose upon the hospitality of her patients many of whom were recovering from St. Nicholas Day festivities. We were on the Kings' Road not far from Brooklyn beside a stream. It was my custom to arise before her and prepare our morning porridge. On that day I added dried cranberries.

"Porridge is ready!" I said into the wagon. Elsje was still in bed. I waited for her, but she did not appear. I looked inside. She was sitting up in bed her hair damp and disheveled. She had a desperate look in her eyes.

"Laudanum!" she said to me. "Get me some laudanum!"

"There must be some here," I said, "we had several bottles."

"There isn't any left, Gerret! I need some."

"What's wrong, Elsje? Are you feeling all right?"

"No, I'm not 'all right,' Gerret. Can't you see that?"

"Why don't we wait until after breakfast? We can stop at Samuel's and get some."

"Go there now! I need it right away!"

I released the hobbles on the mare and rode to Brooklyn. My stomach sank when it struck me: Elsje had been taking much more laudanum than I knew! We both were aware it caused an obsessive craving in some people. Now it appeared to me as though it happened to her.

To my utter frustration, Samuel refused to give me any laudanum. "Bring her here," he said. "If there is something wrong with her I can treat her. No, better have a servant take the fast coach to fetch her."

I gave the coachman directions then waited at the Megapolensis house. When the coach arrived, Elsje didn't acknowledge me. She was trembling and bundled up with blankets and was in a daze. A servant carried her into the house. I followed.

Samuel blocked my way saying, "I'll take her from here, Mr. Snedeker. I'll do everything possible for her. You best be on your way."

"But she needs me!" I said.

"What she needs is a physician and a regimen of rest and appropriate treatment. Surely you understand that."

He closed the door and left me standing alone on the stoop. I felt like an innocent. How could this have happened without my knowing? I had seen my father's compulsion to drink, why didn't I see it in her? I was with her every day! I stood for several minutes in shock unable to think straight before I turned to get the wagon.

So much had happened to her: the grief and pain of her patients on top of her own losses. How could anyone bear up under all those burdens? No wonder she buried herself in a shroud of secrecy and numbed herself with laudanum.

———————

Two days later I returned to see her. A servant from the Islands greeted me at the door.

"I've come to inquire about Miss Nyssen,"

"She is resting, sir."

"Is she well?"

"She gets best of treatment from the Doctor. I cannot say how she is."

"May I enter so that I may see her?"

"Sorry, sir, but the Doctor says she is not be disturbed."

"But I am her intended," I lied hoping to gain access.

"So sorry." he repeated.

"Would you be so kind as to deliver my greeting to her and express my concern?"

"I'll give the message to the Doctor, and he can give it to her."

Once again I asked Tom to write a letter on my behalf expressing my concern for her and promising to see her soon. I delivered it myself and again was denied a visit with her. I had no assurance or confirmation that she ever saw it. My mind kept returning to how she looked when I last saw her being carried into Samuel's house: dazed, unaware of her surroundings, trembling, and entirely at the mercy of others.

"I've got to do something for her!" I said to Tom as we shared a meal. "Maybe I could organize her patients to appeal to Samuel to let her see others. If he won't listen to me then maybe he would to them."

"Perhaps," Tom replied. "But wouldn't her patients say she should obey the orders of her doctor just as they had done for her? How can we just assume that there is something wrong with what Dr. Megapolensis is doing for her?"

"But, Tom, how can it be good for Elsje to be separated from the people that love her?"

"You don't know that. He is far more educated than us about such matters."

"I could break into the house at night and see for myself how she is doing. It wouldn't be hard to do."

"You aren't English are you!" Tom smiled. "We English are quite strict about the rights of property owners, and we now live under English laws. If they found you doing that, you would be severely treated by not only Samuel but by the authorities as well. Are you sure you want to risk that? Of what help could you be to her if you were in jail?"

That December was cold and snowless, and as the solstice approached, I applied myself to sharpening tools and mending fences at my farm. It wasn't a lot of work, and I put my mind to what I could do to get to Elsje. I concluded that my first step was to see what her sisters thought could or should be done.

"You can't see her either!" I said astounded when Hannah said she was rebuffed as well. I had arrived unannounced to visit her sisters and their husbands. Their parlor was bathed in light and warmth from the dancing fire and the twenty-four candle chandelier above us. As we drank ale from our tankards I asked, "How can they refuse her sisters?"

"It is a difficult thing," Theodorus said, "but it is for the good. Nothing else matters except that she get better."

"How can seeing her kin harm her? Surely you see this is ludicrous," Hannah said to her husband. They obviously had had this conversation before.

"Quite to the contrary," Theodorus responded exasperated with his wife. "The fact is that she continues to struggle, and Samuel says that nothing should be done to unbalance her. Her situation is stabilizing, and that is a hopeful sign."

"How do you know?" I asked.

"My father has seen her. After all, he is her pastor. He told me about how she is doing."

"Surely he would understand that Hannah and I would be no harm to Elsje," Mary said. "Couldn't he persuade Samuel to let us see her?"

"You know I'd like that, Theodorus," Hannah said to her husband.

"My dear, I know it is hard to understand," Theodorus spoke sitting in a large fancy chair that was obviously his favorite. The leathered seat was higher than the chairs we sat upon, and he looked down on us all. "But matters like these are best left to the people who know how to care for her. And right now anything new or out of the pattern that has been established would be upsetting." Behind him, on the wall, a dark portrait of his Father's colleague, Rev. Megapolensis, looked directly and sternly at us no matter where we were sitting.

Mary looked at her hands in her lap apparently unwilling to further challenge her brother-in-law.

I was not deterred that easily.

"Perhaps since he is your father-in-law, Hannah, you could appeal to him?" She was still a faithful church woman. "You could suggest to him that you want to be a zieckentrooster, and you want to try it out by reading the Holy Scriptures and his sermons to her. Certainly, he wouldn't object to that!"

"I can do that. What a grand idea!" she said.

Hieronymus finally entered the conversation and said, "I spoke to Rev. Polhemus once about Elsje, but he ignored me. I could go again and be more demanding."

"He should listen to you," Hannah added. "You give generously to the church and the consistory is looking for money to build a home for the pastor and open up the chancel for worship."

Before Hieronymus could answer Theodorus said, "I'll talk to him. As his son, I think I have the most influence. I'll share with him the idea of you being Elsje's zieckentrooster, Hannah. And are you willing for me to tell him of an offer from you, Hieronymus? To help pay for the new parsonage?"

Theodorus looked around the room, and we all nodded our approval. When he looked at me, I said, "It's a good first step. But that is all it is. I'm certain we are going to have to do more. But all of you need to know, I'm going to continue to search for ways for me to see her."

Theodorus stood, ending the conversation. "So it is decided then. We have a plan." He started banking the fire. It was time for me to leave. But I now knew I had partners in my concern for Elsje.

Nineteen

Elsje

My mind was on a single path: laudanum. Where could I get more laudanum? How could I use what was reserved for patients? When could I take more? Not once did I think that laudanum had become my master.

"Samuel and I have it under control," I said to my Hannah when she asked about dependence on my 'tonic.' "I need it to get past this hard time after the tempest. Of all people you should understand that."

Samuel made sure the dosages I received were measured carefully. For that, I am grateful because laudanum is deadly if not used correctly. I was blind to the fact that that man was giving me just enough to keep me dependent on it.

After taking the laudanum, I sat contentedly by the window of my room and relaxed into a calming fog. At night I slept soundly without night terrors. I daydreamed about walking the woods looking for plants with my father, walking with Gerret on an orchard path, or playing draughts with Alice. Their ghosts were my companions.

When the fog lifted and the dreams faded, I paced anxiously hungering for more laudanum. Samuel brought a spinning wheel into my room, and when I saw it I exploded. "How can you bring that thing here! Don't you know I hate spinning? I won't stand for it being in my room. Take it away and don't try to make me do things I don't want to do."

Later when I reflected on my reaction, I was taken aback. This was entirely unlike me. But then I recovered another memory: carrying a spinning wheel out of the house after the tempest. No wonder I was upset by seeing another spinning wheel. To this day I whenever I see a spinning wheel I feel unsettled.

My maid, Machteld, was my age, and she became a close friend. When I asked her how she came to be in Samuel's house, she said, "I'm related to him. He is my cousin. His father, my mother's brother, is Johannes Van Mecklenburg, Uncle Johannes changed his name to Megapolensis when he came to New Amsterdam."

"Why did he do that?"

"My mother says he liked power and authority and as a child lorded it over his sisters. When he came to New Amsterdam, he apparently thought that having an aristocratic Greek name would make him appear dominant and commanding."

"It worked for him. He was the most formidable person in New Amsterdam after Director Stuyvesant. So why did you come here, Machteld?"

"My parents have eight children and four adopted orphans, so there are always young ones running around our house. When any one of us comes of age, we have to leave our home to make way for new young ones. Uncle Johannes visited us when I was sixteen and unmarried and invited me to America. He entranced me with stories of the New World, and he said I'd have my choice of husbands. Since I had to leave home anyway, I thought it would be an exciting adventure to be on an island with many eligible men."

She was endearing and very open with me. Our attachment grew by the day.

How I longed to be like Machteld: young, energetic, charming and healthy with her whole life ahead of her. Compared to her I felt like an old, scarred woman who had experienced too much sadness and loss in her life.

She pressed me further after I told her about Gerret and the orchard kiss.

"What about him?" she asked. "He must be interested in you."

I hesitated.

"You can tell me, Elsje."

"It might have worked once with him but now...?"

"Yes?"

"Look at me, Machteld. He is in love with the young girl he once met years ago. I'm not that anymore and never will be."

"You're only twenty-four, Elsje! You're not old. You're sick and going to recover."

My eyes fixed on a wilting flower in the window and a storm brewed inside me.

"Oh I'm so sorry, Elsje," Machteld said when she saw my eyes wetting. "I'm intruding. Please forgive me."

———

During the two months I was at Samuel's house, I had few visitors: my sister Hannah who was my zickentrooster, and of course Rev. Polhemus. When Hannah visited, she tried to encourage me by telling me I was improving. But I knew I wasn't. Sometimes memories would push me over the brink despite the medicine, and I would stay in bed all day.

My sister's lives seemed perfect in every way: they were married, had their own homes, and had children. Even though we shared the same tragic loss, we were worlds apart.

"I'm in the best place possible," I said to Hannah after she had read the Scriptures to me one day. "I'm thankful to God to have Samuel caring for me."

"I'm glad too, Elsje. He seems to know what he is doing. How soon can you get out, visit with Theodorus and me ... maybe even start doctoring?"

"I'd like that," I said. "I would love to feel useful again. But the timing is in God's hands."

"Elsje, certainly there is something more we can do for you. Perhaps bring you to our home or for a walk along the shore."

"It's taking a long time to get back my balance back. I tried right after the tempest to doctor on my own ... well, I did have Gerret. But without Father, it wasn't the same. Oh, I don't know, Hannah, I have storms inside, and say things I regret afterward. I don't know anything for sure anymore."

"What does Samuel say?"

"He says that I'm doing as well as can be expected given the circumstances. I haven't asked him when it will all be over, and I don't think he knows."

"Can I bring you something or ask to have someone else come with me next time?"

"I have everything I need right here. He provides for my every comfort: a room, a soft bed, the best of food, and attending servants. We converse about the newest advances in doctoring."

But there were many times I longed for Gerret and his absence saddened me. I knew that Samuel was sheltering me from anything that would disturb or excite me too much. Still, I thought Gerret would do anything he could to see me. Perhaps I had hurt him by not telling him about my need for laudanum. We had been so honest with one another before that.

On another occasion, Hannah asked, "But, Elsje, what about the life you had before? Father was so proud of you. What would he think of you not doing doctoring anymore.?"

"He would be glad that I'm safe and content," I said. "And maybe Samuel and I can be doctors together someday."

"Are you truly happy, Elsje?" Hannah said. "You sit in your room all day. Is that what you want of your life?"

I refused to acknowledge the truth in what she was saying. Did I know it at the time? I think I did, at least in part. But like a man in the desert too long all I could think about was my thirst. Everything else faded in importance.

After her visits, I rang my bedside bell for Machteld.

"Isn't it time for my tonic?" I asked.

Twenty

Gerret

In the fireplace of my small, uncompleted cabin I built small fires in one corner and sat on a stool, pipe in hand, staring at the flames. I lost interest that winter in doing the work on the farm. Without Elsje I wondered why it mattered anymore. I ended my day early despite the pressing need to prepare for the Spring planting.

The plans I made with Elsje's sisters were successful but only in part. Theodorus persuaded his father to let others go with him when he visited Samuel Megapolensis' home, but the only people permitted to do so were Theodorus and Hannah. Their reports were not encouraging.

Elsje was apparently calm but not communicative, sitting alone in her bedroom looking out the windows. They said her eyes had circles under them, and her body was thin. She spoke with an emotionless slur. She held Hannah's hand but they only talked about unimportant matters: the tea they were drinking, the weather, or the birds outside. Their visits ended when Samuel or one of the servants brought Elsje her medicine and said something like, "It is time for her to rest. She's had quite enough excitement for one day."

After one visit Hannah told me the unthinkable. "Samuel said, 'I'm going to marry your sister as soon as she gets well.' I didn't know what to say."

"Did you ask Elsje how she feels about him?"

"She said he gives her everything she needs, but she doesn't know her mind."

Married! How could she agree to marry the son of Rev. Megapolensis! She despised the man for his attacks on her. How could she be attracted to a life of wealth and leisure with Samuel?

I tried to see her the next day.

A servant girl answered the door at Samuel's house, and I asked to talk to the man of the house.

"Which one?" She asked. "Rev. Megapolensis or Dr. Megapolensis? They are both here today."

I told her the doctor who was treating Elsje.

"Ah, Mr. Snedeker," Samuel said when he came to the door. I hadn't seen him since the day Elsje was taken to the house. "To see Miss Nyssen again, I presume? Come in. Of course, you can see her!"

I was taken aback by his change of heart. He showed me into the parlor where the old Reverend was sitting at a desk.

"Father," Samuel said to him, "you remember Gerret Snedeker?"

"Of course, I do, Jan, the tapper's son. Forgive me for not rising, young man, I'm unsteady on my feet." His voice was thin and soft, not like the one I had heard bellowing from the pulpit.

With a trembling hand, he motioned for me to sit on a wooden chair. His walking cane hung upon it, and I placed it on the floor as I sat down. I was awed and nervous to be in the old man's presence.

Samuel said he would let Elsje know I had come to visit.

"I'm translating the Scriptures, you see," the Reverend said. "For the Mohawks. No one knows their language as well as I do so the translating isn't all that difficult. But it is a lengthy undertaking. I've time now since I'm no longer the minister of the church in New York. Gave that up to do this which is just as important wouldn't you say? I'm still saving souls."

I nodded my head. Lacking anything better to say I asked, "What passage are you translating now?"

"The story of Saul and David. Sad that the old king who had done such great things went so mad. It was the jealousy, you know, that did it. He couldn't abide David's youth and beautiful music. I know for a fact that jealousy can make a man do just about anything. But God destined David to greatness. Nothing stands in the way of God's design, not even our jealousy and madness."

His head twitched as he spoke.

Samuel entered the room. "She will see you now. Follow me." He offered no explanation why I could visit Elsje now when I couldn't before.

We went upstairs to a back bedroom. Elsje was knitting in a rocking chair with a blanket over her lap. Her back was to the door, and she faced out one of the two windows in the room. Outside a blue heron walked slowly through the edges of a salt marsh stalking his prey. A full white bonnet covered Elsje's head and shielded her face. She didn't turn as we entered even though it was quite obvious that we were there. I walked to her and faced her.

"Elsje! How are you?"

A long thread of yarn snaked its way from her lap to a skein on the floor as though tying her down to this place. Her face was drawn, her skin pasty white, and her eyes sad and sunken. She lifted her eyes from her knitting and held the needles upright like pointed stakes in the ground protecting a castle.

"Gerret," she said, "thank you for coming." I strained to hear her weak voice.

"Of course," I said, "nothing could keep me away." I glanced over at Samuel who stood in the doorway looking at us. He did not react to my statement.

Elsje's eyes teared up.

"It pains her to remember the past," Samuel said. "We try not to remind her."

I ignored him. "Are you getting better, Elsje? Are you well treated?"

"I am," she said. "I'm safe here." She paused then continued, "I'm eating better."

"And taking your medicine," Samuel interjected.

"Yes, I couldn't do without that," she said.

"Could I take you for a walk? Perhaps just the two of us?" I asked.

"I'd like that."

"I'll go with you," Samuel said, "just to be on the safe side."

"No, Samuel," Elsje said. "I'm ready for this conversation. I'll be all right." She stood reaching for my arm to steady herself.

She went down the narrow, steep stairs toward the front door placing her feet carefully on each step. I descended before her ready to catch her if she fell. Samuel was right behind urging her to go slowly and hold the banister.

We passed the parlor, and the Reverend observed us keenly, his eyes flashing at Samuel.

The house sat on a gentle rise above a marsh circled by dry and bent grasses and plant stalks killed by the winter cold. We walked on a trail around it with a gray winter sky hovering over us. There was no snow, but our feet crunched the frozen plateaus of ice along the trail. On a knoll beyond the house, a flock of fifty or so sheep grazed in small groupings.

I asked Elsje to tell me how she was.

"I have everything I need here, Gerret. I'm doing as well as could be expected. I'm stronger than I was." She hunched her shoulders from the cold under her thick cloak and dark blue scarf. I could see her breath in the air.

"I'm glad to hear that, Elsje."

"Samuel says I was exposed to too may ill humours from the putrid places I went and the dying bodies I tended. I was contaminated by the poisons, and my spirit was afflicted by what happened to my family. I've spent the winter purging and restoring myself."

"But I was with you, Elsje. We experienced the same things, and I didn't get sick."

"Not everything, Gerret. Your family didn't die in the tempest. And you didn't attend to the sick as I did."

She was right. "But you are getting beyond those things now?"

"I think so," she said. "Most of the time."

We walked in silence. I watched her unsteadiness and thought about her slowed speech. I'd seen this before when my father drank too much. He developed a temper; Elsje was depressed in spirit and body. She didn't look restored in any way or free of what controlled her. I encircled her shoulders drawing her close to ward off the cold.

"And the laudanum...?" I asked.

She shrugged off my arm. "Why does everyone think I don't know what I'm doing?"

I hesitated, giving her a moment to recover.

"Are you beyond me?" I had to ask.

She didn't answer right away apparently trying to catch some faint thought. Our path turned away from the marsh toward the pastureland.

She pointed to the sheep on the knoll. "Those sheep will be sheared in a few weeks. They'll be naked and vulnerable. I've been sheared in the middle of a cold winter."

"But you can grow back your coat and recover what you once were?"

"Yes, I trust I will. But it can never be the same, Gerret. We might wish it could be, but it can't."

"Then we'll start a new life different from the past. I love you, Elsje, and I'll do anything to make you better and happy." I faced her and surrounded her hands with mine. "Anything."

She softened. "I'm scared," she said.

"I know." I looked deeply into her eyes. "I'll protect you."

"Can you protect me from the wrath of God? Can you absolve me of my sins?" She said sadly.

I couldn't respond to that. I waited for her to go on.

"Can you keep me on the regimen and balance my humours and restore me to health?"

"Of course, I can. You tell me what you need and I'll do it. Just as we did when I cauterized your foot."

She continued, her voice gentle, "You need someone to manage your home and be your wife. I'm not capable of that, Gerret."

"You may not be now, but you will. You're a strong and gifted woman. You'll get over this."

"Oh Gerret, I'll fail miserably at raising children like I did with Alice."

"Elsje, I will do everything in my power to give you exactly what you need. Our love for each other will make anything possible. I can't live without you."

"I don't think I can make you happy as you deserve. As much as we care for each other, it can't overcome what has happened. We are different people now. I'm far less than what I was."

"You are not, Elsje! You've not lost any of your wisdom or ability to help others. And you are still as beautiful as ever. Perhaps more so because of your courage."

Finally, she said in a resigned voice: "Samuel already gives me all I need or have a right to want."

"Samuel! Elsje, he's taken you away from the life you love. He's holding you prisoner and keeping you sedated. I came here before and hadn't been allowed to see you."

"Samuel's been kind to me."

"You know he wants to marry you? I don't trust him, Elsje, and neither did you. Remember? Come away with me and we'll get you free of all this."

I was talking to someone in a dense fog. She couldn't fathom what I was saying. "He doesn't love you, Elsje! Certainly not like I do. That must count for something."

"You mean everything to me, Gerret. But I couldn't burden you with the kind of wife I would be. Please, please move on without me. Have a family. Marry someone who will give you exactly what you want and need. That would make me happy."

"You can't mean that, Elsje, not after all we've been through together. Life with another would never work because I am in love with you. What I need is you, Elsje. The rest doesn't matter."

"It will in the years ahead. It will all matter very much, and I won't take that away from you. Go, Gerret. Make a life without me."

The western sky was turning black with roiling, threatening clouds. I offered to carry her to the house. I would carry her anywhere, anytime, for whatever purpose. But she refused. We slowly made our way back and the first large drops of rain splattered us.

Samuel scooped her up when we reached the house. He said to me, "How could you keep her out in this weather? She's wet and cold!" With that, he took her inside slamming the kitchen door in my face.

When I reached my home that day, the rain had ended, and the still air dripped with moisture. I paused at our wagon which I had parked on the other side of the road in full sight of the house. The winter winds had tossed and twisted the tall, dry grasses that grew through the spokes its wheels. The lettering with Elsje's name was peeling. The plank sides were split, and rain had trickled inside. A sparrow darted through one of the gaps next to my face startling me.

Of what use was this wagon now? She was never going to need it. We would never again travel together to treat patients. If she did marry Samuel, then anything between us would be over. Perhaps he was far better suited to her than I. I was a simple man living on a not very well tended farm. And Samuel? Well, he was far, far more.

I looked into the wagon where we once were so close. The rear floorboards had rotted where water had entered. Vials and jars on the shelves were dust covered, and there was a foul smell from a potion that had gone rancid. I picked up the jars one by one to find the offending one. I angrily threw the bottles I inspected out the wagon letting them break or spill on the ground outside. One after another, faster and faster they flew through the dank air. I didn't look at them now. I threw them away without regard to their usefulness or value. I ripped out the shelves and cabinets and tossed them outside.

I paused when I reached the bed where we had slept together. I kicked it with my boot to dislodge it, but it remained firm. I used both feet smashing it as hard as I could until I felt a sharp pain in one of my ankles. The bed did not budge.

In a fury, I pulled apart the sides and roof of the wagon and exposed everything to the outside air. Panting from my efforts and with my hands red from rusty nails I piled the remnants of the wagon and went inside for embers from the kitchen fire.

When the bonfire burned itself out, I stared at what I had done. Like Elsje, I had my own barren piece of land which marked a life now gone.

With my ankle wrapped tightly, I limped to Tom's house through the silence and the fog. I saw not one creature along the way.

I offered my farm to Tom.

"What are you going to do?" he asked.

"I don't know. I have to get away from everything."

"Gerret, you can't just run away!"

"And what would you do?"

Tom didn't have an answer. Neither did I.

I could accept that it was going to be different between Elsje and myself. But I couldn't believe that our relationship was over, that she was going to marry Samuel, and that I had to start another life without her. No, she was not herself when she spoke, and her questions of me were so unreasonable no one could have answered them. When she was free of whatever was controlling her, she would recover. Then, and not before, she and I would choose how it would be between us.

I went to Hannah's house. She, her sister Mary, their husbands, and children, were gathered around the hearth. Our conversation to turn to Elsje.

"We've done everything we planned," Hannah said. She seemed pleased with the outcome.

"But," I said, "nothing has changed. She is still in the same condition with no sign of improvement. How long are we going to let this go on?"

"We can't rush these things," Theodorus said. "It has just been five weeks since she came down sick and only three months since the tempest." He looked at the two sisters, "Weren't the two of you saying just before Gerret arrived that your grief is harder now than before?" They both nodded.

"You see," he continued. "It takes time. I suggest that we best leave well enough alone."

"Nothing is 'well' about what is happening to her," I said. "She'll get worse if something doesn't change."

"But how can you know?" Theodorus said. "None of us have the doctoring knowledge that Samuel has. You may not like what he is doing but does any one of you have a better solution?"

There was silence. No one looked at anyone else.

"I do." I finally said. "We should rescue her from Samuel's house and bring her here. We'd take away that foul medicine and give her all the love we can. And when she starts to get better we'll all figure it out together."

"You mean, kidnap her?" Mary said surprise in her voice.

"I mean, free her from the man who has already kidnapped her."

"I've thought of that," Hannah said. "If I was in her position that is what I might want."

"We should act soon," I said glancing at Hannah in gratitude.

"Wait a minute," Theodorus raised his hands to calm us down. "Let's not do anything rash. We aren't Willem of Orange liberating an occupied Netherlands. We are talking about Elsje, and she is not in prison. She is under the care of a trained physician. My father visits her and gives her the Gospel of our Lord as a salve for her wounds. Hannah sees her, and she has seen you, Gerret. It is beyond my comprehension that we could do any better for her."

The others looked at their laps not willing to contradict Theodorus. Mary studiously concentrated on her knitting which rested on her white apron. Hannah circled the rim of her beer stein with her finger. It was decorated with a fleur-de-lis superimposed with the letter '*M*'. The coat of arms of the Megapolensis family.

Hieronymous finally spoke, "Theodorus, I understand what you are saying about Samuel's knowledge of doctoring. But why are you so sure about him? Gerret has a point. She hasn't improved much."

"I just know, that's all," Theodorus said with finality. There a sureness about him that left me thinking that he knew more than he was sharing.

I wished I could have found a way to formulate a plan with Elsje's family. Obviously, Theodorus who acted as the head of the family had decided nothing was to be done. I didn't want to upset Elsje's sisters and I was fed up with their lack of drive to do something. So I let the matter go.

We all watched the fire for a time then talked about the latest scandal on the island: the arrest of a cooper who had been caught stealing pigs and chickens then selling them along with his barrels to ship factors.

No one talked about my proposal further.

———

I devised my own plan after that. I would find out everything I could about Samuel's house, who went where and when, what Elsje's movements were, and how I could gain access to the house and her. Once I knew those things I'd figure out what I could do next.

Across from Samuel's house on King's Road, several families were constructing houses. Brooklyn was rapidly growing, and new people and buildings were appearing daily. I hired myself out at the construction sites: digging foundations, erecting walls, and sawing planks. The sound of saws, hammers and shovels became background noise to my observations. Among the workmen, I thought I was invisible to anyone inside Samuel's house.

One drizzly day in mid-January when rain was constant, we were abandoning our work early for shelter somewhere else, I gathered the last of my tools under a partially finished roof. The rutted and muddy road was impassable for anything but the sturdiest of wagons, and I did not look forward to walking home in the muck. "The time has come," I said to myself and with determination I splashed my way across the road to Samuel's house.

A big man with wide shoulders and muscles that bulged under his shirt answered the door. I recognized him as one the household servants that often left the house for errands

"Would the master of the house offer me shelter until the rain lessens?" I asked while rain dripped from my face. "He knows me. I am a friend of Elsje Nyssen who is staying here."

I was invited into the parlor and told to wait. The room I remembered when I had been to dinner with Elsje in the house. Damask curtains hung neatly aside each of the three windows and a wool rug with a design of prancing peacocks was on the floor. The wooden tables, chairs, and desk were polished and bare.

When the servant returned, he was carrying a dry set of clothes with him. They were those of a gentleman made from fine silk and wool complete with vest and jacket with lapels. "Place your clothes in this basket," the servant said, "and I'll put them by the fire, sir. To dry out." He left me to do my dressing.

The fancy clothes were for someone taller and thinner than I and would obviously not fit. The breeches were narrow at the waist, so much so that I'd never be able to button them. The gleaming white stockings were so large they would bag around my knees and ankles. The long sleeves of the white ruffled shirt would go far past my fingertips.

I refused to take off my dripping clothes and sat on one of the chairs with an embroidered seat. I relished leaving my wet mark on them. Through the window, I watched streams of water flowing off the roof and puddling on the road.

Samuel entered briskly, towering tall and imposing over me as I sat sunk into the cushion of the chair.

"Best to be out of this wet weather wouldn't you say, Mr. Snedeker?" He shook my hand as though we were old friends meeting after a long absence. I stood and squeezed his hand with confidence and strength.

"Thank you for the shelter, Mr. Megapolensis. It's one of those days no one wants to work outside."

"Glad to oblige," he said. "You didn't want the dry clothes?"

"No, I'm comfortable with what I have on." I went right to the point, "How is Miss Nyssen."

"Of course, you are concerned for her," he said raising his eyebrows to show surprise at my bold start to our conversation. He looked down at the floor under his expensive chair and saw the small pool of water underneath it. "But let's not talk here ... it is so ... formal. Follow me."

I walked behind him out of the parlor and down a corridor that led to the back of the house. We passed the stairs that led to the second floor where I had visited Elsje three weeks before. The servant blocked my access to the stairs as though he was a guard before a jailhouse cell.

I examined the back of Samuel in front of me. He had a run in his white stocking below his leggings. One of his highly polished leather shoes was scuffed deeply, and its golden buckle was askew. I reminded myself that he was a man like any other man. He had no special powers I did not own and despite his education and family background, he still had to sleep at night and piss into a chamberpot. He was no better than I.

He faced me when we reached the kitchen. Ahead of me was a door leading outside to the drizzling rain. It did not have a lock and could be easily entered from the outside. To my left was a passageway without a door that led down to what certainly was the cellar. It's darkness made me feel uneasy. I tried to inch my way further into the warmth and safety of the kitchen, but he was in my way.

"We can talk here," he said. "Your ... wetness won't matter on this floor."

"In that case, let's sit down," I said trying to take some control. I nodded my head toward the kitchen and the sturdy wooden chairs that surrounded the table. I had to get away from the cellar door, and I wanted a table between him and me.

"Of course," he said as he spun around and walked away from me. I went to the table but he entered an adjacent room that I presumed was the pantry. I sat and examined the room. It was close to dinnertime, and the only evidence of food preparation was a steaming pot that rested on the hearth before the fireplace. The counters that surrounded the room and the cabinets above and below were smooth and lustrous as though they had just been sanded and polished with wax. Lit candles in sconces on the walls glittered their light on cabinet surfaces. Where typically food, bags of grain, kitchen utensils, bowls, and pots would sit upon the counters, there was nothing but shiny countertop. Why wasn't the kitchen busy with servants preparing a dinner?

Around the fireplace pokers, ladles and tongs hung from hooks in the surrounding brick. They were precisely spaced and not touching each other, and the shape of each one perfectly fit the shape of its neighbor. They were so clean they looked newly forged. This kitchen appeared as though it was never used. I felt out of place in all the neatness.

I steeled my resolve knowing I had to be strong for Elsje. The wood on my chair was unforgiving, and the rungs on its back protruded uncomfortably on my spine.

Samuel returned carrying two clean white cotton towels which I presumed were meant for me to dry myself or to clean the water I had left behind on the floor. Instead, he hung one towel on the back of the chair that sat opposite me. The other one he folded neatly, put it on the seat of the chair, and gingerly sat down careful not to let his clothes touch the chair itself.

"Mr. Megapolensis, may I call you Samuel?" I said forcing an informality to make him feel equal to me. He nodded but lifted his chin disdainfully as he did so.

"I'm worried about Els ... Miss Nyssen."

"Of course, we all are," he said.

"When I saw her three weeks ago, she was weak and wasn't her usual self, and from what I hear from her sisters, she's not any better. "

"Yes, well, these things take time you know."

"What things exactly?"

"She has suffered an enormous loss, and her grief is deep. Her humours are out of balance. Time is the best healer, you know."

"And laudanum I suppose you are going to say."

"Yes, and laudanum. It softens her feelings of loss so she can recover."

"Samuel, everyone has lost someone they love, and they don't need laudanum."

"Yes, but it certainly can help when tragedies are as horrendous as the one experienced by Miss Nyssen."

"Difficult or not, I know that surgeons and barbers say that laudanum is never given for any length of time and that it can be fatal. Elsje is dependent upon laudanum and is in danger because of what you are giving her."

"Those things do happen. I'm very careful with the dosages."

"I'm sure you are, but she is taking too much and for too long." I knew that I was going to have to challenge him on this at some point. My palms were clammy.

"Ah, and you are an expert on such things?"

"No, but I know what is right for Elsje, and it isn't what you are doing to her."

"Mr. Snedeker, laudanum can make a person tired and occasionally look even sicker. But it is for the best. I give her laudanum precisely because it allows her body and mind to rest while she recovers. Why would I keep giving her laudanum if not for a good reason?"

"I don't know. But imprisoning anyone as innocent as her is wrong in the sight of God."

"You are joking, right? Listen, Gerret. May I call you Gerret?" he spat out my name mocking me. "You know nothing about the sight of God. How can you invoke the name of the Almighty to me? Are you the only one who knows what God has ordained to be good and right?"

I had touched a nerve and broken through his calm demeanor.

"When it comes to her, yes I do. I want you to release Miss Nyssen so that she can be properly cared for." I had launched this ship and wasn't going to be stopped.

He laughed. "Release? She has nothing to be released from. She is free to go whenever she wants."

"She is not getting any better and can't just leave on her own," I insisted. "In her condition, she doesn't know what she wants."

"And you do?"

"Yes," I said with confidence. "Yes, I do know what she wants ... and needs."

"What exactly is that?"

"She wants to be healthy and go back to doctoring." I felt a gust of wind in my sails.

"Ah, she told you this?" He was smiling.

"I know this."

"What makes you so omniscient when it comes to her? You the keeper of a dilapidated farm who doesn't know how to read or write?"

"We love each other, and I know her better than anyone else."

"Let's see," he said. "You were with her for two months in that makeshift wagon while she was busy visiting patients? And that qualifies you to know everything about her?" He leaned back in his chair his arms behind his head.

Beside us, on the table, several cooking knives were nestled neatly in a wooden holder their handles exposed and vertical for easy access. They were the only objects on the table other than the pumice stone beside them. I eyed the large knife with a polished bone handle.

"What matters," I said looking directly at him, "is that she be healthy and free to do as she pleases. But you control everything in her life." I was steering the ship now.

"In my house, she is under the best of medical care with servants to attend to her every need. That is the way she will get healthy. And as for her freedom and happiness, those will come with time."

"It is taking too much time," I said pointedly. "She will recover best when she is surrounded by family and those who love her ... and away from this terrible medicine and regime that you are forcing upon her."

"You don't think I care for her, Mr. Snedeker? You think I'm doing all this for her for no reason at all? Perhaps I love her as much as you do. Have you thought of that?"

I lowered my voice and spoke with venom: "You're doing this to control and own her. Not love her."

"Is that so? Be the first one to know: we have posted our marriage banns. Elsje is going to marry me. Not you."

I thought he was bluffing, but my heart froze anyway. "She doesn't love you. I know that for a fact. She loves me and always has."

"What has love got to do with it? She and I are perfect partners. Look at this." He produced out of his inner coat pocket an official looking document. "It is our marriage banns," and he pointed to where Elsje had supposedly signed it. He knew I couldn't read. I was a pawn in his game. "This will be posted at the Staed Houis when I get back from the business I must do in Beverwyck."

He paused relishing my shock. I saw a flash of light from a flickering candle reflected off the polished handle of the knife.

He continued. "You will never be on her level. She and I were equals since we were children. When we're married, she will go back to doctoring and have a proper place to practice medicine. Not some gypsy wagon going from town to town like a market fair amusement or some charlatan with sham herbs and potions."

"You are forcing her into this. That's underhanded and dishonorable!"

"What I do and why I do it is none of your business is it? I'm a physician, and a minister of the Gospel and I don't need to justify myself to you or anyone else."

"Yes. You. Do." I spoke punching out my words as though they were cannon shots aimed at a pirate ship. "Elsje Nyssen is a precious gift from God and the good Lord has seen to it that I am the one to love her and watch over and protect her. So, yes, you do need to be accountable to me for what happens to her. God has chosen me to be her protector and provider. I will not allow you to imprison or drug or control her."

"Ha! Look who now thinks he knows everything God intends! And what do you have in mind to do about it, Mr. Snedeker? Are you going to be the brave knight that rescues the fair maiden from the evil lord?"

"I will tell the schout what you are doing and have him call you to account."

"Oh, you will go to the Brooklyn schout will you? Are you talking about my nephew, Adriaen Mecklenburg? All right, have him investigate. We can count on him to get to the bottom of this." My ship faced an armada of enemies.

I abruptly stood up, took the knife in my hand, raised it threateningly, then thrust it point down on his perfect, shiny table. It pierced the hard wood and stood rigid. The gash it made would be there a long time.

"I will not let you do this!" I said.

Startled by my actions, he said sharply, "Perhaps you can start your glorious mission by leaving this house where you are no longer welcome now or ever."

"Not before I see her." My hand was still on the knife.

The candles and the air between us were still. The sound of steady rain punctuated the silence.

Slowly Samuel arose from his chair meticulously folding the towel from the seat of the chair. He avoided my stare and walked to the hallway where his servant was still guarding the stairs. "Otto," he said, "tell Machteld I need to see her in the kitchen."

Moments later I heard a woman's footsteps coming down the stairs. Samuel did not introduce us. I assumed she was a nurse for Elsje. "How is she, Machteld?" Samuel asked her.

"The rain is stopping, and she is less anxious. I think she is solidly asleep."

He thanked her and dismissed her with a wave of his hand. Turning toward me he whispered the victory in his tone clear: "We wouldn't want to wake the maiden would we?"

Of course, I wanted to wake her, gather her into my arms and carry her out of her prison. I wanted to get her as far away as possible from this man.

The evening was descending through overhanging, wet, black branches when I walked out the front door. The day was done, and the road was dark, but I was not finished. Before I had even stepped off Samuel's stoop, my next step to free Elsje came to me with crystal clarity.

———

Early the next day, I went to the ferry and eventually to the Stadt Houis on Manhattan where the new English government had its offices. To my good fortune, Governor Nichols was receiving callers, and I joined the line of people who also wanted to see him. The English Governor, in office only two years, had quickly become respected and liked for his fairness and wise judgments.

I was told to wait outside, and I sat on the half-circle stone battery that supported three cannons pointed out to the sea. A brisk January wind chilled me, and sharp, irregular stones poked me where I sat. The other petitioners waited with me and with frosty breaths we chatted about our hopes to be summoned soon so we could be near a warming fire.

After an hour of waiting, my name was called. I sprinted up three flights of stairs to the Governor's office thoroughly ready to lay my case before him.

The room was long and narrow, the air warm and stuffy. Everything was designed to show wealth and power. Two walls were lined with books of all sizes some of them as large as a table top. I was seated next to the large tiled fireplace with an exceptionally tidy hearth. In the center of the room was an enormous table strewn with papers, maps, and inkwells. A candelabra of perhaps twenty or more candles lit the surface. Two men were at the far end of the room conversing privately. I started to remove my overcoat.

"No need to take off your coat," a tall, thin man said to me. His pointed beard and formal carriage were instantly familiar. It was Cornelius Van Tienhoven who had been the Secretary for Director Stuyvesant. For many years he had meticulously recorded every petition, decision, and judgment about all matters in the colony. Seeing him there pained me. In all likelihood, he had shared with Governor Nichols what he knew about my family and me, especially my father, and therefore prejudiced the Governor against me.

"You won't be long," van Tienhoven said. I pulled my coat back over my shoulders.

The Governor sat at a spacious desk tucked in a dark corner away from the windows. He was younger than I expected and sat with his back ramrod straight as befit a soldier in the good favor of the Prince of York. He looked up at me and nodded to van Tienhoven.

"I'll be translating," van Tienhoven said. "Tell us why you are here." There was an impatience in his voice.

I related the story of Elsje's imprisonment by Samuel and requested the Governor to force Samuel to release her. Van Tienhoven translated what I said into English with far fewer words than I spoke.

"Mr. Snedeker," van Tienhoven spoke the Governor's response, "I am taken aback by what you are asking and by your story. It cannot have been more than a fortnight ago that I gave permission for them to publish their banns."

I was shocked. So it was true what Samuel said about their marriage.

"And they both came before you to ask for the permission?" I asked. I couldn't see how Elsje in her condition would be able to make the journey across the East River from Long Island.

Van Tienhoven answered me directly, "Mr. Megapolensis came with Theodorus Polhemus I recall. I wrote down the record of the Governor's permission as I do every transaction in this office. Would you like to see it, to settle your mind?"

I shook my head, "But if she wasn't present how do you know that Miss. Nyssen approves of the union and that she is not being forced into it?"

"I don't," the Governor replied through van Tienhoven, "but in the absence of her parents who would customarily give permission and because she has no surviving male relative, the only one I could to turn to was her sister's husband, Mr. Polhemus. He endorsed it. But Dr. Megapolensis comes from a respectable family. I have no reason to think that he is doing anything underhanded. I believe he has her best interests at heart." Tienhoven had a cat's smile on his face.

Theodorus gave his permission! How could he after the conversation he and I had earlier with Elsje's family? Theodorus might have refused to rescue Elsje, but I thought, in the end, he would keep peace in the family by going along with their plan for Elsje.

"But doesn't what I am saying to you give you pause and argue for the necessity of investigating the matter further?"

Van Tienhoven spoke without translating for the Governor: "Mr. Snedeker, their engagement has been proclaimed in the Church according to our Dutch custom and no opposition or hindrance came against them. Their banns of matrimony are confirmed. I recorded it myself."

"Proclaimed! Where? Why haven't I heard of it?"

"At St. Nicholas Church here in New York."

"But they reside within the parish of the Dutch Reformed Church of Flatbush. Surely it needs to be proclaimed there as well. I know there will be opposition to it from more than myself." I trusted that Elsje's sisters would speak for her.

There was a quick exchange in English with the Governor. "They are to be married here, not on Long Island. The presiding minister will be the senior Rev. Megapolensis," van Tienhoven translated.

Of course, the snake Samuel and his father had everything lined up.

"Our hands are tied, Mr. Snedeker, he is her protector now," van Tienhoven said on his own.

"Protector? What about her right to decide herself? She is an equal to any man in New Amsterdam."

"That may be your Dutch custom," the Governor said through van Tienhoven, "but we are under English law in this colony. Women are subject and must be obedient to their husbands, even their husbands to be. Miss Nyssen is living under the bonds of marriage, and Mr. Megapolensis has both the responsibility to care for and protect her as he determines. I have no power or reason to intervene in the affairs of that relationship. Is there anything else, Mr. Snedeker?"

The Governor would do nothing. I glared at van Tienhoven feeling the bile rising inside me. He and the Governor were already looking at a sheet on the desk. I guessed it was from the next petitioner. I mumbled a bitter thank you and left.

My exit from the building was blocked by a crowd listening to a Company officer speaking on the staircase above them. Unable to leave, and with my thoughts in turmoil, I stood with the crowd. I wanted to make sense of what just happened and think through what I could do next. But the words of the speaker distracted me.

"It is the best offer the Company has ever given," he shouted in an excited voice. "You can't afford to turn it down. And don't hesitate," he continued, "this offer will only last until the ship sails in three days. And who knows? If you don't take it you may be pressed into service and have to sail anyway... without the reward!"

"What is he talking about?" I asked the man nearest to me.

"Both India Companies are offering a bonus for anyone who signs up as a sailor for their ships. Now that the war with England is over, they are expanding their trading routes and need men. They will take anyone."

Sailors were poorly paid, and their families had to rely on charities to make ends meet. A bonus for signing was unusual and attractive. But it wasn't the money that tempted me. What was I to do with the bonus? It was the escape it offered. Was there any reason I couldn't just leave everything behind and take this offer?

I squeezed my way out of the crowd as it thinned and made my way to the ferry. The usual January wind had died down, and a clear, twilight sky promised a night of deep winter cold. People had retreated from the frigid air into cottages that blinked their lights in the darkness. I was the only person on the ferry as it made its last crossing of the day.

After spending the night at the Ferry Inn, I went to Amersfoort and talked to Hannah. As Elsje's closest sister she was my last resort. If I had no partners in trying to free Elsje, then all would be lost.

She already knew about the marriage banns and that her husband, Theodorus, had given permission.

"But I thought we had all agreed that it would be better for Elsje if she was with her family?" I said.

"We did," Hannah admitted, "but recently we've been allowed more visits with her. So she is with her family, in a manner of speaking."

"We also agreed that what Samuel was doing with her was not right."

"We did. Well, Theodorus wasn't in full agreement. And he is my husband, and in the end I had to agree with him. Samuel is a doctor, and he does provide everything Elsje needs. What good would it do, Gerret, if Elsje was freed of Samuel only to end up with a family that is torn apart by disagreement? Once they are married, Samuel will be family."

"Oh, Hannah, I'm certain that I am the one intended for Elsje, not Samuel."

"I'm sorry, Gerret. I truly am. You'll make a good husband for someone else someday. I'm certain of it."

When I left her, I took one last look at her house and saw a fancy letter 'M' on the gable. "That's strange," I said to myself. "It should be a 'P' for Polhemus." With that thought, came the realization of whose house this was, and that there was much more to Hannah's change of heart than preserving family unity.

My suit of Elsje was over. But I didn't have to live with the pain of being near her or near the places that reminded me of her. It was torture imagining her with Samuel walking the same roads I walked, sharing her bed as I had, forcing her to be his wife when she should have been mine, preventing her from being the doctor she wanted to be.

For my sanity, I had to escape all reminders of her.

———

On the day before the ship departed, I carried my sailor's bag filled with my belongings down Pearl Street to my old home on the other side of the fort. I knocked the heavy brass knocker shaped like a ship's anchor. My sister Christina opened the upper half of the door.

"Gerret!" She leaned out the opening and gathered me into her arms with the lower door between us. "It is so good to see you! It's been so long!"

My sister had been taking care of my children since their mother died. It was a common practice to have them reared by relatives when their parents couldn't, and I was grateful to Christina and Jochem for doing so. They were wonderful parents to Jan, Griet and Christian who treated them as their own mother and father. I was the "uncle" who came with presents so they liked my visits. I was proud they seemed so healthy and smart, but my feelings for them were always tinged with sadness that we weren't closer or living together as a family. I'd seen the children little over the years and when I did my visits were brief. It always seemed I had little time before the last ferry to Long Island left the wharf.

I returned her hug and reached in and opened the door. We caught up on the happenings of our family. Then I said, "I'm off on a new adventure, I'm sailing tomorrow."

Her eyes opened with surprise.

She fussed over me as though this would be the last time I'd see her. "Do you want some tea? I have just made apple olykoeks … you want some to take with you? The children will be home from their lessons soon." The delicious smell of fried bread and cinnamon filled the air.

While we waited for their arrival I asked Christina to show me their rooms upstairs. My old bedroom was being used as a nursery. "He's sleeping," Christina whispered showing me the cradle where a tiny boy with wispy hair was asleep on his back. I stroked Christian's hair then asked my sister, "Can I hold him?"

"Of course."

I slid my hands under him and lifted him to my chest. His arms flopped behind him, but he didn't awaken. His skin felt soft when I touched his face, and was pink as a peony bud. I paced the room a few times then returned him to his bed.

"And the other ones have this room." She opened the door at the far end of the hall that led to where my sisters had slept. "Griet's bed is there," she said pointing to a bed with a frilly quilt piled high with dolls. "She will be excited to see you. And Jan's is there. He shares the bed with our son Jacob. Christian sleeps in the trundle. The three boys are inseparable and are the terrors of the house!" She twinkled and laughed as she said it. "Griet gets the worst of it. They tease her mercilessly, but she's a fiery one and holds her own with them."

I was pleased that she seemed to enjoy my children so much.

They arrived late in the afternoon from their lessons, and I went to the front door to greet them.

"Jan! Griet!" I shouted, delighted to see them. Jan was six and Marrietje was eight. They both stood still and stared at me. I knew I hadn't seen them for many months, but their reluctance surprised me.

I knelt down to their level. Griet inched her way behind her brother's back clutching her satchel tightly. She was always a shy one. I reached out and hugged them. Behind them my sister's son Jacob stood staring at me. Jan saw my duffel and said, "What's in the bag?"

"We'll see soon enough. How are you, Jan?" I looked at him at arm's length still holding his shoulders. He looked older than I expected. I could see his impatience to get to the presents.

"Fine," he said, and he wiggled out of my hold and went to the duffel.

"All right let's see what we can find inside." I drew out two packages wrapped in light rope and an old cloth. "Here," I said handing them to the two of them.

Jan rapidly untied the cloth. Inside was a two-foot high table with legs ready to be screwed into the bottom. The top was inlaid with pearls and colored wood in an elaborate design. "It's from Portugal, and it's a treasure! I bought it right off a Portuguese man-o-war just for you."

"Here," I said to help him. "Let's screw in the legs." He let me do it for him. "Now," I said, "lift the top."

When he did so, music started playing. "It's Buxtehude," I said. "He's the most famous musician in Europe. Have you heard of him?"

Jan looked at me as though I was from deep Africa. It dawned on me that an eight year old boy wasn't much interested in a pretty table or even music. Nevertheless, he seemed pleased to be its owner.

He gave me a thank you hug. He showed the table to Jacob and the two of them retreated to the back of the room and started examining the inside of the box.

I was pleased and hoped that the table would remind him of me when I was gone.

Meanwhile, Griet stood unmoving with the package I had given to her in her hands.

"Let me help you," I offered but she turned around and walked briskly to Christina.

"Go on, honey, let him help you." But Griet shook her head, so Christina knelt down, and together they opened the package.

"It's a purse!" Christina said with practiced excitement.

"Made out of snake skin," I said. "From the jungle in Brazil! Isn't it pretty, sweetheart?"

Immediately Griet dropped the purse without opening it or examining it. And she stepped away in alarm.

"She's deathly afraid of snakes," my sister said. I had forgotten that detail. "But it is a very attractive purse."

Later I saw Jan and Jacob using the legs of the table as swords, and they were sparring with each other. I no longer knew my children, and they didn't know me. When they grew up, I was sure to be only a distant memory.

I left glad I had visited them, and all but certain I would never see them again. My sailor's bag did not feel any lighter.

The next day in mid-February I boarded a Company ship destined for waters far from the Americas. I abandoned Long Island and everything and everyone there. When the ship left the wharf, I cast off the final line that tied us to land, and watched the wake of the ship as the only home I'd ever known disappeared.

Twenty-One

Elsje

Two months after I was taken to Samuel's house, I awakened early one morning to an overcast, cold day and a knock on my bedroom door. The house servants who cared for me, including Machteld, entered only by my permission. Assuming it was one of them I told the knocker to come in. Mary and Hieronymous, Hannah and Theodorus, and to my additional surprise Michiel Pauw, whom I hadn't seen since my days in Gowanus, all entered my room. Behind them Machteld peered at me saying, "I'm sorry, Elsje, they pushed right by me. I couldn't stop them!"

I looked at them astonished by their presence. I pulled up the quilt to cover my night clothes. "What ... what are you doing here?"

"We need to talk, Elsje," Mary said.

"All of you ... now?"

Hieronymous turned to Machteld. "Would you bring us spiced tea please?" he said authoritatively to her. Unaccustomed to taking orders from anyone but Samuel or me, she fumbled momentarily before she left the room.

He then picked up my empty chair from the window and sat down next to my bed. He took my hand in an intimacy we had not shared before. Apparently, he was to be the spokesman.

"Elsje," he said softly, looking at me. I averted my eyes embarrassed by his continuing touch. "You know we all love you and want the best for you."

I looked to my sisters pleading for them to explain themselves and this intrusion.

"I know you are wondering why we are all here," Hieronymous continued. "Hear me out before you say anything."

I didn't know what to say.

"I've been an elder on the Church consistory for several years. Two months ago we had a discussion about how to maintain the purity of our Dutch Reformed faith. There are so many more, shall we say, wayward religions allowed since the English took charge. Not to mention religious charlatans and pagan healers. We are having a hard time keeping the Elect on the true road. Well, that is neither here nor there right now, but during the discussion Rev. Polhemus said, and I quote him: 'At least we don't have to worry about the Nyssen girl. We have her safely put away.'"

"Safely put away?" I said.

Hieronymous continued, "I was shocked, and after the meeting, I asked Rev. Polhemus about it. He said he meant was: 'you were sick and weren't going to get any better.'"

"'How can anyone know that?" I asked him. "And what did he mean 'she is put away?'"

"He fumbled for words and said he was 'glad that you were back in the fold of the true Church and that you've reformed your ways by no longer meddling with unholy practices and medicines.'"

Hieronymous looked to Theodorus who was looking out the window. But Theodorus said nothing.

"Elsje," Hieronymous continued, "I don't believe him. I think you are being deliberately detained here to keep you from doctoring."

Hannah spoke up, "We believe Samuel isn't treating you to make you well. He is keeping you from all the good you can do for others, or as he would put it: all the 'damage' you would do!"

How did they come to that conclusion?

Machteld returned to the room and passed around cups. She poured the tea, and each of them fiddled with their cups and the milk pitcher.

"We've no sugar in this house," Machteld said. We all knew why. Reverend Megapolensis had preached often enough about the sin of sweets.

Machteld leaned down and whispered to me, "I'll bring your tonic after they are gone."

There was silence as my visitors gingerly sipped their hot tea. Machteld stayed in the room.

Finally, Hannah, Hannah whom I loved and trusted the most, said, "We've come to take you away from here, Elsje."

"What?" I managed to get out. Were they going to force me to leave? So that is why they were in my bedroom! They continued in rapid fire statements before I had a chance to think or to speak.

Hannah: "It is for the best."

Hieronymous: "We have the perfect place for you."

This conversation was preposterous! How did they know what was best for me? My anger about them meddling in my life surged forth, and my face got hot. I pursed my lips and flashed my eyes but said nothing. I would let them have their say, and then they'd leave.

Hannah: "Samuel won't be able to object. We'll take you before he returns from New York."

So Samuel couldn't stop this before it went any further.

Michiel Pauw spoke for the first time: "We're building a new asylum for the infirm and aged in Gowanus. And we're recruiting the best doctors from the Netherlands."

Did I need to be in an asylum?

Mary: "The doctors will know how to get you healthy and once you get you better, Elsje, you could work there too."

Hieronymous: "You are too good a doctor to let that go to waste!"

Michiel: "Yes, we'd like for you to assist at the asylum. Just as you helped my servants when you stayed with us."

Hannah: "And Mr. Pauw said he would build you a house when you no longer need to live in the asylum." Michiel nodded in agreement.

Machteld timidly spoke up, "I don't think Uncle Megapolensis or Samuel will like this."

Of course, they wouldn't, but if what they were saying were true?

"We have a routine that is important for her," Machteld continued. "Samuel is the best-trained physician on Long Island and has a precise healing regime for her."

Hieronymous: "That may be, but he is not the only one who knows what is best for people."

Machteld overwhelmed and powerless before the forces in the room, quieted.

Mary: "Tell her why, dear. Tell her about the money."

Money?

Hieronymous: "It's complicated, Elsje, but it boils down to this. Rev. Megapolensis is a wealthy man. One wonders how someone who preaches against the evils of wealth could have become so rich himself, but there it is. He has used his money and his position to dictate many things: where and when to build a new church, who the pastor of the new church will be and what he preaches about, what the consistory does about one matter or another. And he decided that you, Elsje, were a danger to the Church. That should come as no surprise to you. He has his son Samuel detaining you so you can do no more damage or sully the purity of the true faith, especially during these vulnerable times. Nobody is willing to challenge him on it because everyone depends on his money."

Hannah walked over to Theodorus who was still looking out the window. She took him by the shoulders and made him turn him around so that he faced me. She prompted him to speak.

Theodorus: "It's true," he said apparently resigned to having to speak. "He has controlled my father since we arrived. Rev. Megapolensis recruited him from Brazil and pays his salary now that the Company no longer does so. Megapolensis money built the church and gave Hannah and me everything we have."

Why didn't I know this or suspect it?

Hieronymous: "But times have changed. Michiel and I have joined to oppose his pompous ways, and together we have the means and influence to do so."

Hannah: "And one thing we are ending is how he and his son have treated you. They treated Father so badly that he had strokes. Remember? Surely you don't want that to happen to you too? That is why we are here."

My mind was spinning. I no longer knew what to think. I put up my hands to stop them. Everything was moving so fast. I felt like I was on an unbridled horse galloping swiftly through a crowded town. Unable to focus on any one thing, my eyes darting from person to person.

Hannah: "I know we've surprised you, Elsje. But we don't have time to wait. The five of us have been talking about this, and we are convinced this is right for you, and for your patients for that matter. Isn't that right, Theodorus?"

Theodorus nodded again though grudgingly.

Michiel: "We have a carriage waiting outside. You have as much time as you need to gather your belongings. It's not that far to Gowanus, and everything is ready for you."

"What? Now?" I was taken aback. I felt like a piece on someone else's chessboard.

Hannah: "I'll go with you, Elsje. For as long as you like."

I looked at them pleading them to change their minds but they each nodded and did not yield.

Machteld spoke, "I'll also go with you. Now, please excuse us. Elsje and I have some things to attend to."

As they left the room, I motioned to Hannah, and she stayed behind. "Gerret?" I asked, "Where is he?"

"He first proposed this, Elsje."

"Why didn't he come with you?"

"When we found out that Samuel was gone for a few days, we decided we had to act right away. Hieronymous sent a servant to find Gerret in Midwout, but he came back without him. He said he was nowhere to be found."

After they had left, I dressed, and as Machteld and I rushed to put my belongings together, I said, "Machteld, you can't go. Samuel is family. What would he say about your part in this?"

"Elsje, you're my closest friend and, to be honest, I've had my doubts about Uncle Samuel's regimen for you. I'm going with you. We're going through this together, and we'll figure out what to do."

Oh, Machteld! Her words were heaven to my ears.

Twenty-Two

Gerret

I discovered that the *"Gouden Leeuwin,"* or Golden Lion, had an extraordinary captain. Jan Lucasz had complete control over all matters aboard the ship, as was custom, but he treated his crew differently.

"I've learned from the pirates," he at the start of our voyage. "They are a happier lot than the seamen on merchant vessels. So, like them, you men will elect your own quarter and sailing masters, as well as your boatswains and mates. Of course as Captain, I reserve the right to veto."

The seamen who had sailed with Lucasz before lobbied to get their favorites elected, and since the rest of us didn't know each other, we voted for the officers they proposed.

As one of eighty seamen aboard the galleon and as a novice, I was assigned to be a swabbie and over the first few weeks, I cleaned every inch of the decks. But at the end our shifts, while the others took their leisure, I continued to work cleaning rails, repairing lines, mending sails, rearranging cargo, manning the bilge pump, or sanding rust from the cannons. I volunteered for the hardest of work, the longest hours, and the riskiest jobs.

My goal was to be so busy that I would not have time to think about Elsje and all that had happened. Eventually, I reasoned, I would be free of my former life and attachments. Liberated to start a new life whatever and wherever it was to be.

Sailors sleep wherever they find a spot that suits them. I went into the bowels of the ship and made my bed in a windowless compartment below the waterline beside casks of rum and on top of stone ballast. I liked the total darkness of the space and the sleep inducing sound of water on the hull. Another novice sailor, Jacob Van Waert, joined me. He slept more deeply than I, and he asked me to wake him when the whistle for his watch was sounded.

One night when the ship was battling high seas, a large ballast stone was dislodged and rolled onto his foot crushing two of his toes. Unable to rise because of his injury Jacob stayed in his berth. I explained to the first mate why he did not muster on deck. Before our shift was done, Jacob had been hauled out of our compartment and locked in a small room that served as the brig when needed.

I flew into a rage in his defense and confronted the first mate. "Did you ask him why he didn't report on deck? Can you not see that he can barely walk! Imprisoning him is barbaric! He has an injury, that's all." My voice got loud, and my words were cannonballs aimed at the first mate.

Other sailors grabbed me and took me aside as the stunned first mate walked away. "Calm down," one of them said to me. "This is the way it is for sailors. He'll be free to leave tomorrow. It's only temporary." Another explained, "There are always sailors who try to get out of work for all sorts of reasons. Jacob will be an example for others even if he doesn't deserve it. Anyway, he will get treatment from the ship's barber better there than the hole where you sleep." It took days for my anger to subside and when it did, I was amazed at what I had done. Never before had I lost control of myself that way.

But that was not the end. The barber gave Jacob laudanum to ease his pain, and I again lost my temper. "That concoction is the Devil's instrument," I said to the barber. "Do you know how evil it is?"

Anger exploded out in me about other injustices as well. I was as sure as could be in the rightness of my causes. Sailors were cautious around me and only Jacob, with whom I had long nighttime conversations, suspected I was not my usual self.

"I don't know why this is happening," I said. "I can't contain my anger. I know I have good reasons, but it's embarrassing how I've been acting."

"It doesn't bother me," Jacob said. "Sailors are used to all sorts of crazy behavior and most of us go mad for one reason or another. Wait till we've been at sea for months and you'll be the sanest one among us!"

"Or I'll be the first one to be sent to an asylum!" We both laughed. It was so good to have someone to talk to.

And there was someone else: Novio.

He was a Spaniard and his greatest delight, other than being creatively wild during drinking bouts, was showing people how to read and write. He spoke Dutch, English, Spanish and Portuguese. After Adriaen Vander Donck he is perhaps the smartest person I have ever met. He wears a broad smile and is always happy to be alive. His brown eyes have a mischievous look that invites adventure. We quickly became friends.

The best part of my time on the ship was sitting next to him under a small lantern that swayed erratically from the heavy crossbeam it's movements responding to the heeling of the ship on the swells of the sea. The shadows of the weak light of its single candle moved back and forth over the crude squiggles I wrote on the tiny piece of paper in my lap. Beside me Novio instructed me.

"The curl goes the other way," he said with a twinkle in his eye. Even in that weak light, I could see his swarthy complexion and dark hair typical of the Spanish. "Nobody will understand a backward 's,'" he said to me. I blotted out the 's' I had written being careful not to use too much ink or paper.

During our lessons, we talked about our lives and dreams. One night when neither one of us was on duty, I said, "I don't want to be what I used to be. I've made too many mistakes."

"Ah, join the company," he said, and he proceeded to tell me about his failures and setbacks and regrets.

"How can you be in such good spirits, when you have such burdens? I can't shed mine."

"It's not what happens to us that matters. Everybody has good and bad," he said. "What's important is how you think about what happens. As a child, my mother took on many lovers. I thought she didn't care for me. I know better now. Those things in my past were not my fault. They just happened."

"But don't you feel you could have done things differently?"

"Of course! But I no longer blame myself. Instead, I'm determined not to do them again. I stumble sometimes but look how good life can be anyway!"

"What if life is hellish?"

"No, no, no!" he said. "Life may have some bad experiences but look at all the good around you. We're sailing the world, seeing new things, the sun rises every day, we survived that storm last week, we can learn, we have friends. God has given us a paradise to live in!"

Novio infected me with his enthusiasm and I told him, "I'm determined to make myself into a new person"

"Fine. A lot of us do that. But what do you want your new life to be?"

"I don't know," I said to Novio. "I could do anything if I could read. Perhaps I could be wealthy enough buy a library of books." I remembered the shelves of books in Samuel's house and at the Governors office. I thought having and reading books meant you had power and prestige. So that is where I started.

Novio was often a topic of conversation among the men. Once when an Englishman and I were preparing to unfurl the fore top gallant sail with our feet on the long ropes, I called out to him: "How did Novio get so smart?"

"Ah wouldn't we all like to be like him!" he shouted above the wind. "I've heard that his father was a Spanish officer when they occupied the Netherlands. He had an affair with a Flemish woman and then abandoned their child when the Spanish were ousted. Novio's mother was so poor he had to make his own way in life."

"And why does everyone call him Novio?" I asked.

"You don't know?" he replied astonished at my ignorance. "Women chase him wherever we make port and he entertains and obliges them! Novio means boyfriend in Spanish."

The next opportunity I had to talk to Novio I said, "You seem to love so many women."

"That I do. They are wonderful company in oh so many ways!"

"But haven't you ever fallen deeply in love with just one. Maybe even think that God has a plan that you be the only one for her and she for you?"

"Oh, yes, I've been certain of that many times!" he said laughing.

"It happened for me," I said and then confided in him about Elsje.

When I finished he said to me, "You're still angry about what happened aren't you?"

"What?"

"You are a man who shows a lot of anger. I've seen you do it many times."

"But I was right about those things ... like the laudanum. It really is a devil's brew."

"That may be," he said, "but you get angry and upset far beyond most men."

His words stayed with me for days and nights. He was right. I had limitless anger toward Samuel and what he did. The knife I thrust into his table was not enough to show my outrage. But Novio also helped me to see that I was angry with my father for loving alcohol more than his family and for forcing me into a life I didn't want. I was still resentful by what Stuyvesant did and how he did it; and at Rev. Megapolensis for his hurtful words and the way he used his money and power to manipulate people.

"What about Elsje?" Novio asked when I told him what I was thinking about.

"I love her beyond all measure or reason."

"Of course you do. That is obvious. But are you not angry with her too?"

"Impossible!" I said. "She is a victim of tragic events and evil people. How could I be angry at her for that."

"I don't know," he said. But he made me ponder that possibility.

My angry outbursts gradually subsided and I went about repairing my relationships with my fellows. Whenever I had free time or when we were in the doldrums I badgered the carpenter to teach me how to repair the yardarms or replace the oakum between the planks; or asked the sailing master how to read maps and mend sails; or talked with any able bodied seaman how to carve scrimshaw or read the weather or whatever skill or knowledge they had. I trained my hands and eyes for the skills I was being taught. Every person on that ship became the schoolmasters I never had.

By the end of my two year contract with the Company I knew my alphabet well enough to write. To save paper and ink I used a tiny quail quill and made my letters as small as possible. My first writings were short letters with crudely written characters.

I wrote to my children Jan, Christian and Griet telling them about my adventures at sea with pirates and flying fish and describing the exotic things I had seen: seals at the Cape of Good Hope, Brazilian tattooed warriors, colorful houses of Curacao, the beauty of Charleston harbor, the shamans of Tortuga. I wished them well wherever life took them.

I thanked Tom Spicer for taking care of my farm on Long Island. When I signed on as a sailor I told Tom that I would sell all I owned to him for a guilder but he refused saying, "You'll return someday, Gerret, and then you'll have a place to come back to. I'll take care of everything and treat it as my own until you do."

"Then you keep all the profits if there are any, Tom, that's the least I can do for all you've done for me. I'll make my own way and perhaps I'll come back and we'll celebrate our successes."

From the beginning I knew that my letters might never reach their destinations. The ships of the Dutch West Indies Company carried only official correspondence of the Company or Church or States General. However many sailors bribed couriers or passengers or slipped their letters into the official boxes of correspondence hoping that the factors at the wharf would overlook their origin and have them delivered anyway.

I thought about writing to Elsje to ask for her forgiveness for leaving her without saying goodbye and reminisce about our time together. But I didn't want to dwell on such things and it would not have been right for me to send letters to a married woman who was not a relative. I had learned from Novio to accept the past as over and done and to love life as it happens.

Over time the other seaman came to not only befriend me but respect me. In Itamaraca when we had a major change of crew, I was elected first mate. "You are respected and you've learned everybody's job," I was told. It was a first mates responsibility to do the work of any sailor when needed.

I descended the plank two years later in Amsterdam with money, self-respect, and a determination to start a new life. By then my angers had subsided and my compulsion to be busy and to learn had become the habits of my life. I couldn't slow down or stop myself from rushing to and fro and from working long hours. Combined with my newly found self-confidence I was certain I would be successful.

Memories of the past still visit me but I treat them as old friends who teach me that I can survive the hardships of life. I do not like what happened and much of what I did. And I'm still trying to accept the past for what it was: a time of youthful exuberances and passions that inevitably had to be left behind. When my heart wanders toward Elsje I say to myself: "Be grateful that you knew her and loved her."

There you have it. That is why I am here with you and not there.

Twenty-Three

Elsje

The asylum was hell. For two weeks the Devil attacked me on every side. I was sicker, far sicker than I have ever been. I pleaded for the Reaper to take me. My body trembled and wracked by waves of hot and cold. I hid under the bed covers, paced the hallways looking for relief, pleaded for the release of death, but there was no escape. People cared for me and soothed me, but there were no comforts to match the afflictions. My desperation for laudanum was sharp and always urgent.

After the worst passed the Devil lurked behind every corner like a cat waiting to pounce and drag me back into the dark hole from whence I'd come. I admit I gave myself to him and yielded to his temptations more than once. I became an expert at stealing from medicine cabinets and taking laudanum from other patients. Even the fear of returning to my hell did not dissuade me. The Devil will shadow me, forever.

He tempts me into his traps by reminding me of the black chasm left by the death of my family. He claps the clouds into thunder, and I'm desperate to hide from falling trees. He points my eyes at burned houses and screams rise within me to warn the inhabitants. He sends the spirits of helpless children to me in nightmares, and I agonize unsuccessfully trying to save them.

But Satan is an old friend, dare I say that? The good Lord strike me down if I'm blaspheming.

He and I know that when I relive the past, I'm likely to give in to him. In an instant, he can drag me to the precipice of his black hole where his evil and hard to resist potions tempt me to give up my life for them. But I've weapons to back him down and keep him at bay. I have an arsenal of distractions, passions, friends and above all wisdom about myself that I can throw back at him. He visits me daily, but I am no longer afraid of him. Or controlled by him.

He is in this very cabin of yours, Captain. Did you know that? I can see behind you a cabinet of bottles. They are medicines are they not?

With Hannah and Mary, I faced the pain of our shared grief. We talked about the fire, the death of our parents and the loss of the children. Our shared strength was sufficient to battle the temptation to give in to despair and hopelessness. I shed tears into the ample bosom of Nana; a Jamaican woman hired as a nurse in the Asylum. She honored my grief and embraced me with warmth for she had lost her three children to a typhoid epidemic.

The angel of my salvation was Machteld. She walked the hour from Brooklyn to the Asylum at least twice a week.

"My journey is doubly good for me," she said. "I love seeing the water but most of all I like being with you."

And I liked her company. We walked the shoreline, swam in the bay, and played endless games of Ruff and Honours. I wanted to be my best when she came and that, I believe, speeded my recovery.

She said to me on several occasions, "I don't want to go back. I love it here."

So I asked her one day, "Don't you like living with your cousin, Samuel?"

"I like him in small doses," she said. "But his ways bother me."

"Why?"

"He is so cavalier as though he doesn't care deeply about anything. He's a wren flitting from here to there and talking incessantly. He acts like the world owes him his pleasures and desires. It is quite tiring."

"I'm sorry, Machteld."

"It still bothers me that he kept you on laudanum for so long. The more you and I became friends the more I realize that what he was doing was not right."

"It wasn't. Did you ever say anything to him about it."

"It's not my place. He's older than I and better educated. But we did talk about it once."

"What did he say?"

"He dismissed my concern and offhandedly said I didn't know what I was talking about. He can be so arrogant and patronizing!"

I smiled. Samuel was like that when we were children.

"I was disgusted by that whole charade of his about marrying you. His goal was to win you over, and he manipulated the Governor and the Church for his selfish purposes. You know, of course, that he beds a lot of women?"

"It doesn't surprise me."

"You were one he couldn't claim by his usual charm, so he used the laudanum to try to wear you down."

"Thank God that never happened. And thank my family for rescuing me."

"Elsje, I hope you know that I'd do anything for you and that I feel terrible about your 'troubles.'"

"Of course I do, Machteld." We always warmly embraced when she left.

I learned later that there were sentinels, slaves mostly, that prevented Samuel from seeing me while I was recovering in Gowanus. Apparently, he came there as an army of one storming the Asylum with his smooth and demanding ways to abscond with me. But he was repelled and eventually gave up his attempts.

———◆———

My family was right. About everything. Eventually, I was free of laudanum and my health returned. It took the better part of a year.

As I improved, I turned my attentions from my problems towards the needs of others. The Asylum for the Infirm and Aged in Gowanus became my home, and my love for caring for patients was reborn in me.

Despite Michiel Pauw's promises to bring the best doctors from Europe to his Asylum, he had trouble attracting anyone to the tiny settlement of Gowanus. The ongoing skirmishes between the Netherlanders and the English made New York seem unsafe. With few doctors in the Asylum, the patients looked more and more to me for advice and instruction. It was soon apparent that I was the most experienced and knowledgeable medical person there. I became the director in all but title.

Over the next couple of years, the Asylum gained a reputation for successful treatments and families brought patients to us from as far as the colonies of New York, Massachusetts Bay, and Connecticut. I was busy day and night, and I could feel the old emotions and stresses bearing down on me once again. My nights were often interrupted by an emergency or turn for the worse in a patient. Rarely did I sleep longer than a few hours. Even during those hours, I was restless, and my mind brooded on work.

I needed help and Machteld came immediately to mind. She had been so supportive and helpful to me at Samuel's house that I asked her to work with me. She readily agreed and became my assistant and constant companion. Our friendship deepened and we confided to each other the things of our hearts.

"What do you think of Cornelius Van Wormer?" she asked me one day. He was a handsome young man who had a severe case of the bloody flux and almost died. His recovery was long, and we had cared for him for weeks.

"Do you mean as a patient or as something more?" I asked, knowing that each eligible man that came to us was an object of speculation for courtship for Machteld.

"He'd be a good husband don't you think?"

"Machteld, you know nothing about him except that he is considerate to his nurses and that he makes you laugh!"

"He is more handsome than John Conklin who hardly knew Dutch at all. And he looks stronger too, don't you think?" There was a twinkle in her eye.

"Oh, you exasperate me! These are our patients, not romantic interests." But she persisted and before long she was announcing her marriage banns with Jan Voorhees who had been a patient at the Asylum after he fell from a tree.

"You need to get married too," she said to me.

"Oh I'm too old for that," I said to her. "In any case, I'm too busy to watch after a man. Who would want me?"

"Of course, you're not too old ... I'm twenty-three and just a few years younger than you! Most women first marry at our ages. And everybody admires you, Elsje. Surely any man would be proud to have you as his wife. What about Gerret?"

When the topic of romance came up, she always asked about Gerret.

"That was a long time ago, Machteld. He is gone from my life. I'm sure he's found another wife and probably has lots of children. Besides, he went to sea and gave up his farm." I had discovered that bit of information from Tom Spicer, our old neighbor, who had seen him off at the wharf.

"That doesn't have to be the end of it, Elsje. You could hire a post boy to find him and give him a message from you."

"Oh, my, that would be expensive! It's not worth it, Machteld, I am content just as I am. Why go to all the expense and trouble for something that probably isn't possible?"

"Because God didn't give us life to live alone. You liked him, you've said so many times. He might still pine for you. You said he was in love with you."

"Yes, and I with him, you're right. Nobody has ever cared for me as he did, except of course my father. Sometimes when I can't sleep I think about those days in his farm house ... they were... magical. But stop tempting me, Machteld, as much as I liked him it is over. Aren't you tending to Mrs. van Geldens childbirth ... ?"

Because she was related to the large and powerful Megapolensis family, the bann dinners held in the weeks before her wedding were many and sumptuous. Her uncle had been the pastor of the church in New York for so long that he had many loyal parishioners who hosted celebrations. I avoided the dinners and counted it as my good fortune that I never saw Samuel or his father until the day of the wedding.

After one such dinner, Machteld came to me still wearing her black Lyons silk dress with layers of pearl brocades and wonderfully sparkling silver thread. She had a huge smile on her face. "I'm so excited. Jan is taking me to the Netherlands for the honeymoon! I'll introduce him to my family, and I'll see everyone again!"

She continued, "Can you do without me for while? Maybe even for a long time?"

I would do anything for her and was pleased she was so happy about returning to her parents.

"We won't be able to go for months and months. Jan has business to wrap up here then we'll be off, and he can start his new venture."

"I thought his business was in the pelt trade."

"Oh it is, or rather it was. He says the beavers and mink and stoats are becoming too scarce to make a living at it anymore. He wants to be a financier, and he will be going to Europe to find partners."

"A financier! Of what? Is he to be a banker?"

"Not exactly. He is using the money he made in the fur trade to invest in merchant ships. It has made him quite wealthy. But pirates have made those investments quite risky. Now he invests on the other side of the hedge."

"The 'other side of the hedge'?"

"Yes, he invests in pirate ships also. He gets his fair amount of whatever they capture. That way he makes money whatever happens on the seas."

I was amazed at the complexities of such things and appalled that respectable people supported thieves and robbers. Perhaps I shouldn't have been surprised. Pirate captains were celebrities, and many were quite wealthy. They boldly walked the streets of New York looking for investors who would bankroll their next adventure.

Machteld continued. "Everyone is doing it today and getting rich. My uncle, Rev. Megapolensis, was one of the first. Even though he was a preacher, his real wealth came from his investments."

"But he is a minister of the Gospel!" I was shocked. "He preached against wealth and luxury and extravagance. I can't believe he invested in pirates to make money."

"He uses his wealth for good things, Elsje. He gives generously to all the Dutch Reformed Churches. He built Rev. Polhemus' church in Midwout and was the major donor to the Deacons house for the poor in Manhattan."

"It sounds sinister to me and an affront to those of us who work hard for our money. I suppose he also supports his family?" I knew the answer to this question but asked it anyway.

"Oh, yes. Almost everything that Samuel has comes from my uncle: his education, his travels, his house, and servants are all paid for by Rev. Megapolensis. And Theodorus and Hannah, your sister, also get money from him."

It pained me to be reminded of that. I loved my sister, but I hated thinking that she and Theodorus were so beholden to the preacher.

"I'm sure you will have a wonderful time in the Netherlands, Machteld. But don't plan on staying there. I need you here! You know I will miss you terribly!"

———◆———

The wedding was held at St. Nicholas Church in New York City. Machteld's parents couldn't give their permission for the marriage because they were in Holland, so her uncle did so on their behalf. I hadn't seen him for several years, and I wondered how I would react to my old nemesis when I saw him. He was to perform the wedding and her cousin Samuel was to escort her. Somehow she had managed to maintain a good relationship with him despite her misgivings about his treatment of me.

The wedding service started with the schoolmaster, topped with his black conical hat with wide brim, reading the epistles and leading the singing of psalms. Machteld entered on Samuel's arm, and when they passed me, he smiled stiffly in my direction. When Rev. Megapolensis shuffled in from the chancel door, I was stunned to see how old the man looked. Using a cane, he was helped by one of the Deacons up the stairs to the pulpit. His right hand shook as he steadied himself on the railing and his left hand was clenched and rigid. His voice was weak as though hoarse from illness yet he was able to read the formula of marriage and receive the oaths from the bride and groom. His sermon was brief and focused on the sacrifices that must be made in a Christian marriage to follow the hard way of Christ. We strained to hear his weak voice.

Because of my responsibilities at the Asylum, I missed the meals given in the days after the wedding. But I hosted the culminating feast in Gowanus. We Calvinist Dutch are known for austerity in many things, but when it comes to festivals and celebrations, we loosen our restraints. Knowing that the Megapolensis meals would not have sweets because they were "from the Devil," we lavished our table with sugar cakes, marzipan, sugared almonds and beans, and tasty cordials. The Asylum bakers outdid themselves with cakes, pastries, and elaborate molded fruits.

To my surprise, Samuel came to our feast. I greeted him cordially at the entrance to the salon where the meal was set out. He asked if he could speak to me privately.

"Of course," I said not wanting to do so.

When the meal was finished, and guests were mingling with each other, he and I went to the solarium.

"You've been very kind to Machteld," he said.

"She is a wonderful girl and deserves all the support she can get. And she is a skilled nurse."

"What you are doing here is very admirable." We were not looking at each other but gazing at the guests many of whom were patients. I remained silent waiting for him to come to whatever he wanted to say to me.

"I have a favor to ask of you," he said.

I smiled thinking that he must be swallowing his pride to be asking a favor of me.

"My father is not well and is getting worse rapidly. He can barely walk, and his tremors make it impossible for him to do much for himself. You saw him at his best at the wedding, but that is not the way he usually is."

"I noticed how frail he has become," I said wondering where this was leading.

"I want you to take him into the Asylum, Elsje. His needs are beyond what our servants can provide. He needs wise medical care. You will let him be a patient here, won't you?"

I was shocked and, I must admit, horrified at the idea of having him in the same place where I worked every day. Then my father's words came to mind: "Elsje, take care of everyone no matter who they are or where they come from."

I promised my father I would do just that. Now that promise had come back to haunt me.

———

The Asylum was perched on a bluff known as "The Heights" and overlooked Gowanus harbor. We placed a bench on the bluff where the view was spectacular. We encouraged patients to sit outside and restore their spirits with the beauty of the water and the distant shoreline of New Jersey. The gulls swooped overhead reminding us that there was another world far from the bandages and medicines that consumed Asylum life. It was my favorite spot whenever I could steal a few moments from my responsibilities.

Late one afternoon, a few months after Machteld left with her husband, I watched the sun setting over the bay. It played hide and seek behind clouds and brilliantly painted the sky with orange and purple colors. The water was still, and a sparkling highway of light shined off the water from the sun to me. At the same time, a dozen rays of sunlight streamed through the clouds heading toward distant parts of the seas.

"If I could walk those sunbeams," I said to myself, "I'd be able to see where Machteld is and what she is doing." I missed her terribly, and I knew when she returned it would never be the same. She would live not with me but her husband. We wouldn't be as close as we had been. Her first attachment rightly would be to her husband.

I was alone. My sisters had their lives that differed from mine, and their attentions were to their families, churches, and communities. We rarely visited one another. I had patients I liked and who might have been friends, but when they healed they returned to their own lives.

That afternoon I sat on The Heights with no one with whom to share the moment. No one to join me in marveling at the beauty. No one to talk about what happened during the day. No one to add warmth to my small room on the second floor of the Gowanus Inn. No daughter to make me laugh and dream about the future.

"Why did he go to sea?" I heard my heart ask. "He knows. He was there when everything happened. He loved me."

I did not know why Gerret ceased his attentions toward me. He left no messages. No explanations. He boarded a ship and sailed away. More than once during the last couple years, I hoped he would walk into the Asylum to find me, and we'd be together. But he was becoming a distant memory of the time before the "troubles." The life that didn't exist anymore.

Until that day on The Heights when the hole in my heart expanded and swallowed me.

"Which sunbeam leads to you, Gerret?" my heart said as I sat alone on the bench. "I'd give up all I have to pay your way back to me."

The rays coming through the clouds were brighter than ever. My longing took feet and walked the highway of reflected sunlight on the water. When it reached the sun, it followed one of the beams eastward traveling into the distance getting smaller and smaller. It seemed to know where it was going.

"Bring him back to me," I said. "Tether him to a line and draw him home."

Twenty-Four

Gerret

A few months after I arrived in Amsterdam, I navigated the crowds in Dam Square shopping the stalls of cloth, pots, farm tools, vegetables, and candles that always that line the streets of the square. Now that I could read, I devoured all writing I could find. When I saw a wrinkled, discarded coranto with the weekly news printed on its folio pages, I picked it up from the cobblestones. It contained an announcement for the New Amsterdam Society which naturally caught my eye. I read its invitation to join the weekly meetings where people shared their experiences and opinions about the trading settlement when it was Dutch.

The Society met at a tavern near the men's rooming house where I shared a room with Novio. After building up my courage to revisit old memories, I went on a Saturday afternoon. In all my thirty-two years I've never been comfortable in a crowd of strangers but when I entered, and they discovered that I'd lived in New Amsterdam most of my life, I was welcomed as an old friend of each one of them. Some had romanticized the New World even though they had never been there. Some had only passed through on trading ships. The few of us who knew the settlement were sought out to tell stories, to give descriptions of daily life and landmarks, and to answer questions about family and friends who still lived there. That first day I was the center of everyone's attention, and they plied me with question after question. I couldn't speak long enough for them.

"Who runs the ferry now?"

"What is the Director doing now that he is disgraced?"

"What is Governor Nichols like?"

"Do you know how doctor Nyssen is?"

"What changes have the English made?"

"Is it worth investing in beaver pelts anymore?"

"Do you know anything about a girl who works the wharves named Antonia?"

It had been over two years since I lived there, so I answered as best I could and mumbled a reply to the question about Elsje's father.

"How do you like living here?" asked an old seaman with leathered, well-tanned skin.

"I'm having the time of my life," I said. "I love the painting exhibitions, especially the ones by Rembrandt. The chaos of the stock market is fascinating. My favorite is the Botanical Garden. I'm in their library as often as I can to read their illustrated books. Did you know they have plants at the Gardens from New Amsterdam collected and sent here by someone I used to know."

"Have you been to one of Dr. Tulp's dissections?"

"No, I've avoided that. All the blood and gore, you know."

I quickly changed the subject: "I've been learning how to do a lot of jobs and learning so much about herring fishing, coopering, and pile driving. I was a shoemaker for a while just like my father. Now I'm driving the animals for canal barges. Good way to learn about people while we walk the towpaths."

"But don't you miss New Amsterdam?"

"Life is hard there. The land isn't forgiving for farms or gardens. And it's pretty chaotic, people moving in and out all the time, the English taking over, the wilden, and you know how awful the pelt trade is now. Sure there are opportunities there for anyone no matter how rich or connected you are. But I like life here better."

I regularly returned to the Society meetings. As I heard others talk glowingly about New Amsterdam, there was born in me longings for my old home. I had expected that I could find my place in the Netherlands, even call it home for the rest of my life. But New Amsterdam was in my blood, and I was curious about my children, our tavern, my farm on Long Island, Tom Spicer and, of course, Elsje.

One of the Society's regulars was a widow who returned to Holland when her husband had collapsed and died on De Heere Street near my childhood home. She was an exceptional cook and prepared meals from crops native to 'America' as it now was being called. We had corn chowder and fried tomatoes and oysters and something she called 'East River bluefish' which are caught in the English Channel in the summer. One day she even brought tobacco from Long Island and we passed several pipes among us. I found that New Amsterdam was not only in my blood but also in my stomach.

Like a migrating bird who returns to its place of birth and nests on the same chimney every year I was slowly being drawn back into my old life.

W as I tempted to go back to New Netherlands? Of course. But my need for income and my dedication to the New Amsterdam Society kept me from the extended absence of several months it would take to travel to America. This was especially true after I was elected President of the Society which was an honor and responsibility I took seriously.

Originally the Society was only a social group, but all of us wanted to send to friends and family in New Amsterdam letters, gifts, tools, construction supplies, and household goods that were not available there. We pooled our resources and hired couriers and rented space on West India Company ships at a discount rate.

As the amount of goods we sent increased we developed our own business for buying, transporting, insuring, storage and shipping. We had clients far beyond our Society membership and were transporting far more than gifts. We started shipping tiles, furniture, fine linens and rugs, clocks, engraving tools, and books; and back to Europe, we took timber, sugar, minerals, cotton, beads made by the wilden, pelts and exotic plants and herbs.

It was complex business, and as President, I was deeply involved in it all. I spent more and more time on Society business and had to limit my work driving the barge canal to just a day or two a week. I had so little income that I borrowed from Society members who said to me, "You should be paid for being President."

Wealthy men had become members of the Society, and they contributed generously to the business. Abraham Van Duyn made a fortune in the early years of the pelt trade before the beavers and minks declined. Jacob Kolf had lived many places plying the lucrative spice trade, but his favorite place was New Amsterdam. Arent Evertson made his wealth as a stockbroker on the West Indies trade and was enamored with the New World even though he had never been there. He was one of the Directors of the Dutch West India Company, and it was a coup to have him as part of the Society.

As our transport business grew, these wealthy men asked if I would consider being the first Director of the Society and receive a stipend as well. The job was perfect. My life had prepared me for all aspects of the work. I negotiated with farmers for specialty foods to ship, with brewers for the best equipment for taverns in New Amsterdam, with apothecaries for medicines, with ship owners to obtain bargains on shipping cargo, and with sailors to become our couriers.

When the Dutch West India Company collapsed from poor management and debt the demand for shipping was higher than ever and former Company investors turned to our fledgling group. They infused us with enough capital to buy ships and purchase warehouses on the Princengracht Canal not far from where my father lived when he was young. Our business, *The New Amsterdam Society Trading Company*, sold shares on the Amsterdam stock market raising even more cash.

A year and a half after the demise the Dutch West India Company those of us who were engaged in the Atlantic trade realized the need to reorganize the Company to compete with the English, Spanish and Portuguese. Thus the new Dutch West India Company was born, and I was chosen to be one of the ten new Directors. If this had happened to me earlier in life, I would have had power over Stuyvesant instead of the other way around. Imagine that! In just a few years I had gone from an immigrant without prospects to a wealthy, powerful man who directed a subsidiary of one of the largest companies in the world.

Of course, I sent gifts to my family and friends in New Amsterdam: the most popular toys to my children, top quality cooking pots and a modern spinning wheel to my sister Christina, and farm equipment to Tom Spicer at half the cost. Giving these presents gave me great pleasure.

I assume people in New Amsterdam knew about my change in fortunes, but I didn't mention that in the notes that accompanied the gifts. I merely wished them the best and told them I remembered them.

Y ou know the park on Middellane just off the Amstel River? The one just north of the new canal? One Sabbath afternoon about three years after my arrival in Holland the New Amsterdam Society met for a social outing in the park. It was warm and breezy, I recall, and we used stones to secure our blankets and baskets from the wind. Rebecca and Karel Boerum, one of the couples that started our group (you know them, right?) brought with them a newlywed couple who had just arrived from New Amsterdam. They had been married in Manhattan and were visiting the girl's parents who lived next door to the Boerums.

The young husband spoke over an hour about how New Amsterdam was the finance capital of the New World and about the complexities of investing. He kept us spellbound about the potential of success for anyone who wanted to make money. I'm sure after his talk several of us invested with him. When he finished, we pressed him to say more about life in New Amsterdam (in the Society refuse to refer to it as New York).

"I've spoken far too much already!" he said. "I better stop."

"No!" came shouts from the audience, "Don't stop now!"

"Let my bride speak. She's lived there several years now."

He introduced his wife, Machteld, and asked her to describe her years with her cousin Samuel on Long Island. When she told us how Samuel and his father had changed their name from Mecklenburg to Megapolensis, we nodded. Everyone had heard about the Megapolensis family.

"But my real life there began when I started working at the Asylum for the Aged and Infirm in Gowanus." Most of us were unaware of the recently established Asylum.

"It is run by the most remarkable physician," Machteld said with a twinkle in her eye. "She's very smart and is familiar treatments unknown to other physicians, barbers or surgeons. She learns from the wilden, talks to ship's barbers from all countries, has her own apothecary and experiments with new treatments for her patients. The medicinal plants she collects for the Botanical Institute in Leyden are highly prized, and she has discovered new treatments that have earned her great respect."

She had to be talking about no one other than Elsje. I smiled pleased to know that Elsje was successful in what she loved to do. Machteld continued briefly about the Asylum and the town of Gowanus excusing her brevity because of her husband's long talk. I approached her afterward.

"Machteld, thank you for what you said. Could you tell me more about the woman who runs the Asylum? I know her."

"Everyone seems to know her."

"She and I were close a long time ago."

"She is such an inspiration to me. I'm so fortunate to have known her as long as I have. Might I ask who you are?"

"I'm Gerret. Gerret Snedeker."

"You're Gerret! Oh, my Lord, the Gerret?"

"Yes, I suppose I am 'the' Gerret. How do you know..."

"Gerret!" She shook her head in disbelief. "Elsje is more than my employer she is my best friend. She has told me all about you."

"She speaks of me?"

She was still shaking her head. "I can't believe I've met you here! We crossed paths once before you know."

"We did?"

"Well we didn't get introduced, but I saw you the last time you visited Elsje. At Samuel's house."

I had tried to erase that day from my mind. "Elsje's nurse? You're the one who ...."

"Yes, told you that she was asleep."

"How is she?"

"She is doing very, very well. Healthy. Busy. Especially now that I'm here and not helping her."

"She is over her ... troubles?" I didn't know how else to put it.

"I know what you are talking about. Yes, she is. I was with her at the worst. It was trying, but she made it through. Now she is in the best of health."

"And living in Gowanus?"

"She and I share an apartment in the Inn on the Asylum grounds. I did most of the cooking and laundry as she is so in demand."

"She's not married?"

"No. No husband. No children."

"I thought ... she and Samuel ... they seemed so ... Didn't they announce their banns?"

"Cousin Samuel! Heavens no!" She laughed and told me that the two of them had had a falling out after the 'troubles' and that they had only re-met recently at her wedding. When she told me about how Samuel had tried to take her from the Asylum, I felt old anger within me. When the moment had passed, I asked, "Is she happy?"

"I think she has made peace with her life. She enjoys her work. Gerret, if I could be so forward, I think she'd like to see you."

"The last time I saw her she told me to live my life without her."

"Have you done that?"

"Yes, I sailed the world and have a good life here. I'm a different person." I paused then said, "But I still think of her."

When I told her about my business she said, "A Director of the Company!" she took a step backward to look at me. "Isn't life full of surprises."

When Machteld and Jan spent several weeks traveling the Netherlands, I tried to think of ways to get free of my work in Amsterdam to go to Elsje. It would be complicated to do so given how busy I was and the slim chance of renewing our relationship. It had been five years since we saw each other, and I supposed she only thought of me as a friend from the past. I did not want to disrupt the life she seemed to love. "No," I thought, "Machteld is being kind by suggesting I be in touch with her."

But my mind couldn't stop thinking of Elsje and possibilities with her. I rehearsed what I would say if we met.

Before Machteld returned home, she came to Amsterdam and asked me, "I'd like to tell Elsje that I met you."

The moment of decision had come. "Tell her I am fine and doing well and that I send her my best."

"That's all? Are you going to leave it at that? Why don't you join Jan and me and go back to New York and see her?"

I paused still uncertain of what to do.

"Write her a letter then and I'll deliver it," Machteld offered. "Be honest. Tell her about your life. The least you can do, Gerret, is keep the door open."

She looked at her new husband, and both of them glowed. "Being in love is a special thing!" she said as she winked at me.

Twenty-Five

Elsje

By the time Rev. Megapolensis came to us, he was a shell of the man I had known. His left arm was rigid and unmoving. When he tried to walk, it was with the assistance of two people so he wouldn't topple over. His preaching voice was reduced to a hoarse whisper, and he formed his words slowly. His hands trembled like jelly, and he was stooped over looking at the floor. I tried to see him purely as a patient and not as the pompous preacher he had been but, of course, it was hard to do so.

Samuel brought him to us soon after the wedding, before Machteld went on her trip to Europe. I asked her to be the primary caregiver for her uncle so I could make my interactions with him as brief as possible. The progression of his shaking apoplexy was unstoppable despite the extracts of willow bark, henbane, and spiraea we gave him. His bed and chair were in one of the smaller rooms in a corner near a window. From there he could look out on the gardens, Gowanus Bay, the small dock owned by Michiel Pauw, and the occasional ships beyond.

At first, he received many visitors: his family, of course, and members and zieckentroosters of St. Nicholas Church. When Samuel came, I avoided him and busied myself in the apothecary or the herb garden. I had not forgiven him for keeping me imprisoned and dependent on laudanum. In any case, as time passed I wanted less and less to stir up old embarrassments and angers. When I did interact with him, I cast out of my mind our past and treated him as the son of one of my patients and nothing more.

Machteld spoke privately to me one afternoon as we were changing the sheets of a bed where a patient had died.

"Samuel visited today," she said.

"I know. How did the visit go?" She knew I was aware of all the visitors that come to the Asylum so she must have some reason for bringing up the subject.

"The two of them argued about you."

"About me?" I wasn't sure I wanted to hear about it.

"I was in the room with them, but they took no notice of me. Uncle Johann was angry and demanded to know why he was in the Asylum with 'that woman,' as he put it. I knew he was talking about you."

We measured the sheets and tucked them in.

Machteld continued, "Samuel said to his father, 'She's a good woman, Father. She was gracious to take you in, and this is the best place for you. You have everything you need here, and you won't get any better medical care in all of the colonies.'"

"His eyes glared at Samuel, 'But I'm not getting any better am I! How can you call her good after all that she has done in her life? I thought I taught you never to trust her. The Devil disguises His work in attractive people. Don't be deceived!'"

"I was taken aback, Elsje, by what Samuel said next: 'I believed you, Father. For a long time. But I'm not sure anymore. There is too much good and compassion and healing in this place. Perhaps she is an angel sent by God to care for you while you are sick.'"

"'The Devil is tempting you. Don't be seduced! It will only lead to your downfall.'"

"He was getting agitated, Elsje, so I placed a wet cloth on his forehead and tried to calm him. "

"You did the right thing, Machteld," I said. "It is not helpful for him to be upset."

"Thanks, you taught me that. But Samuel wasn't willing to let his father rest. He said to his Father, 'She deserves to know.'"

"Uncle Johann forced his voice to whisper as loud as he could and said, 'That one doesn't deserve to know anything.' He closed his eyes and turned away. You know that way he has of shutting down a conversation and retreating into himself."

I nodded.

"I turned to Samuel and asked, 'What were you talking about? Know what?'"

"He grumbled apparently in frustration and said, 'Just the rambling of an old, sick man reliving his past.'"

"Forget about it, Machteld, the past is past," I said to her.

Several months later Machteld left on her honeymoon, and I assumed more care of her uncle. I had a male assistant who tended to his private and personal matters, but I was in his room more often than I liked.

Early one winter morning as the sun shone its warmth through the window I searched for a sweater for him in the drawers of the small bureau that held his personal belongings. In the bottom drawer, under his heavier clothes, I happened upon a silver hairpin with the seal of Holland attached to it. My heart stopped as I saw the familiar object that I held. It was black with tarnish, but there was no question about where it came from.

"Where did you get this?" I asked the old man who was sitting in his chair.

He was silent and refused to acknowledge my question. He had a habit of doing so when he didn't want to talk.

"I know you can speak! Tell me where you got this pin!" I knelt down to his level and waved it in front of his eyes so he couldn't avoid seeing it. He said nothing.

"This is Alice's hairpin, isn't it?" I thought none of Alice's belongings had been recovered after the tempest. The hairpin had been her prized possession and the only object that would tie Alice to her mother, Jannette. I was stunned.

I tightened my fist around the hairpin and brought it to my chest. I closed my eyes. Charming Alice with the bright eyes and fetching smile. With thin blonde hair clasped by her shiny hairpin. And Jannette, gone long ago and still a hole in my heart.

I faced the old man. With my heart pounding I said with clenched teeth, "You son of a whore, how did you get this?" He deserved that language rare as it was for me to use it. "Where did you get this? Alice was all I had for God's sake!"

He smiled. Not a soft smile but a wry one. He looked at me silently as anger raged within me. Then he said in a voice stronger than usual but with an edge to it, "You don't know what happened."

"What do you mean? Of course, I knew what happened. I was there!"

He stared at the floor his head trembling. Seconds past. I stood before him demanding an answer. Finally, he flicked his eyes at me for a second.

He whispered, "It was for her."

"What was? For who?"

"I did what was right." His voice was weakening, and his eyes were closing. He seemed to be speaking to himself.

I was desperate for him to answer my questions but he was withdrawing.

"You've got to speak! For the love of God Almighty talk to me!" But he had gone into himself. His illness a shield against my demands.

I stared at him willing him to say something, but he did not acknowledge me further. I clutched Alice's hairpin closer.

I knew it was futile to demand more of him, so I turned my back to the old man and left his room. There was one other person who might know what he knew. His son, Samuel.

I went to the stables where the carriage used to transport patients was parked. I ordered the liveryman to make it ready, and we drove northward to Brooklyn heading straight for Samuel's house.

I rapped loudly on the front door and demanded to see Samuel.

When the servant had fetched him, and he saw me on the front stoop, he said, "That's a worried look. Is everything all right with Father?"

"Walk with me!" I demanded.

He fetched his coat and joined me. Together we headed down the King's Road toward the ferry and the Inn where my old friend Miriam used to live.

"What is your father hiding from me?" I asked Samuel.

"I don't know what you are talking about. What makes you think that?"

"This!" I said. I showed him the hairpin. "This belonged to my niece, Alice. How did your father get this?"

We walked in silence for a while.

"You were never meant to know," he finally said.

"Know what?"

"That Alice was rescued from the fire."

"What?" Everything in my body stopped. My breath was motionless.

"Alice is alive," he murmured.

I stared at him. My mind spinning. "Alive?"

"Yes. In Holland."

"She is? And ... and you kept this from me?"

He took a deep breath. "I know how this sounds but we did it for her."

"You 'rescued' her and kept her from me, the only mother she ever knew, and you say you did it for her?"

He was silent then said, "Her mortal soul was in danger with you. We made sure she was baptized and raised by a good Christian family."

"Are you saying that because she was not baptized you stole her from me to save her soul?"

"She was raised by my aunt and uncle in Amsterdam who made sure she was brought up in a wholesome family and the one true faith."

"What! You thought I wasn't a good mother, so you took her from me?"

"You used pagan practices, Elsje. Wilden and popish ways and God only knows what else. You didn't bring her forward for Christian baptism. And her mother was a fornicator. Somebody had to step in if her life was to be redeemed."

I shook my head in disbelief. There was no arguing with this man or his father or their warped ways. I took a different tack.

"How is she?"

"She is fine. How old would she be now? Fifteen or so?"

"Thirteen." I could never forget how old she was.

Thirteen years. Did she look like her mother Jannette, slim with blonde hair? Did she still attract a crowd with her fetching smile and outgoing personality? I could still clearly see her in the marketplace drawing people to our booth.

"Does she know anything about where she came from or about me?"

"She was only five. I've seen her a couple of times since ... well, since she went to Holland. Nobody talks with her about the early years."

"She doesn't know who her real kin are?"

"She's adopted, Elsje. Many of the children in my aunt's house have awful circumstances that made them orphans. Auntie M has chosen not to talk to the children about their past. Alice's kin are the people she now calls family."

"How ... could ... you?"

"Theodorus knew about it too," he said as though that would make it more acceptable.

"My brother in law, Hannah's husband?" I was astonished.

"He's the one who found her in the kindling box."

I wasn't sure I could trust whatever he said to me.

"It was her hiding place, remember?" Samuel said. "She survived because she hid in the brick cubbyhole during the tempest." I tried to picture Alice in the box with destruction all around her.

"Theodorus and his father found her there."

"Why didn't Theodorus just bring her to me? I was her mother after all."

"I know you are going to find this hard to believe, Elsje, but we are all beholden to my father. He is a forceful and rich man. He was obsessed with you. He thought that you and your father were the worst corrupting forces in New Amsterdam. Certainly, you know that."

Of course, I did. Everyone knew that.

"And you were in no shape after the tempest to care for anyone. You were in shock and not in your right mind after the deaths. You would have been a poor mother in that state."

"After the tempest, we needed to be with each other not separated."

"Elsje, you ran away after the fire and went to Gowanus where you encountered even more tragedy. Certainly, that is not what a sane mother would do. We feared you would take Alice with you, and she would see more devastation and suffering."

This man had no heart.

"That is not all. Do you know about Johan?"

"Johan?"

"My dead older brother. He was in an accident when he was young. Your father should have treated him but instead took him to an African healer where he died. My father was devastated by the loss of his first son and blamed your father for Johan's death."

There had been many families over the years who blamed him for one thing or another, or me for that matter, especially when a loved one died. It was part of the life of being a physician.

"I was told you were there when it happened."

I struggled to enter the fog of the past. "The boy caught in the wagon wheel in front of our house...?"

"It rankled my father that Teunis Nyssen had a child that was healthy when his son was taken from him. When your father refused to accept the blame and continued to treat patients even after my father exposed him from the pulpit, he gave up on him and focused on you. "

"But that doesn't make sense. I had nothing to do with it."

"Yes, I know. But my father quoted the Bible: *'The iniquity of the fathers shall be visited upon the children, and upon the children's children, unto the third and to the fourth generation.'* You paid for your father's mistake, Elsje. My father singled you out in the pulpit in the hope that you would repent of the ways of your father. And when you didn't he went to the next generation to try to save your family. "

"By taking Alice from me."

"Yes, he was frustrated that he made no progress with either you or your father. He was trying to save someone in your family and prevent Alice from being exposed to your corrupting influences."

"Nothing ever justifies taking a small child from her family! She was so young and innocent, Samuel!"

"He ordered us to find a way to rescue her from you. 'To redeem something good from that family' is the way he put it. And he proudly kept the hairpin as a reminder of the good he did with Alice. 'My biggest success' he said."

In front of us on the road, a robin cocked its head. We stopped to look at the first signs of spring. In an instant, it drove its beak into the ground and pulled forth a worm and held it captive. The worm writhed but was doomed.

It had to be more than saving her soul. He was trying to punish my father and cause him pain, just as he had experienced loss and pain.

"And who were we to contradict him?" Samuel went on. "He was the authority on eternal life and how one should live this life to get there. He was my father, and I needed his support. We all did. Theodorus and Rev. Polhemus and I knew that if we didn't obey him, he wouldn't support us."

"I cannot believe how selfish you all are!"

"It was a long time ago."

"As though that excuses everything! It may be a long time ago for you, but I've been living with her loss every hour of every day!"

We watched the robin gobble the worm and fly off to a nearby tree.

"Are you telling me about this now just because I found the hairpin?"

"Elsje, my father is old and sick. We both know he will die soon. You carried the burden of his attacks, and I have been controlled by him all my life. But once he is gone, we will both be free. Perhaps it is time to face the truth of what happened and put it behind us. You should know about Alice."

I felt like I was walking with the Devil and the sooner I was out of his company the better.

"I have a question for you, Samuel. Why did you keep me in your house for so long?" It was finally time to ask him the question.

"You know as well as I that you can't quickly remove laudanum from someone who is dependent upon it. I planned to wean you from it gradually. And when you continued to demand the laudanum, I hoped to keep you on it long enough that you'd return to the Church and respectability, and to me."

"And if I did I'd be your trophy! And how pleased your father would be that you accomplished what he couldn't," my voice had an edge. Then I said mockingly: "Look at that great man Samuel! He converted the Devil's maid-servant, stole her daughter, and made them both good little Christians."

It was his turn to say nothing.

"You announced our marriage banns without my permission! How could you?"

"That is not true. You said you needed me and that you wanted to stay in my house. I took that to mean that you were willing to be my wife."

"Wife? I needed you to give me laudanum not to be my husband. And, of course, I wanted to stay there. Anyone dependent on laudanum wants to stay where there is a free supply."

"You're right, Elsje." His voice was softening, and a wall was falling. "I thought I could anchor you to me, and you'd come to love me. You are the only woman I've ever met who was my equal."

There was no way I could forgive him.

"Didn't you have feelings for me, Elsje?"

"Whatever I felt about you was shattered by what you did to me. And, no, I have no 'feelings' toward you. You and your father disgust me."

He was about to say something and chose not to.

"Who took her to the Netherlands?"

"My father did. My aunt and uncle adopted her and raised her as their own. Alice is their daughter."

I twinged when he said that.

Then I remembered that Samuel's aunt and uncle were Machteld's parents and that she was now in Holland. She was with her adopted sister, Alice, my daughter.

Twenty-Six

Elsje

J an and Machteld were in Europe for well over a year. During that time I brooded over whether I should go to Holland and find Alice or whether I should let her live the life others had destined for her.

I refused to have anything more to do with Rev. Megapolensis. Others cared for him, and I gave no attention to his needs. When it came to him, it didn't matter what I promised my father about caring for everyone. I also kept my distance from Hannah and Theodorus not knowing what to say to them about Alice. For all I knew Hannah was as much in the dark about what happened as I was. And confronting Theodorus wasn't going to help anything.

Machteld returned glowing from her experiences in Europe. On her first night home, we drank tea at the tiny table in front of the fireplace where we had once lived together. After she had described places she had seen I asked her, "Tell me, Machteld, do your parents have a child at home named Alice?"

"Why, yes they do. She is the oldest at their home right now. You know they have many adopted children?"

"Yes, you mentioned that before. Tell me about Alice."

"She's smart and pretty, and even a little flirty especially with men. Everyone likes her. Why do you ask?"

I told her about the conversation I had with Samuel. She looked at me wide-eyed, her mouth open in surprise as I revealed who Alice was.

"I knew nothing about this, Elsje," she said. "We don't talk about the past in my parent's house."

"I have to see her, Machteld."

"Of course, you do! You should go right away. She is old enough now that I think my parents would allow that to happen. But how will you tell her, Elsje? I'm sure she will be shocked by what you'd reveal."

"I'd tell her the truth, that's all. She could decide herself what she wants to do about what I say."

"She is a mature young lady, Elsje. You'd be proud of her."

Tears came to my eyes.

"Would you want her to come back with you?" Machteld asked.

"I don't know. I don't know what I want. I want her to be happy."

"Well, she's happy now. She has young men who are interested in her, and she is the smartest girl in her studies. I told her about America and she said, 'I love the adventure of new places!' I think she would like to know and see where she was born."

That thought pleased me. What would it be like to have Alice, the alive Alice, with me?

"And I have a surprise for you, Elsje. Something I brought back from Holland." She handed me a small box with edges worn and dirty. "Sorry it is so tattered," she said. "The travel you know."

I opened the box and inside were several bulbs in dry straw.

"Guess what they are," she said to me.

"Flower bulbs, obviously."

"Of course, but guess what cultivar they are."

"I have no idea, Machteld. You will have to tell me."

"They are tulips. Admiral Sneds."

I looked up at her bewildered. Of course, I remembered that tulip and to whom they belonged. I still had dried petals in my Bible from the ones he had left at our house.

"He is all alone, Elsje. Never remarried."

"Truly? You met him and talked to him?" I asked.

"At the New Amsterdam Society."

She told me about the Society and how Gerret was there the day her husband spoke.

"You obviously must have talked about me since you brought me his gift."
"He thought you were married to Samuel!"
"Samuel?" We both laughed about that.
"He thought I was married and so stayed away?"
"Well, ... yes. But he also said you told him you didn't want him. That he should have a life without you."
"He did? I would not have said something like that! He saved my life after the tempest."
"You said a lot of things you don't remember, Elsje, when you were in your troubles."
"There is a letter." She handed me an envelope. It was sealed with the mark of the Dutch West Indies Company.

———◆———

My very dear Elsje,

My heart filled with a freshening wind when Machteld told me that you are happy and well. After all these years nothing could have cheered me more than to know you are doctoring and caring for the patients to which your lovely compassion has always lead you.

Elsje, my love for you is deathless. I am anchored to you by chains even Providence cannot break. I have sought, with all the powers of reason God has given me, to understand why we are not together. Please know, my love, that I departed from you under an assumption that has proven to be false. It was my sincere prayer that my leaving would allow another to whom I assumed you were married to give you all you needed or desired. Please forgive me for my sad and wrong conclusion that led me away from you. And look past my many other faults that may have been the cause of your hurt and our separation. How I wish I could go back and wash with my tears the stain of adversity and loneliness I may have left on your happiness. But I cannot. Neither can I make amends for my absence from you while you faced the misfortunes and joys of life that Machteld told me you have had.

The memories of the blissful moments I spent with you are as real to me today as when they happened. I feel most grateful to God for those moments and have imagined how they might have continued had our lives been joined. I cannot have any claim upon God to ask Him for His favor, but a spirit stirs within me that tells me that we may be able to rekindle what we once had. Offer me one word of encouragement and I shall instantly fly to you at hearing it. Perhaps the burdens of your duties may instead allow you the freedom to travel and to chance a renewal of our relationship. I shall await your invitation or arrival every week. Machteld knows the places where I may be found.

But if Providence does not bring us together, Elsje, never forget how much I love you and that it will be your name I shall whisper when my final breath is spent. In life and in death I belong to you, and it is, and will, be my spirit that dances with the wind that blows your hair and flickers the candle in your darkest night.

Elsje, let us not mourn what we did not have. Rather join me in lifting praise to Almighty God for the delights He graciously bestowed upon us.

I am yours now and always.

Gerret

Twenty-Seven

Gerret

" **A**lice, remember when we first met? You came to the Society meeting, and you looked so fresh and young. We have a lot of older visitors but you on the other hand ... "

"It was embarrassing! People surrounded me eager to know who I was and why I was there."

"Oh, you liked it! We do that to everyone new. We hunger for anything about New Amsterdam, and we hoped you would be able to feed us some morsels."

"I disappointed them, didn't I? I didn't know anything about America."

"You didn't disappoint me! We both discovered many new things."

"I came to learn about where I was born and found out I have family I never knew about."

"That's what we think. We don't know for sure."

"Who else could it be? The timing works out perfectly: I was five years old when I was adopted, and you say it was the same year as the tempest. I came from New Amsterdam. I vaguely remember the crossing and the ship. My name is Alice, and you say I resemble her."

"It is sad how secretive your parents are with you and your brothers and sisters. Everybody should know their kin."

" *'The truth will come out'* they say. I would have found out one way or another. They didn't count on cousin Samuel to write to me that I was born there. I wonder why he took so long to tell me? He said he was proud of what he did and wanted everyone to know that he 'saved' me."

"You know that I don't trust your cousin. He may have some hidden motive why he wrote to you."

"Yes, it's pretty obvious how you feel from what you've told me about him."

"He took quite an interest in you, didn't he?"

"He was exotic! When he or Uncle Johannes came to visit, they were especially interested in me. I had them to myself. My sisters and brothers teased me about it."

"It sure seems to add up. We'll only know for sure if she comes."

"I wish I knew about this when Machteld was here. I have a hundred questions to ask her. At least I have her to thank for telling me about the Society. Otherwise, I never would have met you. She makes New York sound fascinating."

"Yes, she knows a lot about life there and Elsje."

"What about you? Would you like to meet her again?"

"Well, yes and no. I can still see her blue eyes, her wisps of hair coming out of her bonnet, her gentle way with people. It would be interesting to catch up with our lives. We went through a lot together, and we could have had a good life with each other."

"Maybe now you will."

"That is a far-fetched possibility, Alice. It's been more than seven years since I saw her. I'm afraid each of us will have changed so much that we will be strangers to each other. Our meeting could be very awkward. My position as Director of the Company could intimidate her as it does a lot of people. Or even worse, I could be attracted to her, and she might reject me again."

"What about me? She may not like me."

"Oh, Alice, there is no way you would disappoint her! Everyone adores you. Even if you were a sea monster, she would like you. She was a devoted mother and doted on you. You were everything to her."

"That is if she is my mother. We shouldn't put the cart before the horse."

"No, we shouldn't."

"Do you remember anything about her or America?"

"You know as you've been telling me about her I've been trying to, but very little comes to mind. There might be something there about a ferry, but it just as well could be a canal here. And a sick old mn, who was upstairs and I had to be quiet for him. It's all so vague."

"And the tempest?"

"When you told me about it, I felt afraid, and my skin crawled. I figured it was because it was such a horrendous story. But no, there's nothing there about a tempest. Well, maybe the hiding place in the oven but I can't be sure."

"Perhaps you'll remember more when we see her."

"So you do think she will come."

"Alice, I don't know. But I'm going to be here in case she does. I told her I would be at every Society meeting, and she could meet me here if she wanted to."

"Why don't you go to America?"

"Oh, it is not easy for me to get away especially for that long a trip. Besides, Machteld said Elsje was thinking of coming to the Leyden Botanical Gardens, and she would have to come through Amsterdam to get there. To be honest, I think the decision about meeting is up to her. The last time we were together, she told me to make a life without her."

"Maybe I shouldn't be here when she comes. It may overwhelm her to see you and then find out about me. Don't you think it will shock her to find me alive?"

"She's a strong woman. She has survived many surprises in her life. I imagine she will be overjoyed to find you."

Twenty-Eight

The Atlantic Ocean
Aboard the *Princess Amelia*
Elsje

I was at the end of my story and none too soon. We were nearing the coast of Wales and Lord willing and the wind permitting we would arrive at Amsterdam in a few days.

As we gathered that night the captain sipped thick black coffee and said, "We need the investments of men like Rev. Megapolensis. Without them, I couldn't hire any sailors and wouldn't have this ship for that matter!"

"I suppose," said the English barrister who was seated next to the captain. "But I wish those investors didn't encourage piracy. Get's in the way of commerce, I say."

"I agree," offered the Dutch ship's factor. "Just imagine the profits if the Company's ships didn't have to write off losses to pirates or hire privateers. We need to protect the commerce that allows you to drink your coffee, Captain, and the rest of us our tea."

"Here, here!" said the first mate who occasionally joined us at supper. "We've lost too many seamen to the pirates even after they've signed on with us and been paid half their wages. Can't take the discipline on our ships and those fools think they'll get rich being pirates."

"Well, there is money in buccaneering," said the captain. "This Megapolensis we've heard about made his wealth backing pirates. One would think he would be embarrassed profiting from piracy."

"Can we blame him? The Dutch are traders. Making a profit is everything for them, and it doesn't matter where it comes from or how it is obtained." The Englishman spoke without a judgment even though the Dutch and English had been rivals and distrusted each other for decades.

"I'll give you that, but he preached about the dangers of wealth and living in luxury. I can't understand how he lived with himself."

"We've heard all this before," the captain interrupted waving off his mate. "So, Miss Nyssen, do you have more to tell of your story?"

"You've been patient with me. I've gone much too long in the telling."

"Not at all. Not at all," said the captain. "You've made the time pass quickly. I gather that once you found out about Alice and Gerret, you decided to travel to Amsterdam to find them?"

"Well, yes. I've struggled with whether I should disrupt their lives or simply let things be as they are. I have a good life in Gowanus, and I'm not keen on changing that and leaving my patients behind. From what I heard from Machteld, Alice is content and I wouldn't want to disrupt or unsettle her. She doesn't know anything about me."

"And Gerret?" the captain asked.

"I was touched by his letter. Obviously, he has hopes for us. To be honest, I don't expect anything to come of it. But I do owe him an apology for what I said to him during my troubles and a thank you for his letter and the tulips bulbs. I don't know what I'm going to do, and here we are nearly on the shores of the Netherlands."

"But surely you also have hopes for a future with him?" the captain asked.

"Ah, yes, of course, I do. Maybe it's finally time to righten the ship, as you sailors say. But where that ship is headed, I cannot say. I don't know what I'm going to do. Can we leave it at that, gentlemen?"

"Well, then, tell us what happened to Rev. Megapolensis," the Dutchman asked.

"I saw him just before we sailed. Mute and unmoving in his bed. His body is wasting away in cachexia, and he is a dead weight, if I can use that term. I don't think he will be that long for this world."

"He never explained himself, did he?"

"No. His mind seems without thought. And, of course, he can no longer talk."

The first mate said, "He made your life a living hell."

"Yes, he did. I don't think I'll ever get over my anger about it. But now he is simply a sick old man at the Asylum. I try to think about the good in my life, and there has been a lot of it. Maybe not what I expected or wanted, but good nevertheless. He couldn't keep that from me. I've prevailed over his scheming."

"What an irony to have you caring for him," the first mate said. "It's like Joseph caring for his brothers who had sold him into slavery."

"I've tried to understand why he did what he did. I'll probably never know. I remind myself that we both had terrible losses in our lives. He lost his son, and I, my father and Alice. How can you blame a parent who has lost a child for how he or she grieves? We all have tragedies and not one of us reacts or copes in the same way. It wasn't right that he took it out on us, but that's what he did. I took laudanum to escape my pain. He was so filled with anger at what happened that he took it out on my father and me."

"That may be," said the Spaniard who had been silent through most of my story. "But wasn't he well motivated by trying to save souls, including yours?"

"No, Señor Villalobos. He justified his unrelenting attacks on us by claiming he was trying to save us. What he did was inexcusable no matter what clothing he put upon his actions."

"I'm with you, Miss Nyssen," the first mate said. "I would have nothing to do with him. I'd probably have pushed him off my ship if he were aboard."

"Well, I probably would have applauded you for doing so. But you know, we are all sinners in need of God's forgiveness. He no more than I. I'm not very good at it, but I'm trying to be as forgiving and compassionate as our Lord, blessed be His name."

"And what about your family?" the captain asked. "What happened to your sisters who survived the tempest?"

"Of course, I've never seen Jannette, Alice's mother since she left us. Mary and Hieronymous moved to Blauvelt north of New York City, and I see them rarely. Hannah and Theodorus are still in Long Island busy with their children."

"Did Theodorus ever apologize for his role with Alice?"

"Yes, he did, and I'm trying to forgive him. He was tortured by his dependence on Megapolensis' money and what he allowed it do to him. Our relationship is cordial."

"And that snake, Samuel. What happened to him?"

"Samuel decided to be a minister and gave up being a doctor. He was afraid I'd expose him for misusing the laudanum on me. Not that anyone would care. There is a desperate need for physicians and people would overlook what he did, especially if I didn't pursue it."

"I would have struck that man down if I were you. Make him pay for what he did."

"Yes, well, I wasn't going to do that. He offered to partner with me as a doctor at the Asylum. I refused even though I needed help. Now that his father is all but dead to the world, Samuel doesn't visit him. I'm glad not to cross paths with him."

"You aren't close to any of the family you have left are you, Miss Nyssen?"

"No, I suppose not. I'm quite alone except for Machteld, who is now with her husband."

"And perhaps Alice," said the Spaniard.

"Yes, I suppose that is so. Perhaps Alice."

Part V
Gerret

Twenty-Nine

Nine Years After the Storm

Amsterdam in the winter is cloudy and cold. This year it was also rainy. Gloom settled over the city and into the spirits of those who lived there. "Not another day of rain!" people said, and many in the Society of New Amsterdam pined for the glorious sunny days in New Amsterdam when the sun glistened off the bay, and the brilliant colors of leaves were illuminated by sunsets. In our more honest moments, we admitted there were rainy days in New Netherlands, but as our exile lengthened, we remembered them less and less.

The ducks and geese gathered in larger numbers than usual and frolicked in the rain. I loved their bobbing and dipping and cheeriness. The concentric horseshoe canals and smaller ones that radiated out from Dam Square were built by that time. The bustling commerce of the city brought thousands of immigrants to Amsterdam and made the demand for new homes high. The loud thud of the pile driver weight lifted by men pulling on ropes was constant all over the city. The noise provided an uneven background rhythm to our daily lives. The tall and pointed frameworks of the tripod pile drivers moved from place to place in a macabre dance with the rhythm of the pounding.

"We have to go to her, Alice," I said after a Society meeting as we did the final clean up. "It's all that matters. Everything else is unimportant." The winter had been long, and waiting for Elsje was interminable. My term as Director in the Company had ended, and though my business was doing as well as ever, others could manage it in my absence. Alice immediately agreed, and we made arrangements for travel to New Amsterdam.

In those days, hundreds of ships sailed the trading triangle between the Netherlands, Africa, the Caribbean and New York. In two weeks Alice and I were in a small barque laden with furniture and Delft tiling. We sailed south to catch the trade winds, crossed the Atlantic, picked up sugar in the islands and made our way up the East Coast of America.

After we passed Sandy Hook and were sailing through the Narrows, I saw my first sight of the city. My heart was racing. The early morning sun made a glittering path directly from Long Island to our ship. Off starboard, the shoreline of Gowanus was bedecked with the light green of early spring. It had been eight years since I had seen Elsje, and it took all my willpower to keep from jumping into the bay to swim to her.

New Amsterdam was not what I remembered. There were no gallows in front of the Stadt Houis, and the battery alongside the Fort was gone and replaced with new houses. From our mooring, we could see that the English were filling the Prince Street canal, and the number of ships moored in the harbor was more than I ever imagined possible.

We disembarked from the rowboat at Peck's Landing. To my dismay, the ferry to Long Island was not running that day as the ferryman was on holiday. Unable to find an alternative way to across the East River Alice and I went to Pearl Street to see my children and introduce them to Alice. The street was now paved with uneven cobblestones, and our sea legs made us unsteady.

Christina greeted us warmly and offered us lodging for the night. "Take Jan's room," she said. "He's been gone for a month hunting beavers, but I'm afraid he might not be having success. If he had, he'd be back by now."

"He's on his own? Who is watching over him?" I asked.

"Gerret, he's a man now! He doesn't need any watching over. He has Mohawk friends, and I presume he is with them." How could it be that he was old enough to do that? I would have to come back later to catch up with him.

My baby, Christian, surprised me even more. "Come," Christina said to the two of us. "Let's walk to the green in front of the Fort. The English use it as market for grain, cattle, and other produce but we Dutch still use it the same as we used to. You'll see what I mean."

A large house had replaced our old tavern. It still looked out on the open space where cadets from the Fort had marched. In several hollows, people were seated on the ground watching bowlers aim their wooden balls at pins. Old men whispered to each other about the skill or strategy of each bowler. The players themselves were quiet except for an occasional cry of despair or victory. This was a serious competition. In my days. we were full of beer and boisterous laughter, and we joshed each other continually.

Christina showed us where young boys were competing. Twelve-year-old Christian was among them, and I recognized the family build: broad shoulders, slim hips, and a shock of blond hair.

When Christina called to him, I was afraid that he was going to turn his back on me again. But he ran to me, put his hands on top of my shoulders and smiled broadly.

"Weren't you a good bowler, Father?"

"I had some skill ... once."

Christian turned around and shouted to his teammates, "He's bowling with us!" Facing me, he said, "Do you know how to spin the ball? I've been dying to learn how."

"Yes, I do." We were inseparable for the rest of the day.

The next morning Alice and I took the first ferry to Long Island. The boat was bigger than I remembered and filled with farm hands on the way to work in the fields on the Island.

Alice's wide eyes scanned everything around us. New York was unpolished and chaotic in comparison to Amsterdam. People were dressed not in the fancy clothes of wealthy burghers but the rough clothes of woodsmen, traders, and sailors.

"So this is the ferry you took after the storm before you found out about the Elsje's house." I didn't need to answer her.

"And this is the road to Gowanus you walked when you went to ask her to be your wife." I nodded. The Island had changed little. There were more farms than before, and the pathway along the salt marshes and coastland trees was worn into a road rutted with two tracks for wagons.

It was a partly cloudy day and rays of sunlight streaked the eastern sky as though guiding us to and shining on our destination. I was coming home after a long, long journey. The Asylum was new, of course, and was much larger than I imagined. It was a square, plain, brick building of four stories without ornamentation. Two black carriages were parked on the circular drive in front. Blooming tulips surrounded by a carpet of blue scilla flowers decorated the garden in the middle of the circle. I recognized several tulips as Admiral Sneds.

"Yes, this is home," I said.

We walked in the front door and smelled the odor of liniment and urine. At the desk, a woman with a bored look glanced wordlessly at us.

I had a lump in my throat, so I motioned to Alice to speak, and she said brightly, "We are here to see Elsje Nyssen."

The attendant looked at us silently for a moment then said, "Let me get the Director for you." She disappeared down a hallway leaving us waiting. On a bench nearby an old women looked at us blankly, her thin white hair trying to cover her balding scalp. We said, "hello," but she only stared at us.

The attendant returned accompanied by Machteld. When she saw us, she ran down the hall and embraced first Alice and then me.

"Oh, my. Oh, my." She said several times. She took our hands in hers. Her fingers were trembling. "Why didn't you tell me you were coming? I can't believe you're here!"

She paused with a terrified look on her face. "You don't know, do you?" she said.

Our blank looks answered her question.

"Come with me," she said, not looking at us. She walked us out the front door into the fresh air and privacy outside.

"I brought her the tulips you gave me, Gerret. They are planted there among the others." Neither Alice nor I spoke.

"She went to find you. It took time to get free of her work, but she was determined to get to Amsterdam. 'You've got to let them know you are coming,' I told her. But she said, 'No, I want it to be a surprise.'"

There was a tremor in her words.

"She went on the *Princess Amelia*. I saw her off at the wharf. Did you hear about it?"

My breathing stopped. Please, not the *Princess Amelia*.

"No," Alice said, "why?"

"It never made it to Europe. We presumed it had been taken by pirates or the English. We were sure that the passengers, including Elsje, would eventually be found or that they'd find their way back here or to the Netherlands."

"You mean you don't know where she is?" Alice said.

She looked at each of us. "Her boat shipwrecked near Swansea in Wales."

What can be said at a moment like this? Alice and I stood dumbfounded. I knew the fate of the ship but did not know Elsje was on it. My body shook. Machteld and Alice encircled me with their arms.

"Let's get a blanket," Machteld said as she escorted me into the building. "We didn't know for a long time so we didn't say anything hoping that she would return to us. She never did. Only two months ago it was confirmed that the remains of the ship had been found."

Thirty

After I had recovered from the shock, I stayed in New Netherlands (this place will always be Dutch to me) and re-established my life where I belonged. Alice stayed with me, and Machteld, now Director of the Asylum, agreed to have her as an apprentice nurse. I moved the headquarters of the Society Transport Company to Long Island. The offices are in the new house I built in Brooklyn, and I own warehouses in New York and on the canal in Gowanus. I have the pleasure of watching my children grow into adulthood and being close to my sister, Christina.

Of course, being here has brought back many reminders of Elsje. It may sound strange, but in her absence, I imagine were husband and wife.

I walk the road along the shore amid the salt marshes and the sparkling bay to visit the Asylum. Alice treats me as her father, and Machteld, who is as close to Alice as she was to Elsje, sets aside a room in the Asylum where we can be alone.

I look at the two young women sitting with me: Elsje's best friend and her daughter, both lovely and kind women. I am surrounded by the best Elsje left behind. It isn't what I had wanted or expected. What of life is?

"I couldn't have made it without you," I said to them one day.

"Oh, sure you could," Machteld said. "Look how far you've come, and what you've accomplished in your life. And you did all that before we even met you."

"I suppose you are right. A lot of my hopes were shattered one way or another. Broken into small, sharp, scattered pieces that cut and wounded me. But here I am, content with my life." My mind wandered to Rev. Megapolensis. He'd been wounded too, by the death of his son. He hid his pain by faulting others and controlling them. And Elsje, whose pain was so great, numbed herself with laudanum. And me? I sailed away as far away as I could to escape the agony of losing Elsje to Samuel.

"You picked up the pieces and made something beautiful out of what was left," Machteld said.

"I suppose, but not without scars. I'm fortunate to have both of you. You are daughters to me."

"I have two fathers, and both of you dislike of Jergen." Alice had seen a beau for a while, but he was far more interested in having his fun than anything else.

"But, Alice, how is he going to provide for you?"

A rush of chill air entered through the open door of our room and targeted itself on the nape of my neck.

"Someone left the front door open," Alice said. "I'll check it."

"You are avoiding me, Alice ... you can do a lot better than Jergen you know."

"I'm serious. We don't want our patients to catch cold," she said.

"I'll do it, Alice, you stay here," Machteld said as she rose from her chair. "I've also a patient to check on."

A minute passed, then two. I shuddered from the chill and turned impatiently to see what was taking so long. Alice followed my eyes. A woman was in the doorway.

A large woolen bonnet hid the face, but I knew it was Elsje. How, I cannot say, for all I could see was a silhouette. That bit of exposed skin glowing with reflection from the fireplace? The way wisps of golden hair draped from under the bonnet? How she stood?

"It's her, isn't it!" Alice bolted from her chair and skipped directly to Elsje. They had a brief exchange, then they both came to me.

I rose and faced Elsje. Our eyes met.

She said, "Gerret."

My heart was pounding. "Elsje, I am ... You ... survived?"

She nodded and said, "It took a long time to recover." She reached out her hand and touched my fingertips. Our fingers intertwined.

Alice interrupted us. "Did you see Machteld? She's my sister."

"I most certainly did." Machteld stood watching in the doorway.

"Alice, I have a present for you." Elsje reached into a pocket of her coat and presented Alice with a small box, unwrapped and tied with blue yarn.

Elsje and I leaned into each other. The length of our arms touched. We watched as the present was opened.

Alice's mouth opened in surprise. "It's my hairpin! I remember it!"

"I hoped you might. You loved that hairpin and wore it all the time."

"Then, you really are … "

"Yes, Alice, I am."

"Gerret …. um, Mr. Snedeker has told me all about you."

"He has, has he?" She looked in my eyes. "Well, I have things to say about him too."

Elsje put a hand on my cheek, and said, "Your eye looks much better."

"My eye? My eye is fine. Why?"

"You had a sty, remember?"

"I do. The day we met."

Then she gave me a precious gift worth far more than all the presents ever exchanged by lovers.

She said, "I want to start over. Please say you do too."

Writer's Notes

Most of the characters in this novel are historical persons although the actions ascribed to them and their situations are entirely fiction. Most locations are also real: Maiden Lane (where women did their washing and men did their courting), Stuyvesant's manor at Company Farm #1, the names of the streets in Manhattan, the early towns of Long Island, Peck's Slip and Fulton Landing, and the Asylum for the Infirm and Aged in Gowanus (though it was built well after the time period of the book).

Jan Snedeker, Gerret's father, emigrated from the Netherlands in 1638 and was one of the few people to be given two of the original land grants in New Amsterdam, one on Pearl Street and one on De Heere Street later known as Broadway. His record of violations for which he was fined was long including public drunkenness, foul language, shorting patrons at his tavern, discharging his gun on public streets, and stealing. But, he was not unusual on that score. Violations and fines were frequent for very many residents of New Amsterdam.

Gerret Snedeker and Wilhelmina Vockes were in fact married, had three children, and she died soon after giving birth to a stillborn son Abraham. Unlike what happens in the novel he married Elsje Nyssen on December 2, 1669, in the Dutch Reformed Church of Flatbush. They had five children, the fourth one being named Teunis (who married a descendent of the Polhemus family). In a will dated December 6, 1669, and signed by Gerret, he appointed Jansen Van Heyreinghe and Jochem Woutersz (Gerret's brother-in-law) as *"tutors and guardians"* for the children of his first wife Wilhelmina Vockes. That document also states: *"The aforesaid daughter Maergrieta* (his first born child) *shall also have a gold ring and a silver hair pin in the remembrance of her mother."* I have taken the liberty with this piece of information and gave the ownership of this silver hair pin to Elsje's sister Jannette and subsequently to Alice (who is a fictional character).

Johannes Megapolensis did change his family name from Van Mecklenburg, but his antagonistic character is fiction. Records show that he spent much of his energies on converting the Mohawks to Christianity. He became fluent in their tongue and wrote books on their language, culture, and religion. Allegedly he was so interested in the Mohawks that he neglected the care of his parishioners. The date and cause of his death is unknown.

His son, Samuel Megapolensis, received degrees in law and medicine and was for a short while an associate pastor with his father at St. Nicholas Church in Manhattan. Samuel returned to Holland in 1668 where he served congregations there until his death sometime after 1700.

The author is a direct descendant of Gerret Snedeker through Christian, the third child of his first marriage.

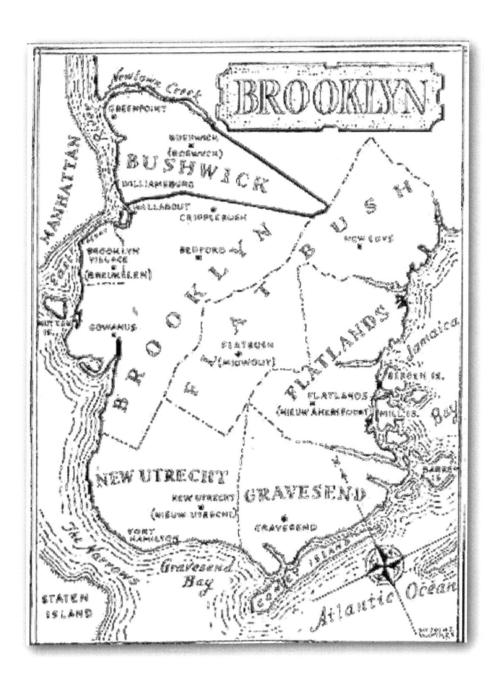

Old Dutch Words and Terms and Locations

Amersfoort Flatlands, Long Island

Beverwyck: Albany, New York.

Bundling Board: A bundling board was a wooden plank used to keep the man and woman separate from one another in bed. Boards might be as long as the bed itself and varied in style. Some rose quite high and created a substantial barrier between the bed's occupants. Others were shorter and largely acted as a symbolic reminder for each to remain on opposite sides of the bed. As a contraceptive device then, the bundling board was not very effective, and extramarital pregnancies were not uncommon in Colonial times.

The Company: The Dutch West India Company started in 1602 by merchants from the Republic of the Seven United Netherlands. On June 3, 1621, it was granted a charter for a trade monopoly in the West Indies and given jurisdiction over the Atlantic slave trade, Brazil, the Caribbean, and North America. It was known by its initials: WIC. As distinct from the much larger and more successful VOC or Dutch East India Company that traded in the Far East.

Classis: A governing body of pastors and lay elders in certain Reformed churches, having jurisdiction over local churches. New Netherlands was under the jurisdiction of the Classis of Amsterdam.

Coranto: Early informational broadsheets, precursors to newspapers that began around the 14th century

Consistory: A gathering of officers, consisting of ministers, elders and deacons, that serve as the governing body of the local congregation and is chosen periodically from the membership of the congregation.

Director General: A person appointed by the West India Company and confirmed by States General of the United Netherlands to be the chief officer of a trading post or colony and given dictatorial power over all aspects of the life and commerce of the colony.

Draughts: an ancient game between two people played on a checkered board. In modified form it is now known as checkers.

Laudanum: Laudanum was made of 10% opium and 90% alcohol, and flavoured with cinnamon or saffran. It was first used by the ancient Greeks, and mostly used as painkiller, sleeping pill, or tranquilizer. It is highly addictive.

Midwout Flatbush, Long Island

Olykoeks: The Dutch word for doughnuts

Orphanmaster: A person appointed by the Dutch East Indies Company to be the protector and provider for orphans in the colony. Usually the care he provided lasted well into adulthood.

Patria: A name often used by Netherlanders to refer to their home state: The Republic of the Seven United Netherlands.

Queesting: A verb used to describe the act of inviting someone of the opposite sex to bed for pillow talk.

Ruff and Honours: an English trick-taking game that was popular in the 16th and 17th Centuries. A precursor to Whist.

Schmervond A traditional Dutch family custom of gathering around the hearth in the early evening before supper.

Schout A local official appointed to carry out administrative, law enforcement and prosecutorial tasks. At times had control over local militia.

Schepens Local magistrates.

Stadt Houis State House, that housed local government and was often the place of public gatherings.

Tercio A Spanish infantry formation of up to 3,000 soldiers.

Tuighuis An 'armory' but could also include a prison or jail as did the one in Amsterdam.

Wilden A Dutch term for anyone that was not Christian. In the New World came to be used almost exclusively to refer to Native Americans.

Zieckentrooster A comforter of the sick. It is a person appointed by a church consistory to visit the sick and read to them the Scriptures and the sermons of the minister.

Made in the USA
Charleston, SC
18 December 2016